THE DRAGON AND THE GHOST

A BEATRIX ROSE NOVEL

MARK DAWSON

AUTHOR'S NOTE

This novel was previously published as Hong Kong Stories (Volume I), comprising the novellas White Dragon, Nine Dragons and Dragon Head. This is an extended and re-edited version of those stories.

PART I

1

Beatrix Rose stepped out of the cyber café and into the mad mêlée of early evening in Kowloon. The sky had been thronged with stacks of black cloud all day, and now it was caught in the hinterland between dusk and night: veins of purple that faded into the grey, like glittering seams of quartz. The plump moon was low above the jagged edges of the buildings on either side of the street, casting a wan glow that strengthened as the thwarted sun dipped farther and farther below the horizon.

The streets of Wan Chai teemed with people at all times, but, with the switch from day to night, the narrow lanes and alleys were infused with a restless madness that became more and more frantic as the minutes passed. The lanterns that were hung from the metal tubes and poles of market stands had been lit, oases of golden light amidst the gloom. Traders exhorted passers-by to sample their goods, pungent food and drink jockeying for attention with knock-off handbags boasting labels from Gucci and Prada.

Beatrix could smell wood smoke, joss sticks, boiling rice and excrement.

Hong Kong.

Heung Gong.

Fragrant Harbour.

Wasn't that a big joke.

She was bustled and jostled, absently allowing the tide of human traffic to carry her along the street. She had no destination in mind, other than the need for a drink —*several* drinks—anything that would help her to forget the increasingly gloomy emails that had been waiting for her in her anonymous Hotmail account.

A man bumped up against her shoulder, knocking her one step to the left. He spilled the Styrofoam cup of tea he was carrying, sneered his disdain for her, hawked up a ball of phlegm and spat it at her feet.

She didn't notice, and wouldn't have cared even if she had. She was distracted, lost in a pit of despair with no prospect of escape.

Isabella was gone. Her daughter was thousands of miles away and she had no idea how to find her.

She shrugged her backpack across her shoulder and kept walking.

2

She found her way to Nathan Road. The signage outside the hostess bars welcomed crewmen from the USS *Nimitz*, the big American aircraft carrier that had been in dock for the past two days, spilling hundreds of men and women into the streets of the city. All of them were searching for the illicit things that were denied them at sea: booze, drugs, and sexual adventure. They were easy to spot; the men with their crew cuts, tailed by attractive young women in miniskirts toting fake Gucci handbags. Beatrix walked by the go-go bars, where lithe women gyrated around chrome poles and men were persuaded to buy overpriced and watered-down drinks with the promise of sex that would often never come.

A little decisiveness returned. She wanted a drink. *Needed* one. She recognised a bar that she had visited before, a week ago, when she had first arrived in the city. The clumsy music of a Filipino cover band blared out of the big speakers in the main room, but she knew that there was a quieter bar at the back where she would be able to drink in relative peace.

She went inside, seeing the dozens of girls—mostly Filipinas from Hong Kong's service community—in tight jeans and short skirts, waiting for a potential mark: businessmen, ex-pats, tourists and, today, eager American sailors. Beatrix knew about these kinds of places. The regular girls would be given a number. If she could get one of the male customers to buy her a drink, she was paid a percentage of the profit. It was brazen, naked capitalism, all the more stark given how close it was to the Communist mainland.

The back bar was quieter, as she had hoped. Once the door closed behind her, the music and the clamour from the main room was more satisfactorily muffled. She looked around. There were three Filipina girls, three Gurkhas who were trying to impress them, and another dozen Chinese men staring glumly into their drinks. She went to the bar, took one of the battered stools, its stuffing held in by a crisscross of duct tape, and looked at the bottles arrayed against the mirrored wall.

She ordered a double gin and tonic and reached down for the fabric backpack. She unzipped it and took out the printout of the email that she had received. There were three pages, a scant reward for the twenty thousand pounds that she had spent to get them. She had hired two private investigators to search for Isabella and they had both struck out. There was no sign of her daughter anywhere. She had known that would be the likely outcome, but that didn't mean that seeing the words in black and white stung any less.

She didn't blame the investigators. She had given them so little to go on, after all. All she had been able to say was that her daughter had been abducted from her home. That was true. But she had been unable to give them the full story of what had happened. She had not been able to tell them that the agents who had abducted her were assassins who worked for Group Fifteen, the classified agency that arranged for the elimination of domestic and foreign nationals who were injurious to the best interests of Her Majesty's government. She could not tell them that she, too, had worked for the Group until information that she had discovered had led to her commanding officer, a man she knew only as Control, deciding that she needed to be eliminated.

This was not a case of a jealous husband who had snatched his daughter off the street and fled with her. Nor was it a stranger, a paedophile, or a people trafficker. Isabella had been taken by the state. They could change her name, erase her records, concoct whatever story they chose. They could send her abroad without fear of being stopped at the airport.

She could be anywhere, with anyone.

She could be anybody.

But that didn't mean that Beatrix was prepared to abandon her.

Couldn't do that.

Had to keep looking.

And right there was the problem. She had money—lots of it—but it was spread around several safety deposit boxes in banks throughout the West End of London. There was no way that she could access any of it. She certainly couldn't go to London. She knew that the Group would be looking for her. She would be arrested as soon as she stepped off a plane. There was a little money in the deposit account that she had shared with her husband, but accessing it electronically would have been the equivalent of calling Control with her coordinates and waiting for him to activate the nearest agent to track her down. The same was true of her credit cards.

She needed cash. But she had no way of earning it. It wasn't that she was unskilled. She was, and prodigiously so. But her talents were very particular. They were not transferable. There was no agency that she could approach to represent her, to find her the work that she was qualified to do. There was the sprawling Hong Kong underworld, but she had no means of accessing it.

She looked at the emails again. Both investigators were prepared to keep looking, but only if their retainers were paid up front. One was requesting £30,000 and the other, £25,000.

Money that she did not have.

She finished the gin and ordered another.

A MAN TOOK the stool next to her. There were plenty to choose from and she sighed in anticipation of the irritation that she knew was coming. He did not speak immediately. She looked at his reflection in the mirror. He was in late middle age, premature wrinkles around his eyes and mouth. He was wearing a bright Hawaiian shirt, stonewashed denim jeans that might have been fashionable for a week during the eighties, and a pair of box fresh white Nike trainers. He wore a hefty gold necklace, bracelets on both wrists and several large rings. He was completely without taste. He reminded her a little of Jackie Chan.

He looked up into the mirror and realised that she was assessing him.

"Hello, Miss."

She ignored him.

"What is your name?"

"No, thanks," she said. "Not tonight."

He frowned and then, realising that she thought he was hitting on her, he blushed furiously. "I am not...please do not think that I..."

"Forget it."

He looked mortified. He took a packet of super length Marlboros from his shirt pocket and offered them.

"No."

"Then at least let me buy you drink."

"I can buy my own drinks."

"You like sake?"

"No..."

He didn't seem to hear her, turned to the bartender and asked for a bottle of warm sake. The bartender turned and bellowed in Chinese to a man Beatrix had observed in the back room, ordering him to bring out a bottle.

"This is not bar for tourists."

"Who said I was a tourist?"

"But you are American?"

"British."

"My apologies. How embarrassing."

"Forget it."

"I am Chau."

He waited, expecting her to introduce herself, but, when she didn't, the colour in his cheeks returned.

She felt sorry for him. "Beatrix."

"I am sorry?"

"My name is Beatrix."

He smiled and then became grave. "This neighbourhood, Miss Beatrix—it is not safe for Western women."

"Thank you for your concern, Mr. Chau, but I can look after myself."

The bottle of sake arrived with two glasses. Chau unscrewed it and poured two measures. He took his glass and held it up. Beatrix still felt irritation at his dumb, oblivious persistence, but the bottle looked inviting, and she was in the mood to drink. She took the other glass, touched it to his and drank. The sake tasted like very dry white wine.

He drank and refreshed both glasses.

"I am sorry. I can see you would prefer to be alone."

"Thank you, Mr. Chau." She raised the glass. "And thank you for the drink."

She got up, took the printed pages and went to one of the spare tables.

3

Beatrix was reading through the reports for a second time when three men came into the bar. The atmosphere immediately changed; the frivolity was sucked out of the room. Beatrix was glad of the papers. She raised the page she was reading and pretended to study it, glancing over the top of it and assessing the newcomers. The men were wearing identical outfits: track suit tops, jeans and white trainers. They had tattoos on their exposed skin.

It was practically a uniform.

She knew the signs.

Triads.

Two of them stood at the door, one on either side, an unspoken injunction against anyone who wanted to leave. The third walked farther inside, looking around the small room with a proprietary air, and went to the bar. He was carrying a small leather satchel and his dark hair was long, reaching halfway down his back. He took the stool that Beatrix had vacated next to Chau and began to speak.

Beatrix was too far away to distinguish the words, and she doubted that her Cantonese would have been sufficient to make much sense of the conversation, but it was obvious from Chau's demeanor that whatever it was that was being discussed was not a subject with which he was comfortable. His interlocutor slouched on the stool in a languid posture, punctuating his words with lazy gestures. He grinned at Chau's evident discomfort, and Beatrix was put in mind of the way that a tiger toys with the hamstrung gazelle that it is just about to tear to pieces.

Not her problem.

She looked down at the papers and started to read them again, from the start, for the third time. Perhaps she had missed something. Perhaps, hidden amid the glum tidings, there was a small nugget of hope. It was all just a question of interpretation.

"No," Chau said, speaking more loudly. "Please. This is unnecessary."

She looked up. The triad had stood and taken off his tracksuit top, and now he was hanging it over the stool. He was wearing a white vest. Every inch of skin was covered in elaborate tattoos: arms, back, shoulders, chest, even to the tips of his fingers. He was big for a Chinese, perhaps six inches taller and a hundred and fifty pounds heavier than Beatrix.

Whatever it was he was proposing to do, Chau was unhappy about it.

The man opened the leather satchel and took out a meat cleaver. He rested it on the bar, reached across and held onto Chau's left wrist. He pressed his hand down on to the wooden surface, took the cleaver, and said something else.

"*No!*" Chau pleaded. "I already apologised!"

"Not good enough."

"Tell him I am sorry. You do not need to do this."

"No, Chau, we do. You know we do. A gesture. It is required."

Chau jerked his arm and managed to free his hand. He stumbled across the room in the direction of the door. One of the men stationed there stepped up and hammered him with a stiff punch in the middle of his face. Chau's legs went out from under him. The man who had struck him picked him up and brought him back to the bar, the second man close behind. The man in the vest took his wrist in his right hand and, reaching out, forced Chau's fingers apart. He raised the cleaver once more.

Beatrix sighed. She pushed her chair away from the table and stood.

"Stop," she said, in Cantonese.

The man in the vest turned to her, an expression of amused surprise on his cruel face.

"What did you say?" he replied, his English heavily accented and halting. The fact that he had replied in English signalled his contempt for her rudimentary attempt to speak his language.

She switched to English, too. "You heard me. He's had enough. Leave him alone."

The man's surprise melted away, to be replaced by scorn and disdain. "Drink your drink, lady, unless you want me to take this and make you not so pretty." He waved the cleaver at her.

Beatrix felt the tingle of adrenaline. She looked at the cleaver, held in a steady hand, and looked up from it into his eyes. There was no pity there. They were the eyes of a man who was used to doling out pain, and unaccustomed to disobedience.

She knew that she stood at a junction, with two ways for

her to proceed. She had come out tonight to get drunk. She had not come to look for trouble. Most of the time, she would have ignored all of this. She could have followed the man's instructions, gone back to her table and the glass of sake Chau had bought for her, and tried to ignore the unpleasantness that was about to take place.

That would be the prudent course of action. The safest, most sensible thing to do. And she could have done that.

Could have.

But if Chau had been irritating, at least he had also been friendly. And Beatrix did not necessarily want to watch what would happen if she left him alone.

And there was this, too: the triad was a bully, and Beatrix did not like bullies.

"I'm sorry," she said, raising her hands. "My apologies."

The man leered at her. "You watch. We speak after."

Beatrix reached across the table for her tumbler. It had a heavy base, made from thick glass.

The triad turned his back to her, faced Chau, said something else, and raised the cleaver to the same height as his head.

Beatrix picked up the glass and flung it, hard, but not so hard as to sacrifice her accuracy. It streaked across the distance between her and the man in the vest and struck him just above his ear. He took a half step forwards, braced himself against the bar, and then dropped to one knee, the cleaver lost from his grip to clatter across the floor.

There came a sudden, shocked, silence.

The remaining two men were stunned into dumbness by the incongruity of what they had just seen. They paused, mouths open, giving Beatrix enough time to take two steps closer to them. The nearest, a man with a discoloured scar down the left-hand side of his face, moved to intercept her first.

Beatrix reached out with her right hand for the stool next to Chau that she, and the man in the vest, had been sitting on. She hefted it, allowing her fingers to slip down the stool, her left hand fastening around the second of the three legs, and then swung it in a hard, powerful arc. The stool splintered against the junction of the man's neck and shoulder, the seat breaking off and bouncing away off the wall. The man had not had the time to raise his arms to defend himself, and the blow knocked him to the ground.

The second man reached for Beatrix, his fingers brushing against her skin as she took a step away from him. She flipped the leg of the stool so that she held it at its thin end and swung it like a baseball bat, catching the man on the temple. The end of the stool's leg that had been wrenched away from the seat was jagged, and the sharp splinters clawed trenches in the man's forehead and scalp. His eyes rolled back and he toppled sideways, his head bouncing off the floor.

Beatrix felt a sharp scratch down her shoulder and back. She turned. The man with the vest was on his feet again. He had a knife in his hand. It was the one that the barman had used to slice the limes for Beatrix's gin. The edge of the blade was slick with blood. Awareness heralded the blast of pain and, as she took a half step backwards, the man stabbed the knife at her. The point of the blade sliced into the fleshy part of her torso just beneath her ribcage. The pain was no more than a sharp sting, but, as she took a second and third step backwards, she felt the blood already bubbling out.

The man grinned at her. He raised the bloody knife and came at her.

There was a sharp pop and the top of the man's head burst apart. There was no time for him to register shock or surprise. One moment his head was there, whole, and the next moment it was not. He dropped to his knees and then slumped straight onto his face. He twitched once, and then was still.

Chau was standing behind him, a fog of blue smoke hanging before the barrel of the little Kel-Tec P-32 that he was holding in his hand. He moved to the man who Beatrix had hit with the stool and, point blank, shot him in the head. The third man was conscious and shuffling away on his knees, his hands raised in supplication. Chau executed him, too, shooting him in the throat and then, finally, square in the face.

Beatrix was confused. She put out a hand to steady herself, but a ripple of pain washed out from the puncture in her side. It amplified, spreading all the way up and down that side of her torso.

She suddenly felt faint.

"Shit," she said.

Chau put the gun into the inside pocket of his jacket and hurried across to her. "Miss, you have been hurt."

"I just need...to sit down," she muttered. She reached out for a nearby stool, but miscalculated the distance between her and it. The heel of her hand slipped off the edge and she fell to her knees, knocking the stool onto its side. She tried to get to her feet, but was assailed by weakness.

Chau hurried to her side and clumsily helped her up. "We must leave. They are triads. Wo Shun Wo. If others come, they will kill you. Please. I help you. I have car outside."

Beatrix lifted her arm so that he could loop his beneath her shoulder. He bore her weight as they stumbled, like a pair of drunken lovers, into the tumult of the main bar and then onto the crazed Kowloon street outside.

4

Chau helped Beatrix into the street. He was slight, an inch shorter than her and of a similarly slender build, but he was wiry and stronger than he looked. He said that his car was parked in the lot around the corner. He bore her weight as they made their way along the packed street, a fast-moving tributary of pedestrians that bumped and jostled them as they passed.

The lot was a temporary arrangement, a wide square of cleared land that stretched between two buildings that were being demolished. Chau had a brand-new Mercedes CLA, shiny and red and hopelessly ostentatious. He blipped the locks, opened the rear door, and helped her inside. She dropped down onto the leather seat, removing her hand from her abdomen to look at it. It was soaked with blood. She felt more throbbing and oozing from the gash and put her hand back, pressing down as hard as she could. She had seen wounds like this before, had inflicted them herself more than once. She knew that she was going to need some help. Unless she got treated, she was going to bleed out.

Chau got into the driver's seat, started the engine, and

screeched away. Beatrix was pressed back into the seat by the sudden acceleration. He drove west on Saigon Street, forging through Kowloon's heavy evening traffic. Beatrix glanced out at the ubiquitous red taxis, the high-end Jaguars and Rolls Royces of the garishly rich, the hatchbacks and the triad-driven minibuses.

They ran up against a queue of traffic gathered at the junction with Nathan Road. He braked and turned to look back at her. "You okay?"

"Been better," she grunted.

"I will help."

Beatrix was tempted to tell him to stop the car and let her out. The sidewalks were thronged with people, a seething morass within which she would be able to disappear after just a few steps. But as she looked down at her side again, at the blood that was seeping between her fingers, she felt the lethargy in her legs. She knew that her body was going into shock. She was losing too much blood. It galled her to admit it, but she needed help. The knife had left a neat and tidy wound that she wouldn't be able to stitch up herself.

Chau looked down, too. "You need to see doctor."

"No hospitals," she said.

"What do you mean? Your side—"

"I don't want to go to a hospital."

I can't, she very nearly said. *I can't go to a hospital.* If the Group was looking for her—and she knew that they would be looking—she couldn't take a risk like that. She knew the reach of the intelligence service was pervasive, and the last thing that she needed was to put herself in a position where her details might be recorded.

She had to stay in the shadows, hidden in the depths, to find out what she needed to know. Only then could she surface with the element of surprise on her side. It was her only chance for vengeance.

"My apartment, then. I fix you up there."

"Where?"

"Five minutes. I take you there, yes?"

She closed her eyes. She felt faint. She knew enough medicine to know what was happening to her. It was hypoxia. Not enough blood pumping around her body meant that too little oxygen was getting to her brain.

"Do not sleep," Chau urged.

"I'm all right," she mumbled.

She closed her eyes.

5

Beatrix was vaguely aware of the car door opening and Chau leaning into the cabin next to her.

"I call friend," he said.

"No—"

"You are badly hurt. Very bad. More than I can fix. My friend is doctor. He will be able to help."

Beatrix wanted to resist, her old instincts still trying to impose themselves, but she had no strength for it and she knew that he was right.

She felt her eyelids drooping.

"Stay awake," Chau urged her. "No sleep."

"Yes," she said. "No sleep." The words felt sticky in her mouth.

Her eyes felt heavy.

Chau shook her gently. "No sleep." He shook her more vigorously.

Chau was speaking to someone in Cantonese. The unfamiliar words came to her as if she were underwater or in a coffin that was slowly being buried.

"No sleep!" Chau said angrily. And then, when she didn't respond, he struck her across the face.

She prised her eyes open. Chau was halfway in the car. How had that happened? He was just wearing a vest. Where was his garish shirt? She glanced down. He was pressing it against her side. The shirt was an obscene scarlet, soaked through with her blood. How could she have any more blood? She had lost so much.

"Talk to me," he said. "Your name is Beatrix, yes?"

Her reluctance to share her personal details seemed frivolous now. *What was the point?* "Beatrix," she said, wondering if she had spoken aloud. "Beatrix Rose."

"My friend is coming, Beatrix Rose. Ten minutes."

"No hospital, Chau."

"I—"

"*No hospital.* Promise me."

"Okay. No hospital. I promise."

She closed her eyes again.

"You must stay awake."

Beatrix knew that he was right, but, despite that, the promise of sleep was too attractive to ignore. She allowed her eyes to close, focusing all of her attention inwards. The darkness seemed to be layered, textured. She felt as if it had substance, and the deeper she delved, the more that seemed to be true. It wrapped around her, warm and pliable and comforting, a cushion for her body and the softest of pillows for her head. She felt someone with her, a presence in the darkness, and, as she looked, she saw Isabella. Her daughter was smiling, her arms held aloft, inviting her mother's embrace.

Beatrix felt herself smile as she knelt down and wrapped her arms around the darkness.

Her dreams seemed to be eternal. The darkness swallowed her and held her, allowing visitations from Isabella and her husband, Lucas. He looked at her with love and forgiveness, but his affection did not excuse the neatly drilled hole in his forehead and the trail of blood that seemed to run and run. She tried to remember what had happened to him, but her memories were wispy fragments, and, as she reached out to collect them, her fingers passed through them like smoke.

BEATRIX WAS AWAKENED by a sound she did not recognise. At first she thought it was a mosquito buzzing around her head. She prised open eyes that were gummed together with sleep and stared up at the false ceiling. She heard it again—an urgent scurrying—and she realised that, wherever she was, it had a problem with rats.

Her repose had not been entirely natural. She noticed a scattering of small glass ampoules on the floor next to her head. She picked one up and read the English translation beneath the Cantonese: midazolam hydrochloride. A drug used for sedation and anaesthesia. She picked up another: metronidazole hydrochloride. Antibiotics.

She was lying on a futon in a tiny room, just long enough for her to stretch out and with barely a foot of space on either side. A cotton sheet was bunched around her midriff, disturbed during her sleep. She was wearing her underwear beneath a pair of mens' pajamas. She sat up, wincing with pain, and saw a foil container of half-finished soba noodles with a pair of chopsticks resting in them. *Had she eaten?* She didn't remember. She was cold, too. There was an ancient air-conditioning unit on the wall, dripping water and wheezing out frigid air.

She got up, the pain almost unbearable. The skin on the left side of her torso felt tight, unusually taut, and, as she raised her arm and looked down, she saw a neat row of stitches that held together the puckered lips of a small inch-long stab wound. There was an enormous bruise, too. It stretched from just above her hip all the way to her armpit.

She remembered: the men in the bar.

The triads.

She probed the wound. It was sore. She pressed with her fingertips and tried to assess the damage. There was no way to tell how deep the incision was, or what structures had been damaged. She remembered the blood. The knife must have caused a haemorrhage. An operation would have been necessary to fix it. *Where had that happened?*

Here?

She edged away from the futon, her arms spread out against the wall to help with her balance. Eventually, she felt strong enough to stand unaided.

She opened the bedroom door.

She was in a flat. *Chau's?* It was tiny. The bedroom door opened onto the kitchen diner. She stepped inside. A sofa bed had been pulled open, a mess of sheets dumped atop it. The bed was empty. The apartment was quiet. She went to a window and pulled back the wooden shutters. The glass had a film of dampness on it, the cause of the rinds of mildew that limned the edges where it met the frame. The room was stuffy and smelt ripe.

Beatrix unlatched the window and pushed it open. The window gave onto a shaft. The poorly tended nasturtiums that drooped from the window box of the next apartment along had attracted aphids and blackflies, and Beatrix gazed through the buzzing cloud to the three walls that completed the deep well. There were air-conditioning units fixed to the walls, lines that held drying washing, and, at the foot of the well below, a jam of green industrial refuse bins. She looked down. It was a vertiginous drop, maybe a hundred feet, and she felt a little dizzy.

She went back into the bedroom. There was a surgical stand in the corner of the room, a saline drip tied around the bracket at the top. There was a wastepaper bin next to it and, inside, she saw three plastic bags. The insides of the bags were slick with thick, globulous scarlet fluid. She retrieved one, saw that it was marked AB positive, and remembered the blood that had poured from the wound. She must have been given a transfusion. There were bloody bandages and surgical pads in the bin, too.

There was a stool at the other end of the futon. Two piles of clothes had been neatly laid out atop it. The first comprised the clothes that she had been wearing when she had been injured; she realised that she didn't know when that was. She picked up the plain black T-shirt that she had been wearing. She held it out and saw the gashes in the fabric, one on the back and one on the side. The garment had been boiled to remove the blood that must have leeched into it, but it was ruined. She tossed it into the bin. Her olive trousers bore a discoloured patch where the blood had seeped in too deeply to be cleaned. She folded them, put them back on the stool and examined the second pile. These were new, a T-shirt and trousers from Gap, matched to the ones she had been wearing. She took off the pajamas and dressed. The clothes fit perfectly. Chau was nothing if not diligent.

He had taken good care of her, but it made no difference.

She couldn't stay here.

The front door was locked, but she opened it and stepped outside. The corridor had a bare concrete surface that was decorated with a repeating oblong design. The walls were bare and the lighting was provided by flickering strip lights. Exterior windows admitted brightness from outside, and the interior windows opening onto the corridor were all barred. Plastic jugs of water stood outside the front doors, and, at the far end, Beatrix saw a painted sign that advertised 'Deluxe Hotel'.

She stepped over to one of the exterior windows. This aspect offered a view of streets that she did not recognise and, in the near distance, the dome and minarets of a mosque she hadn't seen before. She looked up and down the corridor, unsure which way to go for the elevators, but, before she could proceed any farther, she felt a terrible wave of lassitude. She had to put her arm out to brace herself against the wall. The pain flared from her side again, a sudden pounding that darkened the edges of her vision.

She was still weak.

Too weak.

She looked back at the open door to the flat.

She weighed it all up.

She knew that she didn't have the strength to get very far. The prospect of just a few extra steps down the corridor was too much for her to contemplate. She was certain that she would collapse.

Could she stay here?

What about Chau?

Whatever else he had done, he had saved her life. He could have abandoned her or left her here to die, and he hadn't. She had been vulnerable and he had cared for her. There was nothing to suggest that would change now that she was recovering.

And she didn't have much of a choice.

She walked slowly back to the flat, went inside, and closed the door behind her. She crossed to the bedroom, undressed slowly and methodically, and lay down in the bed again. She was asleep within moments.

J ackie Chau drove around the block three times before he was satisfied that the building was not being observed. He was on Kai Hing Road. It was on the southern edge of the Kowloon peninsula, part of the extensive dockside and within close proximity of the Kwun Tong Bypass. The area was home to a large concentration of warehouses and businesses that profited from the goods that were unloaded from Hong Kong's unusually deep natural harbour.

The night was dark. The street was lit by two unreliable lamps and the fat gibbous moon overhead. He turned off. He backed into the narrow alley at the rear of his premises, the car pointing out and the engine still running. He glanced in the mirror. There were two men outside the complex of warehouses, both smoking cigarettes. He thought he recognised them. Men dressed in the uniforms of the import/export business that was based two warehouses down from him. He knew Donnie Qi could very easily have left a couple of lower ranking triad members —*maa jais*, or little horses—in the vicinity to wait for him to come. But he had already postponed this visit for a week. The *Dai Lo* must have suspected that he would run. Chau knew that Donnie Qi respected his intelligence. He had to hope that he respected it enough to conclude that he wouldn't take such a foolish risk.

Because it was a risk.

A foolish, *stupid* risk.

But one that he had to take.

He would just make sure that he didn't stay for long.

He left the door of the Mercedes open, collected his little pistol from the seat next to him and made his way to the building's back door. He heard the cawing of gulls from the docks, but paid them no heed. He walked quickly. He had to pass along an alleyway, an unlit shortcut that was full of trash and huge cat-sized rats that thrived on the scraps tossed out of the neighbouring warehouse that was used to smoke fish. He reached the door. A drop of stale water from an antiquated air conditioner fell onto his head. He unlocked the door and, his nerves jangling because he knew that it would creak, pulled it open.

The warehouse was quiet and dark. He paused in the doorway, listening hard, but he could hear nothing save the familiar drip of the tap that he had been meaning to fix for weeks. He knew the inside well enough to leave the lights off. He made his way, slowly and carefully, along the aisle that was formed by racking that held his cleaning products and equipment, finding his way to the stairs that would lead up to his office.

Thinking about Donnie Qi prompted other recollections. Regrets, too, and the sure knowledge that he had arrived at this juncture because of a series of increasingly poor decisions that had been motivated by greed. Chau had owned this business for five years. He had been doing well. He had a series of reliable contracts with small commercial landlords that paid a decent amount each month, enough to live on, even in an expensive city like HK. He had a nice apartment in Kennedy Town, he had been able to afford the payments on the Mercedes, and there was enough money to treat the Tsim Sha Tsui hookers he frequented to nice gifts and treats on their birthdays.

Running the business was hard work, but it was a comfortable, reliable, secure life.

He could have maintained that life for as long as he wanted, but he had been greedy. He had been approached by a first cousin who said that he had a job that he might be interested in. Chau had known very well that the boy, a callow youth called Liang, had been associating with the local triads. He had heard that it was just a case of a youngster looking up to the glamorously tattooed criminals and their money and status, but he had been quickly disabused of that notion. Liang was a *maa jai* and very much part of the crew. Normally, Chau would have eschewed the invitation, keeping his fingers crossed that his rebuttal wouldn't be regarded as a snub. But he had looked at the boy, remembering the buck-toothed kid who now drove a Lexus and spent money like water, and he decided that he wanted some of it for himself. No, the prospect of making some quick, easy money was attractive, and he had been unable to resist.

More fool him.

Liang had introduced him to Donnie Qi. He was the *Dai Lo*, a medium ranking underboss of the Wo Shun Wo triad. Donnie presided over his part of the Kowloon underworld from the back rooms of the Jade Lotus karaoke bar, a seedy dive on Yau Ma Tei. Chau had been invited to visit him in the club. It was accommodated within a large basement beneath a supermarket, with peeling posters in the lobby advertising the neighbouring twenty-four-hour saunas, massage parlours and clip joints. A rickety shoebox lift descended to the club, where television screens were fixed to the walls and microphones littered the tables. His audience with the *Dai Lo* was quick and satisfactory, with the job put to him in simple terms. An 'unfortunate incident' had taken place in a property that Donnie owned, and the resultant mess needed to be cleaned up. He would pay him $2,000, ten times what he would normally have charged for a day's work. Did he want the business?

Chau had said yes.

He had driven his van to the property. It certainly was unfortunate. The bodies had been removed, but the evidence of what had happened there was still plain to see. Chau knew, figuratively, that death could be grisly. He liked the American TV shows that specialised in this sort of thing, but he had never been called out to deal with something as repellant as this before. There was blood on the furniture and on the walls; there was a splash on the ceiling and dried, crusted blood in the grooves between the floorboards. He knew, from experience, that the nickel-sized stain on the carpet would not be the worst of it, and that there was likely a two-foot stain on the floorboards beneath.

He had been right.

Chau had spent an entire day on the cleanup and Donnie Qi had been pleased with his work.

Pleased enough that more work had followed.

It went well for the first year. There was a steady stream of business: blood to be scrubbed and scoured from the back room of the Jade Lotus where Donnie Qi's discipline was meted out, the occasional amputated body part to be disposed of at the city dump.

There had been seven bodies to make disappear during that time, too. Those were the longest days. He had invested in equipment more suited to the task: non-porous one-time-use suits and gloves, filtered respirators and chemical-spill boots. He bought biohazard waste containers, including 55-gallon heavy duty bags and sealed plastic containers. He bought a supply of luminol to disclose hidden bloodstains. He bought hospital grade disinfectants, industrial strength deodorisers, heavy duty sprayers, long scrubbing brushes and a wet vacuum. He had even bought a fogger, to thicken cleaning chemicals so that they could get all the way into tight or restricted spaces, like air ducts, for odour removal.

His first "full" cleanup had come in the second month, after he had earned their trust. A man who had been in the life had decided that he would prefer the company of his nubile young wife. He did not listen to the warnings that leaving was impossible and so both he and the girl had been murdered as an example to others who might also question the bonds that tied them. Chau had arrived when the bodies were still warm. He had been deputed two *maa jais* to help and, at his direction, they had dismembered the bodies so that they could be dropped into bin liners and incinerated. They took disinfectant and used it to clean all the blood away. They found it everywhere. It was on the walls, on the floor, in between the boards. Brain matter had been scattered on the walls, and now it had congealed so hard that they needed to scrape it off. There were tiny bits of bone fragment that had become embedded in the furniture. They removed all of it. The linen and fabrics that had been soaked in blood were taken up and bagged, ready to be burned. They had cleaned the apartment until it was spotless. Chau heard later that Donnie Qi had moved one of his mistresses into the place the day after he had finished.

He learned a great deal. He saw how each cleanup was different, how each presented different problems that needed to be addressed. Some—the ones that featured bodily fluids—needed to be treated carefully so that the risk of becoming infected with a blood-borne pathogen was minimized. These men and women did not always live the cleanest lives, and Chau had no interest in collecting an unpleasant gift from them. He learned how quickly it took blood to dry and congeal into a thick jelly that he would have to scrape away. He learned how someone who was shot in the chest would not bleed as much as someone who was shot in the head; in the case of the former, the lungs would suck the blood back into the body.

Chau developed a rapport with Donnie and was pleased to be invited to share a drink with him at the club. Chau was too wise to think that this could be a social call, expecting that he was going to be offered a bump in pay to keep him exclusive since he had heard there had been interest in his services from rival bosses. He had been wrong. Over a very pleasant meal, Donnie had suggested that he was having a problem with a mistress, Lì húa, who was too savvy and cautious to be drawn into a position where she could be disposed of.

Donnie Qi had described his dilemma and then, with cunning gleaming in his eyes, he had suggested that perhaps *that* was something Chau could assist him with?

"Lì húa does not know you," he had said. "She has not seen you before. She will not suspect."

Chau had been offered $25,000. He knew the offer was not one that he could very easily decline, and he had considered it. He had watched Lì húa one afternoon, following her from her apartment to the Pacific Place mall. She was beautiful, tall and striking. He thought about how it could be done, and decided that it would be simple enough. Donnie Qi was right. She did not know him. She would not see him coming. He tried to rationalise it, too—how she must have known the possible consequences of becoming embroiled with a man like that. *It was her fault*, he tried to persuade himself. If it wasn't him, it would be someone else. He would do it quickly and mercifully, rather than the unpleasant death that might visit her if Donnie was forced to put one of the other Wo Shun Wo on the job.

Chau tried to persuade himself that it was better for everyone concerned that he accept the commission, but, in the end, his morals—rendered more flexible over the course of the last few months—were still not supple enough to allow him to agree.

And so he had said no.

And no one said no to Donnie Qi.

9

Chau opened the door to the office and went inside. There was enough moonlight coming through the window to find his way across the small room to the desk. He unplugged his laptop and put it into its bag. Then he knelt down beneath the desk and pried up the loose floorboard. There was a hollow space between the floorboards of the office and the ceiling below, and he reached down into it until his fingers brushed against the cellophane-wrapped bundle that he had hidden there. He clasped it and brought it out. The banknotes wrapped in the plastic sheath were worth $27,725. He put the bundle in the laptop case, replaced the loose floorboard, and stood.

He looked around the little office and allowed his thoughts to settle on the first time that he had seen it. He had moved the business here after he had secured his biggest commercial client, and he remembered how excited it had made him feel. It seemed a long way off, now. A different time. He doubted whether he would ever be able to come back here again.

He knew that there was no way he could stay in Hong Kong.

He had already decided that he would have to leave.

He would make sure that Beatrix Rose had recovered—he owed her that much, at least—and then he would leave. He would take a junk to the mainland, and then he would head deep into China. He had relatives in Fushun. He would be able to hide out with them. He was not naïve enough to think that Donnie Qi would forget him, nor that his reach would not extend into China, but he would invest some of his funds in plastic surgery and a new identity. He had the capital to do it. He could start again.

He froze.

Was that a noise?

He listened at the door, closed his eyes and concentrated everything on listening as intently as he could, until he decided that his mind was playing tricks. He picked up the case, descended the iron stairs, and hurried through the darkened warehouse to the back door. He paused there, scanning out into the alleyway beyond. The taillights of his car glowed back at him and he chided himself for leaving them on. He tightened his grip around the handle of the pistol and jogged to the open door. He tossed the bag into the back, threw the car into first, turned out onto the road, and, without another backward glance, sped away.

10

Beatrix awoke.

What was that?

She lay still for a moment. She had not woken naturally. She was groggy, but awareness was returning quickly. She blinked her eyes, and then reached up to rub the sleep away. She was in the bedroom. The surgical stand loomed above her. It was closer than she remembered. *Had it been moved?*

There.

Again.

A noise.

She heard the sound of a door open and close. She looked around the bedroom for a weapon and saw the chopsticks, picked one up and clasped it in her fist. It was far from ideal, but, if she needed to defend herself, it would suffice.

She opened the bedroom door a crack and looked through.

She saw Chau.

He was at the breakfast bar, laden down with a pair of

heavy grocery bags.

He was wearing another lurid Hawaiian shirt, ice-white jeans and brightly polished sports shoes. His back was to her. Her first instinct was to leave. She felt stronger. Chau hadn't seen or heard her. She could disable him without much effort; choke him out or knock him senseless. She could kill him if she wanted to be confident that the loose end he represented was tied off. She had already compromised herself beyond a level where she could ever possibly be comfortable. To have been laid up here, unconscious and defenceless, for God knows how many days? That was anathema to her. She had an opportunity now to minimise the damage. She could take a taxi to her hotel, collect her go-bag, head to the airport and leave the city.

She weighed it up for a long moment, feeling the strength in her arms, her fingers opening and closing, but then she closed her eyes and discounted it.

There was much too much uncertainty for her to be comfortable with what had happened to her. But one thing was incontrovertible: he had saved her life.

She opened the door and cleared her throat. He dropped the bags in sudden shock, turned around and gave her a rueful smile.

"You surprised me."

She checked the room. Just him.

"You are awake."

She nodded, still cautious.

"How do you feel?"

"All right."

He indicated her side. "The wound?"

She touched it, prodded it a little. "Sore, but better."

"And your back?"

She had forgotten about that. She flexed her shoulder,

then reached around and probed with her fingers. It was sore, too, and she felt the rough bumps of additional stitching. "Just a scratch."

He shook his head. "You are not fine. My friend, the doctor, said you had serious internal bleeding. Very serious. And you lost a lot of blood."

"You transfused me."

"He did. Three bags."

She looked down at the shopping bags and the food that had spilled out. Chau followed her gaze and knelt to pick up a piece of meat wrapped in greaseproof paper.

"Want some breakfast?"

CHAU HAD BOUGHT *DIM SUM*. He had dumplings, or *gao*. They were filled with vegetables, shrimp, tofu and meat, and wrapped in a translucent rice flour skin. He had steamed buns, together with meatballs, pastries and small rolls. There was a pot of *congee*, the mild-flavoured porridge that had been cooked until the rice had started to break down. She said she would take a bowl, and he doled out a serving and offered her aduki beans, peanuts and tofu as toppings. She ate quickly, realising that she was even hungrier than she thought. She cleared the plate and took two of the steamed buns, identified by Chau as *bao*.

Chau asked if she was finished and, when she said that she was, he took her plate and stood it in the sink. He boiled a kettle of water.

"*Yum cha*," he said, indicating the kettle. "Tea drinking time. I have oolong, jasmine, chrysanthemum. You like?"

"Jasmine," she said. "Thank you."

She watched as he set to work. He was fastidious about

it. He poured the boiling water into two *gaiwan*, lidded bowls for the infusion of tea leaves, and then let it stand for three minutes to cool a little. Then he took a handful of jasmine pearls and dropped them into the *gaiwan*, steamed the brew for another minute, and then handed one to her.

He put both hands around the vessel. "You drink like this," he said. He used the lid to block the jasmine pearls and sipped the liquid with long, noisy slurps.

She looked at his performance sceptically.

"You must drink it like that," he explained, without embarrassment. "The air bubbles you make when you slurp —they enhance flavour."

She gave a gentle shake of her head and sipped the tea a little more decorously.

"How long have I been out?"

"A week. My friend says it was better that you sleep."

"You drugged me."

"He did." He shrugged. "I am sorry. But he said it was best."

"What did he do to me?"

"It was a deep wound. It damaged your chest wall. Blood was gathering and needed to be removed. He drained it with tube."

A thoracostomy. Beatrix knew that she had been lucky. The knife had penetrated the musculature that protected the vital upper abdominal organs beneath. A thoracostomy was the opening of a hole to drain the blood from the pleural cavity. She would have died without it, but it wasn't a difficult procedure and it was relatively discreet. Once the blood was drained, the major risk to her recovery would have been infection. And provided that the thoracostomy tube was sterile, there was a low risk of that.

"He did all that here?"

Chau pointed to the sofa. "There. How do you feel?"

"I'm fine."

She reached for a pastry and felt a jolt of pain from her side.

"It hurts?"

There was no point in pretending otherwise. "A little."

"My friend says you must rest."

"He does?"

"He says another week."

She laughed grimly. "Impossible."

"A week, and then therapy."

"I can't afford that."

"He says you are lucky to be alive. The knife missed your vital organs. But you lost a lot of blood."

"I can't stay here," she insisted.

She tried to stand, but, as she did, she was buffeted by a deep, debilitating wave of lethargy. Not again. She had no strength in her legs and, unable to resist, she dropped back down again.

"Please, Beatrix Rose. You must rest."

"I can't. I have things to do."

"Nothing that cannot wait."

"I have to—"

"Stay here today," he insisted. "Rest. One more day, please. We will see how you feel tomorrow, yes?"

She leaned back against the wall. She could have made it out of the flat. She thought that she could summon the strength for that. But she didn't know where she was. Hong Kong suddenly seemed very big and very confusing. She could barely remember where to find her hotel. Chau's suggestion became more attractive.

"*Please*, Beatrix. It is for the best."

"One day."

11

She slept again. The dreams returned, but they were not as vibrant and real as she remembered from before. Lucas was in them. He was standing on a beach. The sand was a bright white, and the sea, washing ashore in gentle waves, was an unnaturally vivid blue. He was trying to say something, his lips moving, but she couldn't hear the words. She recognised the beach. It was in the Maldives. They had visited the islands on their honeymoon. She looked down and saw two rows of footprints in the sand. When she looked back up, Lucas was standing ankle deep in the water. She tried to take a step to him, but she couldn't move. The tide continued to roll in, the waves coming faster and deeper, the water reaching up to his waist, then his chest, and finally his neck. She reached for him as the water rose again, filling his mouth and then rising above his head, submerging him.

When the waves rolled back again, he was gone.

She looked to the beach.

There was only one set of prints.

WHEN SHE AWOKE AGAIN, the bare window was dark save for the reflected glare of neon from a sign somewhere outside. She sat up and remembered, more quickly this time, where she was and what had happened to her. She reached down to the wound in her torso and pressed against it. It was still sore, but she thought that the edge to the pain had gone.

She rose, bracing herself against the wall. There was definitely more strength in her legs. She felt grimy and unclean. She hadn't showered for... She tried to think, but she had lost track of the days. *A week?* It had been a while, however long it was.

She walked carefully to the door and went into the main room beyond. Chau was sitting in a seat with his back to her, watching an old Bruce Lee movie on a television that Beatrix had not noticed before. He hadn't heard her. She stood in the doorway for a moment, quietly looking around the room and reasserting everything in her mind. Her eyes settled on the TV and she watched, absently, for ten seconds. She recognised the film. *Enter the Dragon.*

"Good evening, Chau."

She saw him jump a little, his hand flapping up to his heart.

"I didn't hear you," he exclaimed.

"Sorry."

"How are you feeling?"

"Better."

"You look it."

"How long this time?"

"Two more days."

"*Two?* We said one."

"You did not stir, and I did not want to wake you."

"No more drugs?"

"No," he assured her. "All natural. I think it is what you needed."

She still felt uncomfortable. The prospect of her lying here, in a place belonging to a man that she didn't know, was against every one of her instincts. She had been right about it when she awoke for the first time. She was vulnerable, and the thought of that set her teeth on edge.

"Are you hungry?"

She was. She nodded and waited as Chau got up and went over to the kitchen. "Sit," he said, pointing at the armchair that he had just vacated. "I make dinner."

The chair was the only one in the flat. She didn't demur and, as he busied himself taking ingredients from the fridge, she watched the film. "You like Bruce Lee?" he asked her.

"It's all right," she said.

"You know, he grew up in Hong Kong?"

"I did."

"He was in gang. The Tigers of Junction Road. In Kowloon. Not far from here."

That made her wonder where she was, but she let the question pass. She did feel vulnerable, but, if anything was going to happen to her here, the chances were that it would already have happened. Chau had looked after her. Trust was something she rarely accorded anyone, and certainly not a man like him, but there was no reason for suspicion. She owed him that, at least.

Chau had left a bowl of chicken breasts in the fridge to marinate in soy sauce. He seared batches of the chicken in a wok, adding chillies, peppercorns, spring onions and peanuts. He made a sauce with *Shaohsing* rice wine, Chinese black vinegar and chicken stock. It wasn't long before the room began to fill with a delicious, fragrant aroma.

"It smells good, yes?"

She conceded that it did.

"It is gunpowder chicken. My mother used to make it for us. It is a dish from Sichuan province. That is where my mother and father came from. They came here to escape the communists. Do you like chilli, Beatrix?"

"I do."

"Very good."

He served the chicken in two pretty bowls. He gave her a bowl and a set of chopsticks. She ate quickly. The food was delicious and she was hungry. Chau sat cross-legged on the floor, eating more slowly, watching her. When she was done, she rested her chopsticks in the bowl and looked at him.

"You want to tell me what happened in the bar?"

He looked down, the discomfort obvious, and pursed his lips. He didn't answer.

"They were triads, weren't they?"

"Yes."

"Are you?"

"I used to work for them," he said. "No more."

She noticed that a third of the little finger on his left hand had been amputated.

Chau saw that she was looking at it. "The Japanese call it *yubitsume*," he said. "Translated, it means 'finger shortening'. It is apology to another—a tradition the triads have borrowed from the Yakuza. You take knife, slice here"—he pointed to the nub above the top knuckle—"and present it to the *Dai Lo*."

"*Dai Lo?*"

"The boss."

"Once wasn't enough for him? He wanted to do it again?"

"If more offences are committed, you take off another knuckle, or if there is no more finger, then first knuckle of next finger."

"What did you do?"

"It is more what I would *not* do," he said quietly. He sipped his tea, hoping that she would leave his answer as it was, but she held his eye and waited until he spoke again. "I chose not to work with them anymore. The *Dai Lo* did not like that. The men he sent were to persuade me to reconsider."

"But you shot them."

"They would have killed you."

"They would have *tried*."

He smiled and nodded.

"But you did kill them. The *Dai Lo* won't like that."

"I already made my decision. I will not change my mind. What I did to them is irrelevant."

There would be no chance to change it now, she thought. That die was most certainly cast. The thought came to her that being with Chau might not be the safest option for her.

"They will look for you?"

"They do not know about this place." He put his hands together and made a respectful dip of the head. "I must thank you for what you did. I am grateful." She shrugged. "It was foolish, but very brave."

It was certainly foolish, she conceded to herself. Now, in the cold light of day, she couldn't really remember why she had allowed her emotions to overwhelm her reason. She was growing sentimental. Soft. It had nearly killed her.

"You had a gun, Chau. Why didn't you show it, tell them to stop?"

"They are triads. You do not threaten triads."

"You'd let them chop off your finger?"

"No. I tried to persuade them not to."

"That wasn't going well."

"No."

"And if you couldn't persuade them...?"

"They think I should apologise. Perhaps they are right. I would have let them do it."

"But you shot them."

"You intervened. A finger would not have been enough. They would have killed you, then me."

She wondered whether it would have been better to let them take off his finger.

"May I ask, Beatrix—do you have hotel?"

"Yes," she said.

"You *must not* return to it. The triads will look for you now, too. They have many sources of information. I think it is not a difficult thing for them to find blonde Western woman, especially one as striking as you."

She frowned. She knew that he was right, that getting herself involved in his affairs would have consequences for her, too. If she had moved quickly, the same night of the attack, she would have been able to return to her room and collect her things. But she had been incapacitated. She was weak, and she would have bled out.

A week, though?

If they were looking for her, they had been handed more than enough time to find her.

But she needed to visit the hotel.

Chau noticed her discomfort. "What is it?"

"I need to go there."

"It is not safe."

"There is something there that I can't leave."

He looked concerned, his brow furrowed and his lips

puckered. Then, he stood and brushed the crumbs of his breakfast from his shirt front. "The hotel. Which one?"

"The Harbour Plaza."

"Then we must go now. Maybe we are still ahead of them."

12

———

Chau led the way to a communal lobby and summoned a single, wheezing lift. They descended ten floors and emerged into a warren of corridors. Chau led the way into the maze, seemingly confident of his direction; Beatrix was quickly lost. There were metres of electrical cable festooned across the ceilings, twisting stairwells that led up and down to who knew where, crumbling concrete and graffiti in multiple languages. They took what she guessed was a shortcut, a concrete passageway that was a shooting gallery for two old Gurkhas with loosened tourniquets around their elbows and plastic syringes discarded on the floor amid the dirt and trash.

"You know where you are?" he asked her as they descended a flight of stairs.

"Chungking Mansions," she said.

"Have you been here before?"

"Not for a long time."

They walked along another corridor lined with small restaurants, touts doing their best to lure the backpackers and tourists to dine at their restaurant rather than the identical joint next door. Steam poured out of noodle shops, and dealers hawked fake Rolexes, dried tiger penis, counterfeit clothes, cheap electrical goods, computers and mobile phones returned by European consumers within their warranty and sold on. A stall offered pirated Bollywood titles. The place had the same complex smell that Beatrix remembered from before: curry, garlic, aftershave, sweat, excrement and rot.

A young man, wearing a red Adidas tracksuit and with both ears bearing diamond stud earrings, pushed away from the wall and walked with them. He took out a laminated plastic sheet that displayed the Rolexes and Seikos that he swore were the real deal. Chau spoke to him harshly and, when he gave up and retreated to his spot, Chau was a little paler.

"Was he a triad?"

"Yes," he said. "A *maa jai.*"

"What?"

"It means little horse. Someone very junior."

Chau was even twitchier as they walked on. Triads were everywhere, Beatrix knew. They ran most of Hong Kong, let alone Chungking Mansions. The odds of one of them recognising either her or Chau were slim. But there was a chance, and the reality of that prospect had spooked him.

"You live here?" she said, trying to distract him.

"Emergency place only. No one knows I am here."

"You have family?"

"Not here. Thank God."

They found a door that deposited the throng onto Nathan Road, a six lane highway that ran the length of the Kowloon peninsula. Beatrix turned back to look at the building. Chungking Mansions were comprised of five seventeen-storey buildings. The top fifteen floors formed a single, imposing, concrete block that had seemingly been dropped atop a neon-splashed two-storey mall. The accommodation comprised guest houses that had been converted from the building's original residential apartments.

Chau led the way to the underground parking lot where he had left his Mercedes. They got inside and he set off.

"You know about triads, Beatrix?"

"What do you mean?"

"History."

Beatrix knew plenty, but she let Chau talk. He said that the triads were formed as secret societies dedicated to the overthrow of the Qing Dynasty and the restoration of the Ming. When the Qing fell, triad societies no longer had a dedicated cause and so they adjusted their purposes. Some became devoted strictly to criminal activities. Others became martial associations. Still others became labour unions and trading associations. Many were some combination of all of these.

"Joining a triad does not mean you are criminal, although most are," he said. "The greatest advantage is that you join international fraternity of like-minded individuals. You can receive assistance and protection whenever you need it. It is like, in America, when people who want job list their fraternity. They hope that the employer is of the same fraternity. You understand my English, Beatrix?"

She kept her eyes fixed out of the window and said that she did.

Chau explained how triad interests were extensive, including protection rackets in the entertainment industry, drug running, prostitution, the control of hiring on building sites, and loan-sharking. He explained how their illicit businesses operated alongside respectable ventures in the property and finance industries.

"And the man who wants you dead? The *Dai Lo?*"

"His name is Donnie Qi. There is nightclub. That is the side of himself that he presents to the world. A sleazy, unpleasant nightclub. It is appropriate, but it is not the whole of it. He is involved in all of the usual things. He is also involved in drugs."

"You said no to him because of that? Because of drugs?"

He shook his head. "That is not why he wants me. I am a cleaner, Beatrix. My business, before all this"—he waved his hand, taking in the madness of the street around them—"I cleaned offices, warehouses. It was simple job. I enjoyed it. I brought order out of chaos. It was satisfying. You know about *feng shui?*"

"Yes."

"That was what I did. It was good *feng shui.*"

"So why aren't you doing it now?"

He pulled out around a taxi that had braked to an abrupt stop. "I was asked to clean for triad. This was different. There had been a murder. Donnie Qi paid me to make the evidence disappear. They offered a lot of money and I was greedy. I did what they asked of me. I did it *too* well, perhaps. There were other jobs. Many of them. And then he asked me to kill woman and make her disappear, and I told him that I would not. That is why he is angry with me."

"There's no one you can appeal to?"

"Donnie is not popular among the other triads, but I am an outsider. You do not appeal, Beatrix. You *do.*"

Beatrix knew that he was holding something back. But they were nearer to the hotel now and she had to concentrate. She zoned out, all of her attention dedicated to their surroundings. Chau noticed and, growing tense, drove on in silence.

He pulled up outside the Harbour Plaza. Beatrix assessed. There was another hotel across the street with an underground goods entrance. She pointed at it and Chau drove, rolling over a bump and then down into the semi-darkness. There was a large wheeled bin next to a laundry van, but no one around.

He turned to her. "What is your room?"

"What?"

"The number of your room. You stay here, Beatrix. You are weak. I go."

She looked at him and allowed a smile to break across her face. He had no idea. It was almost cute.

"You are laughing at me," he complained.

"No, I'm not. It's just that you've been making assumptions about me."

"It is dangerous, Beatrix."

"You don't know anything about me, Chau. Really. Not the first thing."

"But you are injured."

"I feel much better."

"What do I not know about you?"

"I'll explain later."

He frowned his disapproval.

She asked, "You have your gun?"

He pulled up the tails of his colourful shirt. She saw the butt of the small Kel-Tec P-32, poking out from beneath his leather belt. She was tempted to take it from him, but there was a chance he might need it.

"Stay here," she said. "Keep watch. I won't be long."

"Be careful. It is the triads."

"I'm not afraid of triads, Chau."

13

Beatrix walked through reception. She moved with confidence, presenting the outward appearance of a guest with no reason to excite the attention of the staff. Her room had been reserved for a month, so there was no reason why they would be looking for her. Her attention was focussed on the other men and women around her.

A family checking in at the front desk, the father patiently explaining something to the clerk as his children ran riot behind him.

Two businessmen reading newspapers in the comfortable chairs next to the bar.

A bellhop pushing a trolley laden with luggage.

She walked through to the elevator lobby and summoned a car. A man and a woman strolled after her, standing a little too close as she waited for the lift to descend. She saw their reflection as the polished stainless steel doors parted. They spoke in English. She stepped in. They followed. She asked them what floor they wanted, having them choose first. The man asked for the third floor.

Beatrix pressed the button, and then the button for the tenth floor for herself.

The elevator stopped and the couple disembarked.

It continued up to the top of the building.

It stopped again and the doors parted. Beatrix stepped out into an empty lobby. It was quiet, the passage of a cleaning trolley muffled by the thick carpet. The lighting was subdued, the corridor darkened further by wooden panelling.

Beatrix turned right and made her way to her room.

She slid her card key into the lock. She nudged the door with the toe of her boot and allowed it to swing open. The room beyond was the kind of anonymous, blandly deco-rated accommodation that could be found in any hotel that catered to businessmen and women the world over. Beige walls, dark veneer furniture, a cream carpet. Designed to be inoffensive. The curtains were open and, beyond, she saw the impressive view over Victoria Harbour.

She saw her bag on the end of the bed, just as she had left it.

She saw her cellphone on the bureau. She was relieved. The locket was draped atop it.

The locket had Isabella's photograph inside it. She had left it there when she had gone out for a drink. She didn't have another picture. There was no way she could consider leaving it.

It was all she had left of her.

She held her breath, listening hard, and edged inside.

The door clicked to a close behind her.

She checked the bathroom. Empty.

She checked the rest of the room that was hidden from the door by the angle of the wall. That was empty, too.

She went to her bag and started to pack away the things that she had taken out. She folded her T-shirts and the spare pair of trousers and laid them inside, then went to the bathroom for her toiletries. She stopped before the mirror, frozen there by her own reflection. She looked tired and there was a haunted look in her eyes that had not been there before. The last few weeks had been impossible. She flashed back, again, to what had happened to Lucas and Isabella. When her focus returned to her reflection, she saw the wetness in her eyes and scrubbed at them before the tears could fall.

She ran the tap, filled the sink with cold water and dunked her head into it, letting the sudden shock send the fatigue away. They had murdered Lucas and she would avenge him. She just needed to find Isabella first, but there was nothing she could do as long as Control had her.

She needed money to change that.

She dried her face. As she stared at her reflection, an idea began to take shape.

She was still staring when she heard the gentle tapping at the door.

She moved as quietly as she could back to the bed. She took out the sheathed combat knife that she always kept in her go-bag. She dropped to the floor, sliding beneath the bed. It had been made up with a valance, the frilled fabric obscuring her from view save a half-inch gap above the floor through which she was able to peer out.

The tapping came again, a little louder and, then, after a short pause, there was the sound of a keycard being pushed into the reader. The lock retracted with a solid chunk, the door opened, and Beatrix watched as three men entered. The first man was wearing an expensive looking leather jacket. The second was wearing a crimson tracksuit and trainers, and the third had a vertiginous quiff that had been dyed with a white streak down the middle. The first man held a suppressed pistol. His comrades were carrying meat cleavers.

The first man spoke, a quick snatch of whispered Cantonese that Beatrix could not translate. The second man opened the big floor-to-ceiling closet and started to rifle inside, and the third went into the bathroom.

The first man walked to the bed.

He paused at the bureau, and she heard the sound of him activating her cellphone. He would look through it for messages or useful numbers. He wouldn't find any.

She slid the knife from the sheath. It had a nine-inch blade made from mirror-polished stainless steel. Her fist tightened around the Micarta hilt.

Beatrix knew she didn't have long. They wouldn't be so negligent as to not check under the bed.

The man walked closer.

Beatrix slithered nearer to the valance.

She heard him taking things out of her case and dropping them onto the bed. She watched his shoes, his right foot pressing up and down on the thick carpet.

She reached out and used the razored edge of the knife to slice through the Achilles tendons of both legs. He fell back, landing on the floor with a heavy thump. She slithered all the way out, and, as he was trying to reach for his legs, she plunged the knife deep into his heart.

The second man turned from the cupboard just as she yanked the knife out of the first man's chest and threw it at him. It was close. She couldn't miss. The blade thumped into his chest and stayed there. The man's hands dropped down to the hilt and started to prod it.

Beatrix rolled over to collect the first man's gun—a silenced Walther PPQ—and fired it. The shot blew the second man's head apart and he pirouetted away into the short corridor.

The cupboard door was mirrored and she saw the third man in the bathroom, frozen there.

She got to her feet and took a step to the side.

The angle changed.

She saw the man.

She fired, two times. The first shot went wide, splintering the door frame. The second tore into his throat. The man's arms went limp as he slumped back against the wall and slid down to his backside.

She knew that she had to move fast. There could easily be others, waiting below. She took her cellphone and stuffed it into her pocket. She secured the locket around her neck and threw the rest of her things into the go bag. She stooped down to the second man, pulled out the knife, wiped away the blood on the duvet cover, and dropped it into the bag, too. She hurried across to the window and yanked it open.

There was a fire escape that ran down the face of the building. She clambered out of the window and dropped down onto the metal landing. She started down the steps as quickly as she could. There was a short drop at the bottom and she paused, wincing at the pain in her side from the jar of the landing, and caught her breath. There were a few pedestrians walking along the harbour front and a telecoms engineer working on a telegraph pole, but nothing that gave her cause for concern. With the Walther hidden from view against the side of her leg, she walked briskly around the hotel to the road. She waited again, looking left and right. If there were any other triads in the area, they were keeping out of sight. She waited for a gap in the traffic and hurried across the road, descended into the underground lot and tossed the bag into the back of Chau's car.

She got in. *"Go."*

He drove up the ramp and merged with the traffic.

"It was all right?"

"Fine," she said.

14

Beatrix proposed that they should go for something to eat. Chau was reluctant, saying that she should rest. She knew that his suggestion was partly motivated by concern for her well-being, but, for the most part, it was because he was uncomfortable with being seen in public. That was good. She wanted him to be scared. The proposal that she had decided to make stood a better chance of acceptance if he was frightened.

He was adamant that none of the restaurants in Tsim Tsa Shui were safe, but, in the end, he agreed on a compromise. He would take her to a place that he knew, deep in the heart of Chungking. The confidence that Chau had in hiding there extended to the hundreds of restaurants that served the thousands of residents and visitors who thronged the corridors.

They accessed the building through a quiet side entrance. Chau regarded the homeless urchins who touted heroin and meth with suspicion, but, once they were inside, he allowed himself to relax. She followed him as he traced a path through back corridors and hidden stairs, emerging at last in Block E. There were a series of establishments along the corridor, each appealing to a distinct clientele. Beatrix saw a group of muscular Nigerians in tank tops and flip-flops. An African mama dressed in a traditional West African dress. Two Japanese backpackers, looking lost and confused. A family of Indians, the father sporting a pair of tight-fitting trousers with extravagant bell-bottoms. A Somali in a long robe. Arabs with their checkered scarves. They passed them all, stopping at the Khyber Pass restaurant. It was in a dreary little corner of the building, lit by blue neon, its menu highlighted by a string of flickering Christmas lights. The proprietor, sitting on a stool outside the entrance, smiled warmly at Chau as they exchanged a few words. The man looked over at Beatrix, turned back to Chau and smiled at him with a lascivious leer that he didn't even try to hide.

Chau took her to the front of the dining room, where the various dishes were displayed in green plastic tubs. There were plates piled with snails, giant crabs, emerald eels, and bloated, wart-studded toads. The final bucket contained a seething morass of brown, chubby snakes.

"What do you want?"

She settled for a bowl of vermicelli drowned in chicken stock, with a fried egg and lettuce. Chau loaded his plate with pork strips fried in crispy batter, a shrimp omelette with garlic, and steamed pak choi in oyster sauce. He paid at the counter and led the way to one of the cheap plastic picnic tables. Beatrix used chopsticks to pluck out the larger pieces of food, and a plastic spoon to drink the broth. Despite appearances, the food was delicious and she found that she was very hungry.

She watched him as they ate. He glanced down at his plate to guide his chopsticks, but his attention was focussed on the stream of people who were passing by the open door. In between bites, he chewed nervously on his bottom lip.

"What will you do now?" she asked him.

"I do not know."

"You'll leave Hong Kong?"

"I have no choice."

"But you would rather stay?"

"My business is here." And then, gloomier, "But that is all gone now."

"Donnie wouldn't listen to you if you spoke to him?"

He laughed. "Three of Donnie's men are dead, and I am the cause."

"No," she said.

"What?"

"Six."

"What?"

"The three in the bar, plus the three in my hotel room this morning. That makes *six*."

He gaped at her. "*You didn't*—"

"You said they would be looking for me. You were right."

"But I don't understand—"

"I told you that you didn't know anything about me."

"But—" he started, before running out of words.

Beatrix leaned closer to him. "You need to listen to me, Chau. *Carefully*. I have an idea."

"That's lucky, Beatrix, because I have none. Please, tell me."

"Donnie Qi is the problem."

He rolled his eyes. "Yes," he said, as if speaking to a child. "Tell me something I do not know."

"So why not solve the problem?"

"How?"

She spread her hands.

Chau laughed. "You *cannot* be serious. Kill Donnie?"

"Why not?"

"*Why not?* Because he is *Dai Lo* of the Wo Shun Wo. Do you know what that means?"

"Everyone can be killed, Chau."

He shook his head vigorously. "Not him. He is impossible to reach."

"If he was?"

"This is foolish."

"You said before that he was unpopular among the others in the triad."

"Yes."

"So they might welcome it if he was removed. Perhaps it makes a problem disappear."

"That might be so, but they will not welcome an outsider making a suggestion like that."

"Humour me, Chau. You've been speaking to someone about him. You didn't tell me his name."

She watched his face as he decided how much to tell her. In the end he sighed and shook his head, resigned. "His name is Fang Chun Ying. He is also a *Dai Lo*. Donnie runs Kowloon around the Jade Lotus. Ying has Wan Chai. He also has a club. The Nine Dragons."

"How do you know him?"

"He and Donnie pretend to be friendly, but they are not. They have competing businesses, both legitimate and illegitimate. Ying has become aware of the quality of my work. Some time ago, he asked me whether I would be interested in cleaning for him. Of course, I say no. I could not. I worked for Donnie. He would kill me if he thought I was disloyal. Ying offered me much better terms, but it was irrelevant. I say no. *Had to*. No choice. "

"And how was Ying about that?"

"Disappointed. He said Donnie was unstable—that he was dangerous to triad—and that my future would be safer with him. He is right, of course. But Ying is realist. He would not press too hard. He knows Donnie would kill me. And he knows, if he offered me his protection and Donnie defied him, there would be problem between them. There was no future in it."

"This Ying," she said. "Can you get in touch with him?"

"Yes."

"Set up a meeting."

"For what?"

She looked him dead in the eye. "How much would you give me to take Donnie out for you?"

"*You?* Are you mad?"

"How much would it be worth?"

She saw the confusion on his face. "I do not know. A lot."

"Thirty thousand."

"What purpose is this serving, Beatrix? Is it joke? You cannot help."

"Chau, I'm going to tell you something about me. I'm going to be completely honest with you, and you would be wise to believe me."

He frowned. "Okay," he said, uncertainly.

"Before I came here, I worked for my government. I was an assassin. I've killed more than a hundred people all around the world. Guns, knives, explosives, my hands when there was nothing else available. You should believe me when I say that I am the most dangerous person that you have ever met."

"That is *ridic*—" he started. As he noticed her expression change, the rest of the sentence died on his lips. "That is... it is... I... You are tourist, Beatrix."

"Those men in the bar. How many tourists do you know

who would have done that? And the three men in my hotel room?"

He started to speak, but, unsure of himself, he stopped.

"It doesn't really matter, Chau. From where I'm sitting, you don't have any option. You could run, I guess, but the triads have a long reach. How far would you get? The mainland? No. That wouldn't work. Even if you got away, you'd *always* be looking over your shoulder. You'd *always* wonder if this was the day that Donnie might finally catch up with you. That's no way to live."

"The alternative?"

"Ying. He's the alternative. If you can get him to agree, then Donnie is in play. Can you set up a meeting?"

"He can't help."

"Of course he can. You pay me thirty and I'll kill Donnie for you."

"But a man like him will be guarded. It will be difficult to get to him."

"Ying benefits with him out of the way. You said that. And he knows him. Maybe he knows where he can be found at a particular time. Somewhere I can get to him. Somewhere he is vulnerable. You can leave the rest to me."

She kept her eyes on him. He looked down at the table, his frown deepening the lines on his already furrowed brow. He put his lower lip between his teeth and bit it, nodded once, then twice, then looked up.

"I can try."

15

C hau waited at the dock as the Star Ferry nudged against the jetty. He looked across the water at the lights of the skyscrapers, reflecting in the blue. Hong Kong was two distinct urban sprawls, one on the Kowloon peninsula and the other on Hong Kong Island. The ferry was an institution, beloved both by tourists who wanted the views of the skylines on both sides of the bay and by the native workers who could not afford the fare for the subway that ran from one side to the other.

The mooring lines were tossed down and knotted around the salt-encrusted bollards. The gangway was lowered, the gate opened, and the passengers disembarked. They streamed down to the dockside and disappeared off to the waiting taxis and buses, others swallowed up by the crowds of pedestrians that thronged the area. It was six in the evening and the temperature was still hot, the air clammy and wet with humidity.

Chau looked around him. Beatrix had said that she would be here, but there was no sign of her. She had explained that they could not be seen together, but that, if he needed her, she would be at hand. He wondered whether that had been something she had said to give him some confidence.

Was she here at all?

Perhaps she had second thoughts.

Perhaps she had left him to his fate.

The boat emptied and the fresh passengers started to climb the plank and go aboard. Chau paid for his ticket and embarked. As he climbed down the steps onto the deck, he saw two men, both tall and rangy, looking at him from the bow of the ferry. He took a place by the rail, gazing down into the green waters that lapped against the side of the boat.

The engines fired, the mooring lines were cast off and tossed back aboard, and the boat set off on its return trip.

Chau looked at the two men and saw another who he recognised, walking towards him.

Fang Chun Ying was a similar age to Donnie. He wore a similar outfit, the one that all triads seemed to wear: tracksuit top, jeans, trainers.

"Chau," Ying said. "This is a surprise."

"Thank you for seeing me, Mr. Ying."

"Of course. How are you?"

"I have been better."

"Yes," he said. "I have heard about your ... *difficulties*. Your relationship with Donnie?"

"Broken."

"Why?"

"He asked me to do something I was not comfortable doing. I'll leave it at that."

Ying smiled at him, but it was not a smile of warmth or affection. His eyes did not smile. Chau knew that Ying was cold and implacable. He was more intelligent and calculating than Donnie, but no less dangerous. One did not ascend to *Dai Lo* without the capacity for unlimited violence. Donnie made no secret of his love of brutality—he revelled in it—but Ying was more discreet, something which did not reassure Chau at all. Ying's reputation was every bit as intimidating as Donnie's and, Chau knew, it was fuelled by burning ambition. He had designs on a senior position within the Wo Shun Wo. Incense Master or Vanguard. Assistant Mountain Lord. They were stepping stones on the route to Dragon Head, the man elected to lead the entire organisation.

The ferry bumped and bounced as it crossed a choppy stretch of water. Chau started to feel a little nauseous.

"Now, Chau," Ying said. "You said that you had a proposal for me. What is it?"

"Your offer. Is it still available?"

Ying smiled again, his thin lips stretching upwards just a little. "If you are as good as I have heard, then, yes, of course."

"I'm better than you've heard."

He laughed, a delicate sound that was incongruous from his mouth. "Your arrogance is well known, Chau."

"Not arrogance, Mr. Ying. *Confidence.*"

He allowed that. "My organisation always has space for talented individuals. Your particular skill is, of course, of special interest. Business is brisk. We would see that you were kept busy. But what about Donnie?"

"If that were no longer a problem?"

"Then we could certainly discuss it."

"Your terms would be the same as before?"

A small smile again. "I will be honest, Chau. Not as attractive as when we first spoke. You were in a stronger position to bargain then. Now, though, you have fewer options. Your difficulties are not to your advantage in a negotiation. I believe I am in the stronger position."

Chau gripped the rail and watched as a corporate junk slid by them in the direction of the island. "So?"

"Half of the previous amount."

"Two-thirds."

Ying chuckled again. "No, Chau. Half is my offer. If it is unacceptable, you can go back to Donnie with my best wishes."

Chau knew that he was caught. He couldn't go back, and Ying knew it. There was no point in driving a hard bargain when it had no prospect of success. "I agree."

"That is very good, Chau. I am pleased. And Donnie? What will he say?"

"He will not be happy."

"No, I should think not."

"He will kill me if he finds me."

Ying shrugged. "Then this discussion is pointless, perhaps."

"No," Chau said. "There is a solution to that."

Ying nodded, inviting him to go on.

"We could remove him as a problem."

Ying's eyebrow raised, just a little. Chau had his undivided attention now. "Are you serious, Chau? Donnie is *Dai Lo*."

"You asked if I am as good as people say. We can treat him as a demonstration."

"You will kill him?"

"And make him disappear. If no one knows what has happened to him, where is the harm?"

"I do not think you have thought this through. You want me to approve his death?"

"Not approve it. The only thing you have to do is tell me

where to find him. Somewhere he feels safe. I'll take care of the rest."

"That is a semantic difference, Chau."

"You are not friendly with him."

"No. But what you are proposing is drastic."

Ying looked out over the harbour. Chau could see that he was considering his suggestion. He knew, too, that his answer would determine the path that his life would take from this point on. There were no other cards to play if Ying turned him down. And, if he decided against him, he knew that there was a very good chance that he wouldn't have very much longer to live. If Donnie Qi found out that Ying had been talking to him, in circumstances where their conversation could only portend bad things for him, he would take grave offence. Ying would not be comfortable with risking Donnie's ire. The best way to demonstrate that Ying was not interested in causing animosity between the two societies would be to deliver Chau to Donnie.

Beatrix Rose was on the ferry somewhere, assuming that she had been true to her word, but, even so, she was just a woman. A peculiarly dangerous woman, perhaps, but a woman nonetheless. What would *she* be able to do against Ying's goons?

Chau's attention was drawn down to the rail. Ying was drumming his fingers against the metal. He was reluctant to prompt him for an answer that he expected to be bad. He knew, for sure, that he had just a few moments of liberty left. He did not want to wish them away.

Ying turned. "Let me think about it," he said. "This is not a trivial thing."

"Of course."

"What will you do in Kowloon?"

Chau exhaled. He found he had been holding his breath. "I do not know."

"I have a restaurant in Tsim Sha Shui. The Golden Lotus. Go there and tell them that Mr. Ying sent you. You will eat and drink well. Be on the last ferry back to the island. We will discuss it then."

16

Chau spent four hours wandering the streets of Kowloon. He started in Salisbury Road, turned onto Chatham Road South and then walked south on Nathan Road. He tarried in the food market, the crazed open-air bazaar where you could, it often seemed, buy absolutely anything you wanted. The place was full of life, with locals and tourists alike jostling for space. The banter of the sellers was loud and intense, and the stalls were a riot of colours. He stopped and bought a lychee from a stall that also sold oranges, pineapples and coconuts, and gazed at the dozens of chickens that had been plucked and hung from metal racks on S-shaped spikes next to beef and pork. He allowed the eddy of the crowd to jostle him along the street until he was deposited before a particularly popular attraction. An old man, so thin that he looked like a collection of skin and bones, was sitting before a basket that writhed with snakes. The man reached a hand into the basket and retrieved one of them, a greenish coloured serpent that was a little shorter than his forearm. He took a knife, made a cut at the back of its head and then, with one firm tug, skinned it. He tossed the skin behind him and dropped the snake, now pale and bloodied, into a second basket where it roiled with the others who had shared its fate, waiting to be cooked and eaten.

Chau flinched. It was difficult not to see the display as a metaphor for his own life. He was one of the snakes, waiting in the basket to be plucked out and skinned.

He wandered to the restaurant that Ying had recommended, but he had no appetite. He wondered, too, how safe it would be. If Ying had already decided to decline his offer, going into a business that he owned did not strike him as a particularly sensible idea. He would be taken out to the kitchen. Perhaps Donnie Qi would be waiting for him there. There would be no 'apology' this time. No amputation of his fingers. They would take their cleavers and hack him to pieces. No, he did not feel hungry. *Not at all*. He passed the restaurant and kept walking.

Chau looked for Beatrix, but he couldn't see her. She had explained that they could not meet until they were back at Chungking Mansions, but she had promised that she would be close at hand in case the meeting with Ying went badly. He was beginning to doubt that. *Paranoia?* Possibly. But why would a woman whom he barely knew want to involve herself in a scheme that would involve the murder of a triad leader? The more he walked, and the more he thought about it, the more it seemed likely that she had abandoned him. *What was he thinking?* He was putting all of his hope in this one woman, and the only experience he had with her had been to watch her attack the three triads who had set about him. It wasn't just naïve; it was foolhardy. She was a *lunatic*, and he had played himself into a position where he had no one to depend upon but her.

He ambled back to the dock and joined the queue of people waiting for the gates to open. He looked around, but he couldn't see Ying. He couldn't see Beatrix, either. As he stood there, shuffling impatiently from foot to foot, he realised how stupid and credulous he had been. He should have fled to the mainland. Donnie Qi might have found him, but his chances would have been better than they were in this insane scheme.

"Move!"

He turned around, fear all over his face. He didn't recognise the man behind him.

"The gates are open," the man said irritably. "*Move!*"

Chau turned back and saw that the man was right. He apologised and shuffled ahead, across the gangplank and onto the ferry that would take him back to the island. Back to Donnie Qi, Fang Chun Ying and the short, brutal fate that destiny had planned for him.

CHAU TOOK the same spot at the rail as before. The lights of the city played out across the rolling waters in long painterly strokes.

He looked around for any sign of Beatrix. There was none. As he swivelled, looking left and right, he saw Fang Chun Ying's bodyguards approach him. They stopped ten feet away. Ying was nowhere to be seen. One of the men brushed through the crowd and took the space on the rail next to him. He had a cigarette in his mouth, the tip flaring red as he drew down upon it.

"There is a place," he said. "A brothel. It is in Tsim Sha Shui. The Venice. Do you know it?"

"I think so."

"Donnie Qi has a girl there. He visits her every week."

"When?"

"*Tonight.*"

17

---

eatrix took the Tsuen Wan line to Mong Kok station. It was eleven when she passed out of the station exit and emerged onto the Tsim Sha Shui street outside. The atmosphere was hectic, a shifting morass of revellers piling into and out of the station. The street was lit by an onslaught of flashing neon that advertised the businesses nearby: the vast bars of Ned Kelly's Last Stand and Bottoms Up, as well as tens of competing dives and nightclubs. She passed through a throng of *gaai bin dong* vendors, their brightly covered handbarrows loaded with an array of aromatic wares. The barrows were lit by paraffin lamps, their warm amber glow filling the street and illuminating the faces of the vendors as they proclaimed why their food was better than the food offered by their rivals.

Beatrix had intercepted Chau as he had disembarked from the ferry. She told him to meet her in a bar that she had suggested and then followed fifty feet behind him to ensure that he was not followed. He had informed her of the opportunity to dispose of Donnie Qi and, after a moment of tactical consideration, she had determined that this was likely to be the best chance that they would get.

She ignored the mad display and followed the directions that Chau had given her. The Venice was on Portland Street, a popular thoroughfare that ran north to south, parallel to the main drag of Nathan Road. It extended through the districts of Yau Ma Tei and Mong Kok. It was a place where high commerce and base human nature existed cheek by jowl. It was dominated by a large business and retailing skyscraper complex, but gathered around it were massage parlours, karaoke joints, hostess bars, cheap restaurants and the brothels of its infamous red-light district. Girls paraded in windows in cheap lingerie. Signs in the windows promised a good time in Cantonese, Mandarin, English, and a host of other languages. Neon signs suspended above the crowds advertised half-naked girls, pouting open-mouthed at the camera, and the promise of live flesh.

Beatrix walked north, passing restaurants with names like Supreme Beef and Brisket and Yokohama Japanese. She passed the Portland Street Rest Garden on her left, crossed over Pitt Street, passed a 7-Eleven, the Sun Shine Centre and Galaxy Wi-Fi, until she saw the brothel she was looking for. She paused on the other side of the street. She surveilled it discreetly, looking at its reflection in the window of the karaoke bar opposite. A large neon sign was affixed to the wall, with VENICE SAUNA written in flashing green next to a representation of a Roman arch. Chau had explained that it was owned by Fang Chun Ying, an outpost amid Donnie Qi's territory. Donnie tolerated it. He patronised it to make a point that he was magnanimous.

She saw that the front door was wide open, with a large man just visible in the neon-tinged gloom inside. Triad security. The building was three storeys tall, with two covered windows on each floor. The street in both directions was busy with idling passers-by, plenty of them drunk and looking for a good time. She saw a loose group of men, their hair cut short in regulation buzz cuts, crew from the *Nimitz* looking for a good time with the Filipina women who worked the clubs. She walked on, the men staggering along the road to her left. She continued for five minutes, turned when the road reached the end, and then came back.

She crossed the street to the entrance. To the right was a small lobby with an open door, obscured by a curtain of beads. There was a flight of stairs straight ahead.

The big man pushed himself away from the wall and blocked her way inside. "What you want?" he asked.

"Mr. Ying sent me."

"For?"

"Donnie Qi."

"You?"

"That's right." She stared him out. "Problem?"

"He didn't say—"

"He didn't say it would be a woman?"

"He didn't say that it would be a *gweilo*. You have no place here."

"You want to call Mr. Ying about it?"

The man grunted, his demeanor changing from hostility to a kind of lazy distaste. "Upstairs," he said.

She climbed the stairs and reached a waiting area. A *mamasan*, dressed in a cheap leather miniskirt and smoking a cigarette, was negotiating with a potential customer. A girl had been brought out for him. She was Asian, and pretty, but he was not impressed.

"White girl," he said, in English, speaking slowly and deliberately. "Not Filipina."

"Russians all busy. One hour. You wait."

The man shook his head. He turned, saw Beatrix, and, as if suddenly embarrassed, he scurried down the stairs.

The *mamasan* looked angrily at Beatrix. "You make customer go. You make him ashamed."

"Mr. Ying sent me."

She harrumphed.

"Donnie Qi."

Recognition dawned, and then bled into surprise.

"Where is he?"

The woman assessed her, wrinkled her nose, and pointed down the corridor that led away from the waiting area. "Room with red door."

Beatrix nodded.

The *mamasan* stepped aside.

Beatrix took the corridor.

onnie Qi stretched over so that he could reach the crystal meth that he had left on the stool beside the bed. He took the baggie and his glass pipe and rolled onto his side. It was good shit, manufactured in an underground lab in the Philippines and smuggled to Hong Kong by the triads. Donnie had bought a pound of it, and, before he handed over his money, he'd had it tested. It was ninety-nine per cent pure. Some of his more old-fashioned colleagues had a problem with selling drugs. But, with ice as good as this—pure enough to bulk out and sell for a serious profit—he knew they would come to accept it.

His woman, Chuntau, reclined on the bed next to him, naked, a sheet covering her from the waist down.

"Got some for me, baby?"

He ignored her, putting a small pile of ice into the bowl and placing his lips around the slender stem. He took his lighter, thumbed the flame, and held it underneath the bowl. The meth liquefied and then began to smoke. He moved the lighter quickly back and forth beneath the bowl, playing the flame across it, and inhaled. He removed the heat, but the meth continued to smoke. He inhaled until his lungs were full, and the meth had started to recrystallise.

He waited for the hit, gazing with absent-minded interest at the 1980s porn that was playing on the TV. It came on him quickly, a dizzying rush that prickled his skin and sent a spasm of delicious energy around his body.

"Donnie?"

He handed her the bowl and his lighter. She was a fine girl. She was nineteen and had run away from a life in Shenzen where the height of her ambition would have been to work in one of the big Foxconn factories, making electrical goods that she would never have been able to afford. Her name meant spring peach and that, he thought, was about right. Big tits, nice arse. Donnie could have taken her away from here, and he had considered it many times. It wasn't as if she had never asked him. He had declined. There was something about the nature of their relationship that gave him particular pleasure. It was no more than a commercial arrangement. He paid, she performed. There was no emotion and no attachment. That, it seemed to him, was one of the reasons why he found such enjoyment in visiting her here. He could make her do whatever he wanted, just by taking out another note from his wallet and tossing it onto the floor with all the others.

There was more to it, of course. It was squalid and cheap and that, he knew, was another reason. It was a ready reminder of his upbringing in the slums not too far from here, and of all the girls like her who had looked down their noses at him. He had been a runt of a child, skinny and nervous, and he knew that they had looked at him and had come to the conclusion that he would amount to nothing. They would not have looked at him that way today. He had money, more than they could imagine. He had power. He had respect. He could buy and sell them, and he did. It did him no harm to be reminded of where he came from. It whetted the edge of his ambition. It made him hungrier to *succeed*.

Chuntau was quiet. He looked over at her. She was asleep.

The meth hit his brain and his eyes rolled back into his head. He slumped down into the embrace of the sweaty sheets, listening to the frantic sounds of the street outside.

He heard the creak as the door to the room was pushed open. He blinked, trying to focus. He saw a white woman with blonde hair and blue eyes, standing there. She was lit by the flickering naked bulb in the hallway, an on and off glow that alternately silhouetted her and then cast her in darkness.

"Who are you?" he said. It was an effort to speak through the torpor of the drug.

She said nothing.

"Wrong room. Get out."

She stepped inside.

Something was wrong, but the cloud in his brain was so thick and cloying that he couldn't think what it was.

She closed the door.

What was it? His thoughts were scrambled, and he couldn't make sense of them. A white woman. He knew there was something that he needed to remember.

What was it?

She took another step inside and unzipped the leather jacket that she was wearing.

He smiled then, propping an elbow beneath him so he could raise his head a little. He grinned, hungry and lascivious. "Maybe not wrong room. Ying sent you?"

"Yes," she said.

Donnie and Ying had clashed lately. The older man was too conservative, almost constitutionally unable to grasp the scope of the opportunities that the new modern world had made available to men like them. He was obsessed with staying beneath the surface, better to avoid the attention of the authorities on the mainland. Donnie knew that the Chinese were corrupt. He had politicked for the triad to open direct lines of communication with them. Ying and his cronies in the old guard had shouted him down, the same way they had tried to stop him from selling meth.

Perhaps Ying had changed his mind. Perhaps this was a peace offering?

He patted the bed. "Come over here."

She did.

Donnie pressed himself into a sitting position. He caught sight of himself in the cracked mirror that was fixed to the wall. He was lithe, muscled, his skin covered in tattoos that were themselves daubed in a sheen of sweat.

The woman drew closer so that Donnie could see her more clearly. She was very beautiful, with porcelain skin and cool eyes. He grinned at her. The ice fired his appetite. He was ready to go again. He saw her looking at the glass pipe on the stool.

"You want?"

"Sure," she said.

As he turned away from her and reached to the stool, he realised what it was that was bothering him.

Chau.

The bar where three of his men had been shot.

The hotel where another three had been killed.

The blonde white woman.

The *gweilo*.

Fuck.

He tried to get off the bed, but the meth was thick and fogging his brain. His legs became tangled in the damp sheet. He kicked the sheet off, but, his balance gone, he fell off the edge and landed on the bare floorboards between the edge of the bed and the wall.

He scrambled to his feet, his back pressed against the peeling paint. The woman had come around the bed. He looked down at her hand. She was holding a syringe.

He was naked now that the sheet had fallen away. He picked up the lamp from the floor and threw it at her, but she deflected it with a sweep of her arm.

He backed up, into the corner, with nowhere to go.

The woman stepped up and thumped her right fist against the fleshy part of his thigh. He felt the prick of the needle and the sensation of something cold, working its way up his leg and into his groin. He felt woozy. His balance deserted him and he tumbled down onto the bed. He tried to roll over—to look up—but he couldn't. All he could see were a series of circles in an ever tightening spiral. The last thing he could remember was the feeling of taking a deep breath of cold, sweet air.

19

There was a place to park the van at the back of the brothel. Chau got out, pulled back the sliding door and collected his bag. He suspected that he would need to make more than one trip, but the large leather satchel contained the things that he knew that he would always need. He made his way across the uneven ground to the alley that ran between the buildings, opening out onto Portland Street at its other end. There were entrances to the buildings on either side, and he opened the door to the Kimberly and climbed the stairs to the top floor.

A woman in a tight leather skirt was waiting there. The *mamasan* pointed down the corridor. Chau followed her directions.

He rapped quietly on the last door.

It opened, and Beatrix Rose let him inside.

Donnie Qi was on the floor. He was naked save for the plastic bag that had been tied around his head.

"Are you...?"

"I'm fine."

"And...?"

She pointed at the body. "What do you think? It's done."

"And?"

"Relax, Chau. It was easy."

He came inside and shut the door. He had promised Ying that he would make a good job of this. Donnie would disappear. This was a very good start.

"He was alone?"

"There was a girl with him."

"Where is she now?"

"The *mamasan* took her away."

"Did she see what happened?"

"No."

"We should be sure—"

"No," she interrupted. "She was asleep. Doped to the eyeballs. She won't remember anything."

"I said no witnesses—"

"No, Chau. She didn't see anything. You'll have to trust me. *Nothing* happens to her. Non-negotiable."

He could see that there was no point in arguing with her. And he was relieved that she was so firm on the matter. He really had no wish to hurt anyone else. "Fine."

Chau opened the leather satchel, took out the folded plastic sheet and spread it over the floorboards. He took out his butchery tools: a meat saw, a bone saw, and two heavy cleavers. In the van were two large rucksacks he had bought from a trader he knew back at Chungking Mansions. They just needed to get Donnie into the bags, and then he could be taken out of the brothel, back to the van and then disposed of.

Chau had a contact at the Goodbye Dear Pets Cremation Centre in Yeun Long San Tin. For a thousand dollars, he could have the body parts incinerated at the same time as the remains of a dog or cat.

He took out his disposable plastic coverall and started to put it on. "You can go," he said to her.

She took off her jacket and dropped it in the corner of the room. "We've got to be quick, right?"

"I said we would be."

"Then I'll stay and help. You got another of those?"

"Yes."

She went into the satchel, took the suit out and unfolded it.

"You don't have to help me, Beatrix."

She put the suit on, pulling the hood over her head. She took one of the cleavers. "Ready?"

20

J ackie Chau parked his van in front of his warehouse on Kai Hing Road, got out and looked around. Caution was habitual now. He had been careful before, but the experience of the last few weeks and the attention from Donnie Qi and his men had made him even more aware of his surroundings and the threats that could be hidden within them.

He undid the padlock, pulled back the hasp and gave a firm upwards yank, sending the roller door up toward the ceiling. He went back to the van and drove inside.

He stepped down and shut the door.

"Chau."

He spun around in shock. Beatrix was waiting for him. She was wearing a black leather bomber jacket and black leather trousers.

"You gave me shock," he complained.

She must have been watching the building. He had thought that he had been careful. But he had quickly come to learn that if she didn't want to be seen, then she would make herself quite invisible. He knew what she was capable of, too—those expressions of controlled violence—and the thought of her hiding in the shadows was not one that was likely to make a man sleep easily at night. It was the reason that he had instantly dismissed the notion of welching on their deal. Thirty thousand was a lot, but there was no amount of money that would have made him comfortable with the prospect of her as his enemy. It would take every last cent that he had, but he was prepared to pay it.

Besides, he had a proposal to put to her.

"Have you got it?" she said.

"Yes," he said. "In the office."

She followed him to the iron stairs. Chau went up first, unlocked the office and held the door open for her. She went inside and he went in after her. The money was in a counterfeit Hello Kitty rucksack that he had bought in Chungking Mansions. It appealed to his sense of humour; thirty thousand US stuffed into a bag that he had bought for ten Hong Kong dollars.

"Seriously?"

"I have another bag if you would prefer."

She took it from him. "You're a funny guy, Chau, anyone ever tell you that?"

"All the time."

She slung the bag over her shoulder.

"You do not want to count it?"

"You know it would be stupid to short-change me."

That was the truth.

"I have spoken to Mr. Ying," he said.

"I hope he was pleased."

"Very pleased. And impressed."

"Well, that makes me happy," she said sardonically. "And Donnie?"

"Gone."

"What are people saying?"

"Many things. That he has been killed, of course. Or that he has been chased away. Some have even suggested that he is working with the police. Much speculation."

"None of which can be traced back to you."

"No. Ying knows, of course, but it is not in his interest to reveal his hand in it."

"Then it's done."

She turned to the door again, about to go. Chau needed to broach the subject now or he would lose his chance. If she left without him speaking to her about what he had in mind, there would be no second chances. She would be gone forever; he knew that for a fact. He would never see her again.

"He said something to me that I thought you might like to hear."

"That's probably unlikely, Chau."

"Will you hear me out?"

She rubbed her palm against her cheek, and, exhaling, leant back against the wall. "One minute. Go."

"Good," he said. "Good. A cup of coffee? Something stronger? I have a bottle of sake."

"No," she said, shaking her head. "Fifty seconds. Get on with it."

He nodded and spoke quickly. "As I said, I have spoken to Mr. Ying. I will be working for him from now on, as you know. There is a lot to do. A man like Mr. Ying—the organisation he works for—well, you understand business is brisk."

"Twenty seconds."

He flapped his hands. "Yes, yes, of course. Mr. Ying explained that, most times, the people that are in the way of the triad's business are easy to reach. But, other times, people can be more difficult. They are cautious; they take precautions. Perhaps they have guards, or they rarely move away from places that can be defended. He said Donnie Qi was easy—"

"Then he should have done it himself."

"—and that others would be more of a challenge. They need someone who would not be suspected."

She folded her arms across her chest. "He have anyone in mind for this?"

"You have made an impression on him, Beatrix. The men in the bar. The men in your hotel room. And now Donnie Qi. He wants me to introduce you."

"That's not going to happen."

"No. I said you would not be prepared to do that. But you still need money, yes?"

She shrugged, declining to answer, but Chau could tell that she did.

"Then perhaps I have a proposal. I will work with Mr. Ying. Front man. He will supply me with the name of the person he is interested in, and I will supply it to you. We can consider each person on their merits. If they are acceptable, then it can be as it was for Donnie Qi. You can do what needs to be done and I will make them disappear."

He stopped, watching her face. She was inscrutable.

"The Chinese have an expression, Beatrix. '*Life is meat.*' Life is temporary. Life comes and goes; it is brutal and it is hard. The men and women who have crossed Ying know that this is a consequence that might come to them. Life is meat. There are no innocents."

She was silent.

"Beatrix?"

She pushed herself off the wall and stooped to collect the bag of money. "I'll think about it."

"We will be able to ask for more," he said. "Thirty thousand is low for something so professional."

"I said that I'd think about it."

She left the office and started down the stairs.

Chau followed.

"Do you want to know what he called you?"

"Not particularly."

"He called you *gweilo*. You know this word?"

She stopped. "Foreigner. It's not a compliment."

"Yes, that is right. But it also means something else. *Gwái* means ghost. He says that he has tried to find out about you, but that he has found nothing. You appear, you do work, you disappear"—he clicked his fingers—"like ghost. It is as I say, Beatrix. You have made an impression on him, and he is not a man to easily impress."

She continued on without answering, but he saw the flicker of something across her face. Interest? Curiosity?

Maybe.

"Mr. Ying will want an answer," he called down after her.

"I'm sure he will."

He followed. "How will I know?"

She zipped up her jacket and turned to him.

"How will I find you, Beatrix?"

"You won't," she said. "I'll find you."

PART II

21

B eatrix followed the man, staying a steady thirty metres behind him. She looked over her shoulder and saw Chau on the other side of the street, adjacent to her, ready to step in should she feel the need to drop back. They were on Lockhart Road, in the historic Wan Chai district that mixed flashy new bars with ageing topless joints. It recalled the image of Hong Kong as a port city that catered to the basest appetites, and it was that reputation, and the cheap beer, that attracted the bankers and professionals from the nearby offices in Central. The newer establishments, swanky and bright, could polish their chrome and glass as much as they liked, but the stain of sleaze would always stick to this part of town. It was a fundamental reason for its appeal.

It was a hot evening, with the mercury well into the upper nineties, and there was a cloying humidity in the air. Beatrix was sweating, but, save an occasional, almost unconscious, swipe of her hand to clear the sweat from her forehead, she gave it no heed.

Her concentration was focused on the man ahead of her.

David Doss was an English ex-pat who had risen to a senior position in a well-regarded international law firm. The practice had made its reputation through its litigation division, but it had developed a considerable banking practice in Southeast Asia with the Hong Kong office as its headquarters. Doss was fifty years old, married with two children, and had, for the last six months, been seconded to work with the commissioner of the Hong Kong Independent Commission Against Corruption. That was an unfortunate career move when considered against the scope of his life expectancy. The posting had led to his name and details being passed to Beatrix.

Beatrix heard Chau's accented English in her ear, "*He goes to club.*"

Beatrix and Chau were communicating via an open phone line, both of them wearing headphones with in-line mics. Beatrix had worked with super high spec Japanese gear before, the kind of receivers and transmitters that were so small they were almost invisible, but they would have cost thousands and she didn't have the hookup any more. This, although a little more obvious, would have to do. Solo surveillance was difficult. Beatrix had taught Chau the rudiments of careful pursuit, but he was still too raw to use hand signals confidently and being able to speak provided her with some useful redundancy and him with the peace of mind that he could always reach her in the event that he was made. So far, it had worked well enough.

She had been hesitant about accepting Chau's offer to work under Fang Chun Ying, but her need for some form of income had given her little choice. Beatrix's talents were valuable in the Hong Kong underworld and the payments on offer were sizeable. This was no time for morality, with Isabella still held by Control and Group Fifteen.

"Wait. He is stopping."

Beatrix glanced up ahead and saw that Chau was right. Doss had stopped at the side of the pavement, reached into his pocket and taken out his wallet. She couldn't very well stop herself, not without giving away her pursuit to anyone who might be watching him, so she turned into Coyotes, one of the most popular bars in this part of town.

"Go ahead thirty metres and then stop," she instructed.

"I know what I am doing, Beatrix."

She raised her eyebrow at that. Two hours of training with her and now he thought he was a professional. She had explained to him that if the target stopped suddenly, he had to keep going. If it was a move designed to flush out a tail, people who stopped at the same time would be made immediately.

It was seven in the evening, and the bar was starting to fill with the *gweilo* workers who had made the decision that, seeing as it was Friday, they would risk the ire of their bosses by leaving the office after a twelve rather than a fourteen-hour day.

Beatrix pretended to occupy herself with an old-fashioned jukebox, knowing that Chau would continue the surveillance from the other side of the street.

She looked around at the men with their shirtsleeves rolled up and the women in their expensive dresses. The atmosphere was awkward, no one quite drunk enough yet to relax, staccato small talk the best that anyone could do. The bar was doing its best to compensate. Music played loud and the Happy Hour drinks were half the price of a bar on Land Kwai Fong. There was an antique dentist's chair at the back. It was unoccupied for the moment, but, when things started to pick up, it would be busy with men and women prepared to pay fifty bucks for the privilege of lying back and having the barman pour neat triple sec and tequila straight down their throats.

Beatrix noticed one of the men at the bar, looking her up and down.

She turned away from him and lowered the bag she was carrying to the ground.

"*He's gone into the drugstore,*" Chau reported.

Beatrix knew a little about the target. He hadn't shown any particular caution, despite the inherent danger that came with a job like his. Perhaps he thought he was above being threatened by the triads he was investigating. Perhaps he was just naïve. It didn't really matter. His sudden halt might have been the move of someone who was trained in detecting a tail, but Beatrix didn't think so. She guessed that he had stopped in the drugstore to pick up a tube of breath mints or a pack of condoms. He had a wife and children back in the United Kingdom, but her quick assessment of him had revealed a man who took advantage of his money and the host of eager local women who were impressed by affluence. He dressed younger than his years, with trousers that were a little too tight, buckled shoes that were a little too ostentatious, and a haircut that was just a little too fashionable.

His attitude would be the death of him.

Beatrix guessed that she had a couple of minutes to dispense with and so, to avoid drawing attention to herself, took a coin from the pocket of her jeans and slotted it into the jukebox. She selected 'Gimme Shelter' by The Stones and made a show of listening to it.

The man from the bar detached himself from his friends and came across to her. He was wearing an expensive suit that most likely cost about as much as a small family car. He looked unpleasantly confident.

"Nice," he said, nodding to the jukebox.

Beatrix ignored him.

"My name's Neal."

She turned her gaze onto him. He had an even salon tan, an expensive clip on his expensive tie, and solid silver cuff-links of a dollar and a pound that showed on the creamy inch of shirt sleeve that was visible beneath the cuffs of his jacket.

"You like The Stones?"

"*He is moving,*" Chau said.

"What's your name?" the man asked her.

Beatrix stooped to collect her bag.

"You're very enigmatic," the man said with a leer that she supposed was intended to be alluring.

She went right by him and into the brightness of the evening.

Beatrix walked quickly until she saw Doss again. He was passing one of the 7-Elevens in the area. The store specialised in alcohol, and encouraged customers to linger outside to consume the drinks that they had purchased. He passed through the clutch of men and women drinking from bottles of Guinness and Peroni and kept going. Beatrix reached the storefront twenty seconds later, looking up and across the street and noticing Chau.

"Stay ahead of him," she said.

She dropped back again, watching Doss's grey hair as his head bobbed up and down in the flow of traffic. Doss was a touch over six feet, still reasonably tall for a man in Hong Kong, and his charcoal grey suit would stand out until he reached The Corners, the intersections of Lockhart Road with Luard Road, and then Fenwick Street. Crowds of busi-nessmen and women were beginning to congregate around two of the more upscale, less sleazy bars in Wan Chai. The first bar, on Luard Road, was Mes Amis. It had an open facade and Doss had visited it when she had scouted him last week. It seemed that it was one of his regular haunts.

They drew closer to the intersection, the cheap neon signs already pulsing on and off and loud music pumping out of open doorways. Rickshaws angled through the tumult, scooters and mopeds overtaking them, bells ringing and engines whining. Girls hovered in doorways, looking for *gweilos* to buy them overpriced drinks. A homeless man slumped in the mouth of an alley, the upturned cap laid out before him scattered with a few coins.

Just as Beatrix was expecting Doss to turn into the bar, he stopped, turned back to face her and fiddled with his mobile phone. Beatrix kept walking, allowing herself to be hidden behind the slow-moving group of secretaries who formed a buffer between him and her. She would have to continue right past him if he stayed still. If she stopped when he stopped, she would risk being made, but he didn't wait long enough for that to be a problem. He turned, slipped his phone back into his pocket, and walked on.

"Here we go," she said.

He slowed again, picking a path through the busy crowd outside the bar, and went inside.

"*What do you want me to do?*"

"Just as we said. Watch the front."

eatrix observed as Chau slowed down and then stepped into the restaurant across the street from the bar. He negotiated with the waiter and was shown to a seat in the window, where he would be able to keep watch without revealing himself to anyone else who might be following Doss tonight. Beatrix, satisfied that the coverage of the front entrance was adequate, followed the alleyway that ran down the side of the building until she reached a door. It was open, standing ajar just enough so that she could see inside to the kitchen beyond. There were two chefs, both preparing food with their backs to her. The room was full of steam and noisy with the sound of the radio that was tuned to Sing Tao, the Cantonese radio station that was a favourite of the man who owned the grocery store where Beatrix usually collected her supplies.

She opened the door, slipped inside, and, after checking that the rest of the kitchen was empty—it was—she turned sharply to the left, went through a set of folding doors and followed the corridor back into the club.

She came across a waiter laden down with a tray of dirty

plates and glasses and stepped aside to let him pass. He paused, looking at her quizzically. She didn't hesitate, finding her way to a flight of stairs and then, at the top, a small lobby with three doors. The sound of discordant singing could be heard through the door that was directly in front of her. The other doors opened into the club's bathrooms. Beatrix pushed open the door to the ladies' and went inside, locking it behind her.

"Chau," she said.

"*I am here. Where are you?*"

"Inside. Where is he?"

"*He has not come out.*"

"Hold position."

"*I understand.*"

Beatrix placed her bag next to the sink, opened it and removed the knock-off Chanel dress that she had purchased from a Kowloon stall that afternoon. She undressed, removing her jeans and T-shirt and folding them neatly, sliding them into the bag. She dropped the dress over her head and tugged it so that it fell smoothly, accentuating her slender curves. She went back into the bag and took out a black wig. She settled it on her head, arranging it so that her blonde tresses were obscured. She took out a lipstick, pouted, and applied it with a careful, steady hand. She withdrew an eye shadow stick and painted around her eyes. Finally, she fetched a dark mascara and thickened her lashes with it.

When she was done, she gazed at her reflection. She hardly recognised herself.

She reached back into the bag and took out a small triangle of paper. The edges had been folded over to form an improvised sachet. She opened it very, very carefully. The powder inside was still there. *Ricin*. Beatrix had purchased the plant from a dealer of herbs in Kowloon. She had planted it next to a crape myrtle that was in the centrepiece of the window box that she had fitted to her windowsill. As the summer progressed, her little castor bean plant, *Ricinus communis*, had burgeoned. It developed red-veined leaves that were shaped like stars and unfolded small red flowers. Its fruit were small coral balls that were covered with spines. Beatrix had harvested the seed pods and crushed them, revealing brown seeds that were about the size of haricot beans.

Ricin had been the poison of choice in Group Fifteen for many years. It was six thousand times more potent than cyanide, twelve thousand times more deadly than rattlesnake venom. The KGB had used it first: the case in 1979, when they had assassinated the Bulgarian diplomat Markov in London. The man died after being shot with a tiny bullet that contained ricin, delivered using a pressurized gas mechanism in the tip of an umbrella.

She had used ricin before, but she had never had to produce it herself. She had put the beans in a solvent to break down the oils and fats, filtering the slurry with water and hydrochloric acid and allowing it to form a powder. A 425 mg dose would be enough to kill most men. Beatrix had more than that. The poison was deadly because it could be inhaled or ingested, was quickly broken down in the body, and was virtually undetectable.

It was perfect.

She folded the triangle again, took a small clutch from the bag, and slipped the ricin inside.

She zipped up the bag and looked around the small room. She lowered the lid of the toilet and stood on it, reaching up to the ceiling. It was comprised of UPVC panels. She probed with her fingers until she found a point of weakness, then pushed up until she separated the panel from its neighbours and opened a small aperture. She stuffed the bag inside, then slid the panel back into place.

She pressed the earphones back into her ears and held the mic to her throat.

"Chau?"

"*Still here.*"

"The target?"

"*He has not come out.*"

"Stand by. I'm going dark."

"*Dark?*"

She rolled her eyes. *For fuck's sake.*

"Quiet, Chau. I'm going quiet."

She removed the earphones and put them and the phone into her clutch, unlocked the door and went outside.

23

S he found her way to the bar. Doss was there, sitting at the same stool that he had chosen when she had scouted him last week. He was a regular, well known enough to the bar staff that they didn't need to ask him what he would like to drink. The bar was growing busy, but he was the only one sitting there. She was able to sidle alongside without too much bother.

The barman turned to her.

"Yes, madam?"

"Gin and tonic, please."

"Which gin?"

"Hendrick's. With cucumber and lots of ice."

The barman nodded, took a glass and filled it with ice. He took a bottle down from the lit display rack, unscrewed the lid and free-poured a generous measure.

Doss turned to her.

"You know your gins."

"Excuse me?"

"Most people drink Hendrick's with lime."

Beatrix smiled, making sure it came across as a little tentative. "It's my one vice."

The barman added tonic and gave it to her with the bill. "Eighty, please."

Doss pointed to the bill. "Put it on my tab."

"You don't have to do that," Beatrix said.

He waved her half-hearted objection away.

"Thank you."

"I'm David." He extended a hand.

"Suzy. Nice to meet you."

She shook his hand. He had a limp, damp handshake. Unimpressive. Weak.

She had investigated his background thoroughly before accepting the assignment. The Independent Commission Against Corruption was an attempt by the authorities to at least make it appear as if effort was being expended in tackling the triads. It was a shameless PR move, but it still had the ability to be a nuisance.

Doss had caused a commotion with one investigation in particular. Ten years earlier, a huge fire had wiped out the Shek Kip Mei Squatter Area, rendering fifty thousand Chinese homeless. The government had awarded a billion dollars' worth of contracts to build new accommodation on the site. The local triads, sensing an opportunity to gorge on the largesse, had swarmed in like sharks around a bloody corpse. They formed dozens of small construction firms and, building cheaply and quickly, were responsible for a good proportion of the renewal work. In order to increase their margins, substandard materials were used. Corners were cut. Rules on safety were flouted, with inspectors paid generous backhanders or threatened with violence in order for the works to be approved.

And then, two years ago, one of the blocks had collapsed

and trapped more than two hundred people amid the rubble. Fifty-three were killed. The press, unusually, found its voice. ICAC was charged with investigating the original contracts, and the early word was that evidence had been secured implicating several very powerful triad figures. There was a rumour that the evidence led all the way up to a Dragon Head, one of the men elected to govern the loosely affiliated organisations. Despite his limp and ineffectual appearance, Doss had proven himself to be a tenacious investigator.

The job had been passed to Beatrix in the same way as the others. Mr. Ying had contacted Chau, and the two of them had met on the Star Ferry in the harbour between Wan Chai and Kowloon. He had provided a name, a photograph, and an envelope that contained two hundred and fifty thousand Hong Kong dollars. Twenty thousand sterling. Thirty-two thousand US. It was a down payment. The second two hundred and fifty would be paid upon completion of the job. Chau contacted Beatrix to provide her with the target's details and her half of the money. Beatrix took over then, running a full scout on the person she had been tasked to eliminate. Doss had been no more difficult than any of the five other men that had been unfortunate enough to cross her path.

He held onto her hand for a beat too long.

"What do you do, Suzy?"

She removed her hand. "I'm in management."

"Here on business, then?"

"That's right."

"What do you make of it?"

She made a show of her guileless grin as she waved her hand about her. "It's crazy, right?"

He turned all the way around on his stool so that he was facing her. "You haven't been before?"

"First time."

"You'll have to let me show you around."

"Oh, I don't know—"

He smiled at her. "I'm sorry."

"No, it's all right."

"You don't think me too forward?"

"Of course not."

She asked him what he did, and he explained that he was a lawyer. What kind of lawyer? she asked. He gave her a five-minute explanation of his résumé that had all the hallmarks of something that he had down pat. He tried hard to make it sound exciting, dropping little hints that he must have imagined would be tantalising to her. She made a show of listening, encouraging him to continue, but she was really assessing the situation. The bar was busy, and getting busier, but she could see no CCTV and there was nothing about the two of them that would stay in the mind any more than any other patron. If there ever was an investigation, she wanted to make it as unlikely as possible that the death could ever be traced back to her. Satisfied that the odds of that happening were suitably long, even if the cause of Doss's death was correctly diagnosed, and even if there was some way of evidencing the fact of this meeting, it would be impossible to attribute it to Beatrix. She was anonymous, a spectre, flitting back into the shadows, hidden among the seven million other souls who were crushed together in the city.

Doss talked for five minutes straight. He was vain and self-important. In the end, he finished his drink, stood, and excused himself to go to the bathroom.

"Don't go away," he said.

"I won't," she smiled. "What are you drinking?"

"I'll have one of your gins. Get one for yourself, too. Tell him to put it on my tab."

"Thank you," she said.

Beatrix watched him disappear into the back of the room and then ordered another round of drinks. The barman delivered their gins and, when he turned his back, Beatrix reached into her bag for the folded triangle of paper. She checked that the barman was still occupied, and then used the mirror to surveil the space behind her. She wasn't being watched. She opened the end of the sachet with extravagant care and, hiding it in her hand, tipped the contents into the gin. The particulate looked like table salt, and it fizzed and bubbled as it was absorbed into the liquid. She took out her cell phone and set the alarm to ring in ten minutes.

She saw Doss come back through the door and concentrated on looking as normal as she could. He sat down next to her.

"Just what the doctor ordered," Doss said, pointing at the drinks.

Beatrix smiled. He took his seat next to her again, collected his glass and touched it to hers. "Cheers."

"Cheers."

She watched as he sipped the drink.

Doss was still talking when her cell phone alarm rang.

She picked it up, pretended to read a message that wasn't there, and frowned.

"What is it?"

"My boss," she said.

He looked concerned. "What?"

"He needs me to go in."

"You can't stay?"

"I'm sorry." She held up her phone apologetically. "He's a bit of a tyrant."

"Shame," he said. He reached into his pocket and took out a business card. He gave it to her. "This is me. If you want a guide to show you around, I'd be happy to do it. Just give me a call."

"Thank you," she said, smiling brightly at him. "Thanks for the drink."

He raised the half-finished glass. "Cheers. Lovely to meet you."

"And you."

He took her hand and tugged it gently. She ducked down to his level and allowed him to kiss her on the cheek. When she looked into his face she saw sweat on his upper lip and moisture streaming out of one nostril. It confirmed that his business in the bathroom had involved rather more than simply relieving himself. That, she thought, might not be such a bad thing. The poison that was already moving around in his blood would induce vomiting and diarrhoea that would eventually become bloody. He would become dehydrated, and that would eventually develop into seizures. Within three or four days his liver, kidneys, and spleen would stop working and he would die. The evidence of other substances in his blood might confuse the correct diagnosis. Ricin was almost impossible to detect in any event, and it looked as if his lifestyle might be usefully obfuscatory. It was all good.

Beatrix made her way through the crowded bar to the

warm street outside. She glanced across the traffic to the window of the restaurant and caught Chau's eye. She stared at him without giving him any other signal that could be observed, and then set off in the opposite direction to that which she had arrived.

24

B eatrix followed Lockhart Road to the MTR station at Causeway Bay. She descended the escalator to the eastbound platform and waited for a train. It was quiet, with a few commuters waiting to head home. These were true Chinese, the low-paid menial workers who cooked, washed and cleaned for the Westerners who lived in the affluent districts around Central. A train pulled into the station. Beatrix opened the case of the cell phone and took out the SIM card. She snapped it in half and dropped it into the trash as she boarded the train.

Beatrix was aware of a few lazy glances of disdain as she sat down. She was travelling in the opposite direction to that which would have taken Beatrix to her flat. It was a habit, long ingrained, that she would run this kind of surveillance detection route to ensure that she was not followed. Her instructor had called it 'dry cleaning,' and had driven into her how important it was. Both she and Chau had followed a similar routine as they made their way to Wan Chai that afternoon. Beatrix had taken the ferry to Kowloon and back, partly to satisfy herself that she was clean and partly because she enjoyed the spectacular view from the boat, the high-rise vistas on both sides of the water as if each part of the city was vying to outdo the other.

She remained on the carriage as they passed through Tin Hau, Fortress Hill, North Point, and Quarry Bay.

She alighted at Tai Koo. People had disembarked along the route and, by the time she reached the station, there were only four other people in the carriage with her. She stepped onto the platform, noted that the only others to disembark had been several carriages back, and satisfied herself that she was black. It might have been unlikely that anyone would have tried to follow her, but that didn't mean that she was prepared to neglect her routine. Chau had been lax until she had demonstrated to him how easy it was to follow the unwary, surprising him outside his apartment with her fingers pressed against his spine. No one— certainly not Mr. Ying, and not even Chau—knew where she lived, and that was a state of affairs that she intended to maintain.

She waited until the other passengers had departed, ascended to the surface and stopped in a store near the station where she knew she could pick up a change of clothes for a few dollars. She bought a new pair of jeans and a black T-shirt, took them to a public toilet and changed. She removed her make-up, took the dress and the black wig and, ensuring that she was unobserved, shoved them into the nearest bin outside.

She dumped the body of the cell phone into an open drain and walked east to Sai Wan Ho. The district was residential, bounded by Victoria Harbour to the north and the mountains to the south. The hill upon which it had been founded had once been filled with squatter settlements, but those had been razed and replaced with expensive new developments. There was Taikoo Shing, redeveloped from the dockyard, and a swathe of reclaimed land that had been filled with private housing estates.

Older buildings, like the restaurants and food stores at Tai On, were farther inland. It was a cheaper area, more affordable for locals. Beatrix checked behind her as she walked from the station, pausing several times to ensure that she was not being tailed. She entered the lobby and then walked past the various eateries, deciding what she wanted to eat. There were food stores that were selling egg waffles, *congee*, fried noodles, fish balls, deep-fried tofu, eggplant and dozens of other dishes. It was a riotous mixture of aromas, each more delicious than the last. Beatrix walked all the way through the building to the café that she knew was near to one of the other entrances. It specialised in cart noodles, served with a delicious soup base and a wide array of toppings. Beatrix chose *wonton*, vegetable and beef brisket, and took the carton to a table where she broke apart a set of plastic chopsticks and set to eating.

She finished her meal, dumped the sauce-smeared carton in a garbage bin, and walked back to the station. It was dark now, the million lights on the other side of the water leaching their glow into the night and casting long-fingered reflections across the glassy waters of the harbour.

There was a payphone outside the station. She took the paper napkin that she had taken from the restaurant and wrapped it around the handle of the receiver so as to avoid leaving any prints. She pushed a dollar into the slot and, covering her fingertips with a second napkin, dialled the number of the payphone at the corner of Kai Hing Road, close to Chau's warehouse.

The call picked up.

"*I'm here,*" he said.

"What did you see?"

"*He came out an hour later.*"

"And?"

"*He was unwell. Very white. Sick.*"

"To be expected."

"*How long will it take?*"

Beatrix was uncomfortable with discussing any of her business over a medium that could be intercepted, even if the precautions they took with this particular arrangement made it practically impossible to eavesdrop on them. Still, her caution was deeply rooted and she let the question pass without answer. "When are you speaking to our friend?"

"*He will call me when he knows it is done.*"

Two or three days, then, she thought. "Very good. Contact me when you know."

"*Beatrix—*" he said as she replaced the receiver.

She gritted her teeth in vexation. No names. *No names.* She knew that he was trying as hard as he could, but he could not prevent himself from making stupid mistakes. He wouldn't have lasted half an hour in the Group, but he was all she had, and, if she wanted to maintain her income, and continue funding the investigators searching for her daughter, she had no other choice than to work with him.

She entered the station, descended to the platform, and took the first train that was heading west.

She thought about Doss.

She had been working with Chau for six months now.

Doss would shortly be the sixth victim of their arrangement.

The men that had been marked for death by her hand had been a varied group. Most of them had underworld connections in one way or another. Beatrix did not ask for the details, but it was quickly apparent when she started to research the targets to assess their habits and patterns, divining their weaknesses and the times when they were most vulnerable. The first had been a member of the Wo Shun Wo who was informing on his brothers to the police. It had been a difficult assignment. The man had been granted police protection, but Beatrix had been able to gather that he visited his mother on Sunday evenings. She had staked out the old woman's flat and, with his escort waiting in the lobby downstairs, she had thrown him out of the tenth-storey window into the rubbish-strewn shaft between one building and the next.

Another man had been responsible for laundering triad money. Beatrix guessed that he had been skimming a little from the top, not that the nature of his guilt would have made any difference to her. He liked to go fishing on his private junk every Tuesday afternoon. Beatrix had stowed aboard and thrown him over the side.

The last one had been messier. Beatrix had broken into the man's expansive apartment in Central, but he had awoken just as she approached him in his bed. She had stabbed him, but there had been a struggle, and she had ended up garrotting him with the electrical flex from the lamp on his bedside table. Chau had been involved in the aftermath, removing the body and cleansing the apartment so thoroughly that there was no trace of what had happened there. Chau was clumsy, gauche, and unsuited to the preparatory work, but Beatrix was prepared to admit that when it came to clean-up, he was the epitome of professionalism.

It was midnight when she alighted again at Wan Chai. She made her way back to her apartment block. She had been on edge for hours, and it was tiring.

She was ready for sleep.

25

Her flat was on Lockhart Road, not far from the bar she had been in earlier. It was only a ten-minute walk to the west before she was in the bustling, neon-drenched heart of Wan Chai, but it was a different world. This was the heart of old Hong Kong. The buildings were a hundred years old, and showing their age. Instead of neon, the small stores advertised themselves with weather-beaten signs that hung above their front doors on creaking hinges. It wasn't the sort of place with any appeal to tourists save those who stumbled out of the clubs and wandered to the east, looking for Wan Chai MTR station and ending up all the way over at Causeway Bay. Skinny cats lounged on windowsills and rooftops, bathing in the light of the moon. Mangy dogs snouted through garbage, competing with rats that were almost as big as they were for the choicest morsels.

The small stores were still open, and the owners sat outside their establishments on plastic chairs, often with pots of tea or bottles of Tsingtao on folding card tables. Others wandered by in traditional Chinese dress. Deliveries were made by handcart and Beatrix had to step aside as one youngster pushed his barrow along, struggling with the sacks of rice that he was delivering to the neighbourhood restaurants.

It was busy and bustling, noisy and alive, and Beatrix loved it.

She could have stayed in one of the shiny apartment blocks in Central or Mid-Levels, rubbing shoulders with the bankers and lawyers and accountants who retreated there at the end of the day, but she had no interest in that. If she was going to have to stay in a place, she wanted to experience it properly. She wanted the dirt and the grit, the stench and stink. She wanted the colour. There was a more practical motivation to her decision to locate herself here, too. It would be harder to find her if she were submerged within this teeming morass of humanity.

She diverted to a late night drinking den that she had visited a few times before. It was off the beaten track and did not welcome tourists. Beatrix nodded to the man behind the rickety bar. They had transacted business before, and he nodded for her to follow him to the small room at the back. It was a storeroom, with stacked bottles of Maotai and Guijing Tribute and Tsingtao, a metal desk with a roller chair, a dirty sofa and a wooden cabinet. The barman was a triad, and the bar had been affiliated with Donnie Qi's organisation. There were two other triads in the room, one of them sitting on the sofa and the other smoking a joint as he leaned back against the wall. The three men all sported variations of the same basic uniform: tracksuit tops, trainers, lots of bling. Beatrix had found the place by asking around. She had not been concerned that she might be recognised. Only Donnie had seen her face, and he was dead.

"What you want?" the barman asked in harsh, rough English.

"The same as before."

The barman went to the cabinet and pulled out a drawer. It was full of small plastic bags, each of which was stuffed with a green-brown material. He opened one of the bags, ripped out a handful of buds and wrapped them in a piece of newspaper.

He held up a finger. Beatrix nodded that she understood, took out a hundred dollar bill and gave it to him.

"Want something else?" He looked to his two colleagues, gave a stagey wink, and pulled out another drawer. He took out more bags, but these contained different substances. Beatrix saw fibrous brown opium, white meth crystals, and small tablets of ecstasy.

"I'm good," Beatrix said. "Thanks."

She turned to go, but the man clicked his fingers twice and told her to wait. "You like the hashish, yes? It good? You ever try opium?"

Beatrix turned back. The barman had picked up the bag with the stalky brown contents and was holding it out to her. His accomplices were watching avidly.

"No."

"I give you. As gift."

She knew that she should leave, that staying here was a bad idea with bad consequences, but she looked down at the opium and found that her reaction to it was more ambivalent than she had expected. Her experience of drugs was limited. She had smoked weed ever since her teenage years. It had been almost medicinal during her service with the Group, easing the pain of the numerous injuries that she had suffered. She had smoked a little more of it these last six months. She had more to forget, more pains to salve, and, when she was high, her troubles receded just a little. But weed was weed, nice but limited, and she wondered whether she might appreciate something more. Something that offered a deeper retreat.

"Come on," the man urged. "Free sample."

Beatrix extended her hand and the man dropped the bag into her palm. "Thank you."

"You like, you want more, you come here, okay?"

"Okay," she said.

She put both baggies into her pocket, went out into the bar and then out onto the street beyond.

26

B
eatrix's building was twenty-five storeys tall. She summoned the ancient shoebox lift. The flat was on the penultimate floor. The elevator opened onto a narrow hallway with two doorways on either side. The shaft was in the centre, with the stairs winding their way around it. She doubted if the hallway had seen a paintbrush for twenty years. The floor was cold stone and the windows were empty, with rusting decorative ironwork taking the place of a pane of glass. There was a door that led out onto a balcony and an open archway led to a large recess, into which years' worth of trash had been stuffed.

She paused, as was her habit, and listened. She could hear the bustle of the street below, and the grumble of a jet passing overhead, but, save that, it was quiet. There was nothing that made her anxious. She had been in Hong Kong for six months and, during all of that time, there had been nothing to make her suspect that the Group was any closer to finding her.

She turned to the other doorway. The flat, which she guessed was identical to her own, was occupied by a woman and her daughter. Beatrix did not pry into the lives of her neighbours once she had satisfied herself that they were not a threat to her, but she had very quickly gathered that the woman was a prostitute. The flat was one of the one-woman brothels that were legal in Hong Kong. Clients would come to the flat, business would be transacted, and then they would leave. Beatrix had seen the woman a few times. She would have been pretty once, but now she was haggard, her emaciated body bearing witness to the meth habit that her hooking funded.

As she stood, staring at it, the door opened.

It was the daughter. She backed out of the door, dragging two large bags of rubbish that were almost too heavy for her to manage. She hadn't seen Beatrix and, as she half turned and caught sight of her, she jumped in surprise. She lost her grip on one of the sacks and it tipped over, spilling dirty takeout cartons and empty tuna cans over the floor. The girl blushed immediately. Beatrix stooped down and started to collect the escaped rubbish.

"No," the girl said. "It is fine. I can do it."

Her English was heavily accented. Beatrix's first thought was to wonder how the girl had known that she spoke it and not Cantonese. They had never conversed before. It made her a little uncomfortable.

Beatrix smiled at her. "It's okay." She collected a chicken *chow mein* can and dropped it into the open mouth of the sack.

The girl sank down to her haunches and quickly gathered up the other bits of rubbish. "I am sorry."

"Nothing to be sorry about."

It didn't seem possible that she could blush any more, but she did.

"What's your name?" Beatrix asked her.

She started to speak, but bit her lip.

"My name is Beatrix."

She would never normally have provided her real name, but the girl was young—no more than twelve or thirteen—and Beatrix felt uncomfortable with the prospect of lying to her.

"My name is Grace."

"Hello. Nice to meet you."

She found a sweet little smile. "Hello."

Beatrix nodded at the trash. "Taking the rubbish downstairs?"

"Yes."

"Where is your mother?"

A quick flash of discomfort passed across her pretty face. "She is asleep."

"And you're not?"

She squirmed. "I have work to do."

Beatrix knew that there was no point in pressing any further. Grace seemed uncomfortable with the subject and most likely wouldn't answer. The woman had probably been hooking all night and the chances were that now she was in a drugged stupor, leaving her daughter to take care of the domestic chores. It was a shabby, unpleasant kind of life for a young girl, but Grace wasn't Beatrix's daughter, and she had long since abrogated any right that she might have had to moralise about anything.

Beatrix stooped to collect her bag and was about to bid her farewell when the girl's face broke into a smile. "Do you like my English?"

She rested the bag on the floor again. "It's very good. Did you learn it at school?"

Her face clouded again and Beatrix guessed that she didn't go to school. "I learn it on YouTube."

"It's excellent."

She beamed with pride. "Thank you." She collected the bags and dragged them to the lift. Beatrix pulled the grille back so that she could get inside and then slid it closed for her.

"Goodbye, Grace."

"Goodbye, Beatrix."

BEATRIX WAITED until the interior door had wheezed shut and the car had started to descend, and then she turned to her own door. She unlocked it and went inside.

There was a single, uncovered window in the sitting room. The view was of the buildings directly opposite, but, behind them, she could see the towering edifices that comprised the business district around Causeway Bay. When she pushed her head close to the glass and looked to the right, she could see a sliver of dark blue from the harbour. It almost counted as a sea view.

The flat was miniscule. The main room was large enough for an armchair and a small bookshelf, onto which Beatrix had stacked the books she had purchased from market stalls in Kowloon: Woolf, Forster, Dickens, and Hardy. The dark wood parquet floor was scuffed and aged. The kitchen was crammed inside what was not much bigger than a cupboard, with a single ring cooker and a sink. The toilet was in a similar cubbyhole, with a shower directly overhead so that you had to sit on it to wash.

The walls bore a variety of documents, maps, photographs, lists of names and addresses, all of them decorated with the felt-tip markings that she had made across them. The photographs were of girls whom Beatrix's investigators had suggested matched Isabella's description. They were all taken with a long lens and, although they all shared superficial similarities—the blonde hair, the blue eyes—she had known immediately, every time, that none of them was Isabella.

She went through to the bedroom. It was big enough for her futon, but only when the last few inches at each end were pushed vertically up the walls. She could sleep by lying flat out, but there was barely any room to spare. The room had a concrete floor that had been stained with numerous unpleasant and noxious-looking liquids.

The bedroom had the only other window in the flat, although the view through the dirty panes was spectacular. It framed the high-rises on Lockhart Road and, behind them, the looming majesty of the Peak. She opened the window to ventilate the stuffy room, leaned out and looked down. She was vertiginously high and, from up here, she could see the squares and rectangles that formed the back-yards of the businesses down below. The spaces were hemmed in by plywood fences and protected from the elements by makeshift roofs that were constructed from sheets of plastic made opaque by years of bird shit that had rained down on them. The roofs had collected the plastic bags, trash and other detritus that had been tipped out of the windows of the building. Beatrix watched the silvery outline of a huge gull as it swooped down onto a bag that must have been a recent addition. It tore through the plastic with its beak, liberated the carcass of a chicken and flapped away with it.

She was tired. It had been a long night, powered by adrenaline, and it was catching up with her. She was not as young as she used to be, after all.

She collected the dope and headed for the roof.

27

T he roof was accessed through a door on the top floor that opened when Beatrix put her shoulder to it. She stepped out into the darkness. The exit was in a raised brickwork housing and the roof was arranged in three staggered levels, all of them littered with all manner of debris. Air-conditioning units whirred and glugged. Discarded trash, snagged on sharp points, flapped and rustled in the gentle breeze. Television aerials, bent flat by decades of resisting the typhoons that tore in off the East China Sea, prickled densely. The motors that raised and lowered the building's unreliable elevator buzzed into life. Fat gulls took to the air as Beatrix stepped out, and the concrete surface was slick with their guano.

Beatrix picked a careful path through the rubbish to the edge of the building. The view was spectacular. The harbour was a palette of black and greys under the looming moon, the skyscrapers on both sides of the water vying for her attention. Rolling away above even those were the vastness of the nine hills that surrounded the city. Local mythology said that they were nine sleeping dragons. They warranted their names.

She drew her focus in a little. The next building, a little shorter than this one, was close at hand, to the east. Windows faced her, some of them lit and uncovered, and, through frosted glass, she saw a blurred figure raise its arms and stretch. She drew closer to the edge, dropped to a sitting position and dangled her legs over the side. Beatrix did not suffer from vertigo, which was just as well. When she looked down, the cars and lorries that were jammed up along the length of Lockhart Road looked small and insignificant. The span between the two buildings was connected by a taut metal wire that suspended some sort of electric cabling. The distance between one building and the next was thirty feet. The pipe was attached to the wire along its length by a series of regularly spaced plastic ties. Beatrix looked down to where the pipe was attached to the parapet by a metal ring. A similar fixing supported it at its destination.

She took the joint from her pocket and lit up. The air was fresh this high up, absent of the smells of the city that she had come to accept as its unavoidable background: the fried meat and fish, vegetables, peanut oil, soy sauce and chilli and vinegar, the sweat of her fellow inhabitants and the faint, but unmistakeable, odour of excrement. She held the joint below her nose and inhaled the pungent scent. She put it to her mouth and drew down on it. She inhaled deeply, right down into her lungs, and held the smoke there. She felt the tension seep away from her taut muscles.

She planted her hands behind her, leaned back and angled her head towards the moon. She closed her eyes and exhaled.

28

C hau had tried to persuade Beatrix to take a cell phone so that he could easily get in touch with her. She had refused. She had no interest in owning a piece of technology that could be used to track her location. When she needed a cell phone, such as when they were working on an operation, she would purchase a prepaid burner and then dispose of it when she was finished. She had set out a procedure whereby he could get in touch with her. He would hide a coded message in a Facebook group dedicated to model boats. She visited a local Internet café every day and, when she saw his message, she would respond with a variation of one of several messages that she had told him to memorise. Each message contained the venue and time for a meeting.

Beatrix saw the message the week after she had poisoned David Doss. She replied, nominating the Lookout Restaurant at the top of the Peak. The message suggested that she would be there at midday, but she set off three hours earlier so as to arrive in plenty of time to check that Chau had not been followed.

She took the MTR to Central Station and walked the short distance to the foot of the Peak. She rode the century-old funicular railway to the top. She circled the area twice, eventually finding a spot in the restaurant where she could watch the comings and goings without being seen herself. She had an hour to wait for Chau. She ordered a latte and entertained herself by drinking in the vast, improbable view. She had travelled all over the world during her career, and the vista from here matched any that she had ever seen. The harbour stretched out between the mainland and the island, crisscrossed by the Star Ferry and the legion of private yachts and junks that plied its waters. The Peak was elevated enough to look down on the stupendous sight of the skyscrapers on both sides of the water, so audacious and lofty that Manhattan was rendered pedestrian in compari-son. It was a crystal clear day, without a cloud in the sky, and she was able to see beyond the buildings to the mountains that penned in the city to the north and, beyond them, the rest of China. It was a view of which it was impossible to tire.

The funicular ascended the side of the hill at a quarter to the hour, and Beatrix knew Chau would be on it. She watched him disembark from the railway and approach the restaurant. She had been trying to teach him the basic elements of tradecraft, but he found the whole thing too exciting, like some cut-price James Bond, and she had not been impressed with his progress. She knew that he found her attractive, and that revealing what she was capable of doing had not soured her to him. Worse, it seemed to have had the opposite effect.

All very annoying.

She sipped her coffee and watched. He stopped, just as she had instructed him to do, and she watched for a sign of anybody who might have been tailing him. She saw nothing.

She switched to a chair that faced the door and waited for him to climb the steps to the restaurant and come inside. He saw her, started to wave before remembering that she had told him never to attract attention to himself, then came over and sat down.

"Hello, Chau," she said.

"I was not followed." He said it proudly, like a child fishing for praise.

"You sure?"

A disappointed frown passed across his brow. "Yes. I—"

"What about her?" Beatrix said, nodding at the pretty girl who had just sat down at a table on the other side of the room.

"She was not... She did not..."

"I know. I was kidding."

Beatrix very rarely joked, and she delivered it with the most deadpan expression that it took Chau a moment to realise that she was making fun of him.

He started to speak, but she cut him off.

"Well?"

"He is dead," he said. "Three days ago. They did not find a cause. Unhealthy living, they say."

"Mr. Ying?"

"He is pleased."

"As he should be."

"He has paid the rest of the fee. I have it." He made an exaggerated gesture at the bag that he had slid under the table.

"Just leave it there when you go," Beatrix said.

"I know," he said with a little flash of indignation. "I remember."

There had been a good amount of money from the work that they had done together. She kept some of it in a safety deposit box ready to pay the investigators who were searching for her daughter back home. Then, she would transfer it in batches from various Western Unions throughout the city. Chau kept the rest for her.

"Did he say anything else?" she asked.

"There will be another job soon. No details yet. He will contact me when he is ready."

"Very good, Chau." He made no move to leave. She sighed. "Is there anything else?"

"You said you would think about having something to eat with me."

"And I was joking, Chau. I told you before. No mixing business with pleasure."

"I would cook, Beatrix."

"Then the answer is *definitely* no."

She was being unfairly harsh. He had previously cooked her simple, homely Chinese food and it was good. But she wasn't interested. She had no interest in companionship. She was quite happy to eat takeout, read, get high, and sleep. She knew that Chau would want to know about her history, and that he would probe and probe until she would have had to tell him about Lucas and Isabella. She had no interest in talking about that with anyone. It was dangerous. More to the point, it was too raw. And his view of her as a glacial, humourless killer was useful. There was no profit in him digging beneath the harsh exterior.

He frowned.

Beatrix rolled her eyes. He was like a child, and she felt bad for teasing him. "The other day, Chau. With Doss. You did well."

She had never praised him before. He smiled. "I am learning, Beatrix."

"Yes, you are. Keep learning. The day you think you know everything is the day you make the mistake that kills you."

He nodded solemnly. "I understand."

"See that you do. Now, we're done. Go back down, get on the train and head away from your apartment."

"I know, I know—"

"And leave the bag."

He stood.

"Be careful, Chau. I'm serious."

"I know, Beatrix. I am careful."

He turned and crossed the restaurant to the exit. Beatrix turned back to the window and watched him walk towards the funicular railway again.

Her life had changed so much that it was utterly alien to her. She was a foreigner in a strange city, a *gweilo*, friendless save for a man she hardly knew. Another world away, her daughter was missing. The only way she could pay for the search that was her only chance of finding her was to kill in the service of the vast criminal network that cocooned the city.

What were a few more deaths on her conscience?

It was too late to worry about that.

It was a small price to pay.

29

Beatrix took out the radio that she had bought from one of the dubious sellers in Chungking Mansions, switched it on and tuned in to the World Service. They were broadcasting a Radio 4 program about wildlife in the Cambridgeshire Fens. It made her think of home and, for a moment, she felt morose. The chill mornings, the fog cloaking the flattened landscape; it could hardly be more different to where she was now.

She went into the kitchen, took a cucumber from the cupboard and sliced it. She took down a glass, collected her bottle of imported Hendrick's gin and poured a double measure, filling the glass with tonic. She had no ice—she had no freezer to keep it in—so she did without. She took the glass and sat down with her back to the wall, staring at the pictures that she had fixed around the room.

She rested the glass on the floor beside her, undid the clasp of the locket she wore around her neck and opened it. She looked at the only picture that she had of Isabella. The photograph was from six months before she had been taken from her. She was happy, smiling widely, her father pulling faces behind the camera. Beatrix stared at it until she felt the familiar lump in her throat. She closed the locket.

She took out her bag of weed and a packet of papers and rolled a joint. She lit it, took a deep draw and rested it on the floor.

She reached for the gin.

And then she stopped.

What was that?

She listened.

She had definitely heard something.

There.

A scream?

She couldn't place where the scream had come from and, in truth, it wasn't unusual to hear the sounds of arguments. The windows of the flats were almost always left open for ventilation and sound travelled easily. The clamour of a violent struggle had woken her last night, and it was a regular occurrence to be disturbed by the neighbourhood cats who somehow made it up to the building's roof.

She collected the glass and sipped the gin. She looked up at the photographs of all the girls who were not her daughter and let her mind drift, a thousand miles away, to England and the memories of happier times.

She took the joint again and inhaled deeply.

30

There came a frantic hammering at the door. Beatrix licked her fingers and nipped the end of the joint. She got up, hurried into the bedroom and collected her Glock 26. They called it the Baby Glock; its size only allowed for a two-finger pistol grip, but its double-stacked magazine still carried ten rounds of 9mm ammunition. She held it in her right hand as she went to the door. She looked through the spyglass and saw the top of Grace's head. The girl knocked again, harder, and then stepped back. She turned her head to look across the hallway to her own door and, when she looked back, Beatrix could see the terror on her face.

She used her left hand to unlock the door and, hiding the pistol behind it, she opened it a little.

Grace was halfway between the two doors. She was rooted to the spot.

"Grace?"

The girl turned. Tears were streaming down her face.

"What is it?"

"Please."

"What?"

"*Please.* You must help me."

"What's happened?"

The words would have gushed out, but for her maladroit English. She panicked as she searched for the words, and more tears came. "The man... the man came... tried to touch me."

"What man?"

"*The man*," she repeated angrily. "The triad."

Beatrix felt her chest tighten with anxiety. The girl was frantic, her breath coming in shorter and shorter gasps. She was going to hyperventilate if she didn't calm down.

Beatrix looked past her to the open door of the flat and knew that the thing she should do—the *sensible* thing— would be to tell her that she couldn't help her, close the door and leave her to whatever fate was waiting for her. But, even as her knuckles whitened around the grip of the Glock, she knew that there was no way she could abandon her to that.

She was a girl, maybe not even in her teens. Whatever it was that had happened in her flat, it had ripped her natural reticence into pieces.

The Chinese were a proud people. To ask a *gweilo* for help? That would have been out of the question.

Whatever it was, Grace had nowhere else to turn.

The pistol was compact and weighed less than twenty ounces, even with the full ten shot load. Beatrix slipped it into the waistband of her jeans, covered the butt with the bottom of her T-shirt and opened the door.

"Come inside," she said.

∾

SHE TOLD Grace to stay in her flat, shut the door and crossed the landing. The door to the opposite flat still stood ajar and, as Beatrix edged up towards it, she thought that she could hear something. She paused, reached round for the pistol, and listened harder.

There.

She was sure now. It was a rasping inhalation, in and out, the sound of someone struggling for breath.

Beatrix raised the pistol, took a breath, and edged the door open with the toe of her boot.

It swung open.

She took it all in.

The layout of the flat looked identical to her own. There was the same tiny living space and the door to what must have been the bedroom. The furniture was cheap, but well cared for, and the place was clean and tidy.

She looked down. There was a man on the floor, scrabbling for the door. His rasping breath was evidence that the effort was difficult for him. Beatrix looked past him and saw the trail of blood that led back into the bedroom. He had dragged himself into this room, and was trying to make it outside.

There was a kitchen knife on the floor. The blade was slick with blood.

Beatrix stepped all the way inside and pushed the door closed.

The man grasped ahead, managing another foot towards the door.

She crouched down.

"Hey," she said.

The man raised his head and looked up at her.

He said something in Cantonese, but it was little more than a whisper that she didn't understand.

She knelt down and, holding the pistol up so that he could see it, gently rolled him onto his back.

She didn't recognise him, not that she had expected that she would. He was in his mid-forties, tanned, his skin prematurely lined by a life that had, at some point, been lived outside. He bared his teeth as he gasped for another breath and she saw a mouthful of snaggled and blackened teeth. He was wearing a garish yellow tracksuit top, expensive denim jeans and white trainers. A triad. Beatrix's attention was drawn to the jacket. There was an incision between his sternum and navel. A large bloodstain had bloomed there and was slowly expanding.

She unzipped the jacket. He was wearing a white T-shirt beneath it, the fabric pierced in the same place and saturated with blood.

She pulled up the T-shirt. The man was in bad shape. A sucking wound. Beatrix could see what had happened to him just by looking. The knife had punctured his lung. When he breathed in, the air entered the opening in the chest and when he breathed out, it was forced out of the thoracic cavity. The right lung had collapsed, and he was breathing with just the left. He was in grave danger, but it was possible that prompt treatment could save him.

He looked up at her.

"*Help... me.*"

She nodded that she understood and, waiting for the gratitude in his eyes, she put the gun on the floor and reached both hands so that they were around his neck. His face washed over with confusion and then, as he realised what was about to happen, blind fear. She pushed down, squeezing as hard as she could, feeling his larynx and pushing down with her thumbs on it. His eyes bulged and his legs gave a buck, but Beatrix was above him and pushing down. He had no leverage and he was weak. The scant strength in his body dissipated and he finally lay still. He gave a final gasping choke as the life faded from his eyes.

Beatrix stood, collected the pistol and shoved it back in her jeans.

She turned.

Grace was standing in the doorway.

Shit.

She hadn't locked the door.

The girl was staring at her. Her expression was inexpressive. Emotionless.

Beatrix got up and blocked her view of the dead man. "What did you see?"

"You kill him."

"I had no choice."

"*Good*. He deserved to die."

There was nothing at all on her face. Beatrix was lost for words. She didn't know how to react.

"Out," she said, ushering the girl onto the landing. She did as she was told, waiting for her there as she closed the door behind her. She pointed to her flat. "Go in there."

"Thank you, Beatrix."

"Go," she said, waving her hand. "I'll be there in a minute."

She was in a spot, and she felt vulnerable and exposed. Where was the mother? If she came back and saw the dead man in her flat, what would she do? And the girl had seen her throttle the man. What was she going to do with her?

First things first.

She took her key from her pocket and locked the door as quietly as she could. There was no other way out.

She went back into the other flat. There was a cordless telephone on the table. She picked it up and dialled.

"Chau. It's me. We have a big problem."

31

She had to give Chau directions to the flat. *That* was annoying. It meant that she would have to move. But she would have had to move anyway, she corrected herself. Beatrix couldn't possibly stay here now that Grace had seen what she had done. She had known that she wouldn't be able to put down roots, but she had been comfortable here.

Oh, well.

Sharks had to keep swimming to stay alive.

She would keep moving.

She waited in the hallway, glad for the hard shape of the Glock pressing into the small of her back. She heard the lift rattle and jangle as it came to a stop on the twenty-fourth floor. She saw Chau's face through the little window in the door. He was alone. She pulled the cage aside; Chau opened the door and stepped out. He looked around, taking in the details, his curiosity at the place his business partner had chosen for herself all too evident.

"Come on, Chau. Move."

"Where is problem?"

She pointed to the flat.

He went through. Beatrix followed behind.

The man was just as she had left him. The blood had stopped flowing, and the puddle that had leaked around his body had started to congeal.

"What happened?"

"The girl who lives here. She stabbed him."

Chau lowered himself to his haunches next to the man's body. He tilted the head and pointed to the purple bruising around his neck. "What about this?"

"I may have helped him on his way a little."

"This is not good, Beatrix."

"I know that, Chau," she snapped.

"Do we know who he is?"

"I don't know his name."

"But...?"

"She said he was a triad."

"That is obvious."

Chau released the man's chin so that his head flopped back down again. He examined his face and, almost immediately, the colour drained from his own.

"You know him?"

"Yes," he said. "I do not know name, but he works with Mr. Ying. He is in charge of girls in Kowloon."

"Makes sense. The girl said he wanted her mother. She's a prostitute. Then she said he tried to touch her. I heard something going on. She screamed. He must have come on to her and she stabbed him."

"This is *very bad*."

"He was going to bleed out, Chau."

"You could not have taken him to hospital?"

She laughed. "And then what happens to the girl?"

"*The girl is not our problem!*"

Beatrix put her boot on Chau's chest and pushed so that he toppled over. She took a step until she was standing over him. "Listen to me, Chau. If you think we are going to abandon a girl to the triads, you're wrong. *Dead wrong.* We are going to help make sure that, as far as everyone else is concerned, this never happened. I'll do that with or without you. But if it's without, then you need to know that we're through. You understand?"

Chau sat up and carefully backed away from her. She had let her temper catch, just a little, and, knowing what he did about her, it had the expected effect.

"Yes," he said. "I understand. I help."

Beatrix reached out her hand and hauled him to his feet. "Thank you, Chau. I knew you would."

He dusted himself down indignantly. "This whole room. It needs to be cleaned. Top to bottom. The blood needs to be gone. And we need to get rid of body."

"What do you suggest?"

"We cannot take him down in the lift like that, can we? We need to cut him up, and then we need to clean up."

"I need to speak to the girl—"

"I will do it," he said. "Is there a key for door?"

Beatrix looked across the room to a low table decorated with a vase of peonies. She saw a keychain and went over to collect it. The key fit when she tried it in the lock.

"Where is girl now?"

"With me. I'll look after her."

"She must not come here when I am working. I know you understand that."

Beatrix did. She knew exactly how Chau would be spending the next few hours. He was talented in removing evidence that might lead to the conclusion that a violent act had taken place in the location where he had been asked to clean. In situations like this, where it was not possible to remove the body from the scene without attracting attention, he would cut it into pieces so that it could be transported less conspicuously.

"You've got this?" she asked him.

"Go," Chau said.

32

Grace was sitting quietly in the chair. She looked up with alarm as Beatrix opened the door.

"It's all right," she said. "It's just me."

The girl's face was ashen and her eyes stared ahead, unresponsive. Beatrix recognised the beginnings of shock.

"It's going to be fine, Grace. I'm going to take care of it for you."

No response. Beatrix felt overwhelmed. She didn't know what to do. She had been a mother, once, but that seemed a hundred years ago now. She had never been particularly maternal, although she loved Isabella with all her heart. The responses and reactions that came naturally to some mothers did not come as easily to her. She'd had to work at it, constantly reminding herself to focus on her child's needs.

"Grace," she said. "That's a cute name."

"My mother liked it."

That was an opening. "Your mother... where is she?"

"I have no mother," she said, before she realised that she had betrayed her lie from before.

"The woman in the flat?"

"*She* is not my mother," she said, with a little heat.

"Then...?"

"My mother is dead. That is my sister."

Beatrix stopped. *Her sister?* The woman didn't look young enough to be her sibling. Whatever it was that she was addicted to—heroin, ice, or crack—had scoured the youth from her face.

Grace looked down at her lap.

"Then where is your sister?"

"I do not know. I have not seen her for a week. And I do not care."

She stared at Beatrix and, without warning, began to weep.

Beatrix hovered before her, unsure once again what she was supposed to do. She knew that she was being drawn into a situation that she might come to regret. But the girl was so pitiful and helpless that it was impossible not to think of her own daughter.

Isabella had watched her father's murder.

She had watched her mother kill.

She had watched her mother *abandon* her.

Beatrix hoped that the men and women responsible for Isabella's abduction would show her compassion, despite the circumstances. This was not so different. Grace was a child confronted by the most obscene situation and unable to work out how to react.

And she was alone.

Beatrix drew the girl into a hug, stroking her glossy black hair with the palm of her hand.

"It's all right," she said. "You're safe."

Grace disengaged herself with a sudden jerk. "I am *not*

safe," she said, her eyes full of desperation. "He is triad. They come for me."

Beatrix held on to her shoulders. "No," she said. "They won't."

"Beatrix. The men he work with, they are dangerous."

"I'll look after you, Grace."

"They are *killers*."

"Grace, you're not listening—"

"No, Beatrix, *you* not listening."

"They don't know what has happened to that man. We will make him disappear. And then we will make you disappear, too."

"You cannot hide from triad. Triad are everywhere. Triad *are* Hong Kong."

"They won't be able to hurt you, Grace. You have my word."

Did she believe it herself?

Not really.

She hoped the girl didn't hear the uncertainty in her voice.

33

Beatrix gave her bed to the girl. Grace was tired, her eyes rimmed with red, and it would be better for everyone if she was oblivious in sleep.

Chau worked through the night to dispose of the dead man. Beatrix had often assisted him during clean-up, but this time she left him to it. She stood guard as he left the flat to go and collect his butchery equipment, returning with his large leather satchel and the large blue plastic sheet that he would spread over the floor to collect the blood when he started to dismember the body. The door to the flat remained closed for the next two hours. She knew that he would be removing the arms and the legs, decapitating the corpse and then bagging up each individual body part in one of the large vinyl bags that he bought in bulk from a Kowloon trader. Each bag would be delivered to the Goodbye Dear Pets Cremation Centre and disposed of.

It was a little after two in the morning when she heard the door open and close and the rattle and clank of the lift as it was summoned to their floor. Ten minutes later, she heard the lift ascend again, and then heard the door as it was unlocked, opened, and closed. This sequence repeated itself four times until, finally, she heard a gentle rap against her door.

She looked through the peephole, saw Chau, and opened the door.

He gave a single nod and stood aside.

Beatrix crossed the landing and went into the opposite flat.

The triad was gone.

There was no sign of blood or any other evidence that might have offered a clue as to what had happened here. Beatrix knew how fastidious Chau was, and that he would have scrubbed away the blood and then used luminol to identify any residue that he might otherwise have missed.

"All good?"

"It is done. I will dispose of him."

"Thank you, Chau."

He gave her a shallow bow.

She turned and walked out of the flat. Chau followed and she closed the door.

"What will happen to girl?"

Beatrix locked the door. "I don't know," she admitted. "I need to think about that."

He paused, his mouth open as if there was something else he wanted to say.

She went to the lift and pressed the button to summon it to the floor.

"Don't come back here," she said. "Use the Facebook page when you need to contact me."

The lift arrived and she opened the door and then pulled the cage back.

"Be careful, Beatrix."

She nodded as he bowed again and got into the lift.

She waited until the car had descended and then went back into Grace's flat. She looked around, opening the cupboards and seeing cans of chicken *chow mein* and dried noodles. There was nothing else, and Beatrix realised that the girl must have been living off just these basic foodstuffs. She closed the cupboards and gazed at the room. Everything was colourless and drab. She felt a flash of pity. The girl's life had been difficult enough as it was, and now it had worsened.

She found a bag in the bedroom and packed it with a selection of clothes that she found. Grace couldn't stay here, that much was for sure. Chau had been correct. They did need to be careful. Beatrix didn't know whether anyone else knew the dead man had been here tonight, but she couldn't assume that he was working alone. There was a chance, at least, that others would come. Grace needed to be gone.

She closed and locked the door and crossed the landing to her own apartment. She laid out two bath towels on the floor, set a sheet over the top and took the cushion from the chair. She locked the door and, staring at it, took the chair and propped it at an angle so that the top was jammed beneath the handle.

She took the Glock and placed it on the floor next to her makeshift bed. It was going to be as uncomfortable as hell, but Beatrix had slept in worse places. She lay down, rested her head, and closed her eyes. She quickly fell asleep.

34

B eatrix woke early the next morning. She carefully opened the door to the bedroom and saw that Grace was still asleep. She took the Glock and hid it in a box of cornflakes and then hurried down to the store at the foot of the apartment block to buy breakfast for them both. She bought *dim sum* and *congee* with pickled vegetables, aduki beans, peanuts, tofu, and meats. Grace was still sleeping when she returned, and she remained that way until the noise of the kettle woke her.

She came out of the room, rubbing her eyes.

"Hungry?"

She nodded.

Beatrix busied herself, taking a plate and laying out the *gao* and *bao* and doling out the *congee* into two bowls. The girl sat cross-legged on the floor and devoured the *dim sum*. She ate quickly, shoving the dumplings and steamed rolls into her mouth with her fingers and then began to set about the rice porridge. Beatrix thought of the drab tinned *chow mein* that the girl had evidently been living off. No wonder she was eating so enthusiastically. Beatrix brought her a cup of tea and then offered her second helpings. Grace finished the rest of the *congee* and, when she was finally done, she leant back against the wall and gave Beatrix a small smile.

"Thank you."

"You're welcome."

Grace looked across the room and recognised the bag that Beatrix had used to pack her things. Perhaps she had been ignoring what had happened last night, but seeing the bag must have served as a reminder. Her chin began to quiver and Beatrix thought she was about to cry.

"You're going to be all right," she said, trying to calm her. "The man is gone."

"But I cannot return."

"No. That wouldn't be safe."

"Then where can I go?"

"Your sister?"

"I told you. I do not know where she is."

And I'm not sure that I'd be happy passing you over to her, Beatrix thought. Whatever the extent of the situation she found herself in, one thing was clear: the sister was responsible for it.

"Do you have any other family?"

"I have aunt. In Tianjin."

Tianjin was two hundred kilometres from Beijing. It was a full day's travel by train and bus from Hong Kong.

"You can get in touch with her?"

"Of course," she said. "I email."

"You could go there?"

"Yes," she said. "But I have no money for ticket."

"Don't worry about the money. Could you email her today?"

She shrugged. "Of course. I use café in road. I know man there. Lets me use Internet for free."

"I'll take you down there this morning."

"She doesn't check her messages every day. No computer at home. She use café, too. Checks every week only."

"That's fine. You can stay with me until you hear from her."

The girl looked at her with a mixture of gratitude and confusion. "Why you do this, Beatrix? Why you so good to me?"

"I have a little girl, Grace. A long way away. I haven't seen her for a very long time. If she was in trouble, I would want someone to look after her, too."

Beatrix took the locket that she wore around her neck, opened it and passed it to Grace.

"She is very pretty. What is her name?"

"Isabella," Beatrix said.

She busied herself with tidying away the breakfast things, turning away slightly so that Grace didn't see her as she bit down hard on her lip.

35

Beatrix was washing the dishes in the tiny sink when she heard a loud impact from the hallway outside.

Grace looked over at her with alarm.

Beatrix dried her hands as there came a second impact and then, as she started to the door, a third. This one was immediately followed by the noise of a door splintering.

Beatrix stood at the door and put her eye to the peephole.

There were six men gathered in the small hallway. They were wearing tracksuit tops and new sneakers. Two of them were carrying meat cleavers. Three had pistols. One had a short-barrelled shotgun.

One of the men, the biggest, addressed the battered door, drew back and booted it again. The wood splintered as the lock tore through the frame and the door flew back, bouncing off the wall.

Grace tugged at her sleeve. "What is it?"

"Get in the bedroom," Beatrix said quietly.

"Beatrix?"

"Get in the bedroom, Grace."

"I—"

"*Now!*"

She glanced back to make sure that the girl was out of the way. She hurried over and closed the bedroom door, then went and took the cereal box from the kitchen cupboard. She opened the flaps at the top, reached inside the box and took out her Baby Glock from its hiding place. The ten-shot magazine was full and there was a round in the chamber.

She went back to the door and looked through the peep-hole again.

Two of the men were waiting in the hallway. The others had gone into the flat. She saw them through the open doorway, turning the place upside down.

They were looking for something.

She stayed where she was, watching.

Her view was distorted by the narrow angle of the peep-hole lens, and restricted by the two men left to guard the hallway. But it was obvious from the urgent, barked Cantonese that she could hear from the apartment that, whatever it was, it was something the triads wanted very badly.

The flat was tiny. It only took them five minutes to tear it apart.

The four men who had gone inside had now rejoined the two in the hallway. They conferred for a moment. Beatrix assessed them. It was obvious that one was senior to the others. He was wearing a white tracksuit top unzipped to the navel. The skin underneath was festooned with tattoos. He wore a heavy gold necklace and chunky rings on his fingers.

And he was *angry*.

She heard the door creak behind her.

She turned back and saw Grace, watching through the crack just as there came a heavy knock on the front door.

Shit.

She waved for the girl to go back inside the bedroom.

The knocking came again, angry and insistent.

She switched the Glock to her left hand, dropped the steel door chain into the receiving plate, unlocked the door and opened it.

"Yes?"

The man with the tattoos was standing in front of the door. She saw the butt of a pistol protruding from the waistband of his Levis. His face was spiteful, with small eyes that were a little too close together and a bulbous nose. He looked at her and a moment of surprise passed across his face. She knew why: this was a poor, unpleasant place to live, not the sort of accommodation that would normally appeal to a *gweilo*.

He spoke in awkward, guttural English. "Woman who live there. You see?"

"No," Beatrix said. "Not for several days."

"Sure about that?"

"Yes. I'm sure."

"Know her?"

"No. Not at all."

The man looked at her. "I good at smelling bullshit, *gweilo*."

"Why would I lie?"

"And where girl?"

"What girl?"

"Girl from flat. Young girl. Where she?"

"I don't know what you're talking about."

"Don't play stupid, miss."

"I don't know what to tell you."

She tightened the grip on the Glock. The man with the shotgun was the one she was most worried about. A spread from short range like this would take the door out and anything that was behind it. He was behind the two men with cleavers. That was good and bad; he wouldn't be able to shoot without taking them out, but, conversely, he was also shielded from her.

The man in charge reached a decision. "Open door."

"Why?"

"*Open door*," he snapped. "Open door *now* or we kick door in!"

"Okay. Take it easy." She pushed the door closed and quickly slid the Glock into her waistband, the cold steel sliding down and nestling against the small of her back. She saw that the bedroom door had closed again.

Taking a breath, she slid the chain out of the receiving plate, let it fall free, and opened the door.

The man pushed it open and hustled inside.

"Take it easy," she repeated.

He looked around the flat. "Where woman?"

"I told you—I don't know her. I don't know anyone else here."

She kept her back to the wall, hiding the pistol. One of the men with a cleaver came inside. The small space already felt crowded. Beatrix felt her options constrict.

"When you last see woman?"

"A while ago. Maybe a week."

The man walked over to the bookshelf and took down Beatrix's copy of *Great Expectations*. He opened it and flipped through the pages. Beatrix gritted her teeth in frustration. This guy was an amateur, and this was an amateur's play. He was showing her that he was in control, that he didn't care about social niceties by invading her space and interfering with her things. Trying to make her feel uncomfortable. It didn't work.

She stretched out her fingers and then made fists.

His funeral.

She concentrated on the bulk of the pistol against her back.

"Girl, then. Where she?"

"I don't know. How many times do I have to tell you? I don't know her and I don't know her mother. I don't know anyone."

"Girl have video. You know about this? You know about *video?*"

"No," she said honestly. "I have no idea what you're talking about."

The man nodded at her answer, tossed the book onto the floor, turned away from her and started to the bedroom door.

Beatrix was all out of options. If they found Grace, they would take her away.

The girl would have no future.

They would probably kill Beatrix, too.

Nothing else for it.

She reached around, pulled the pistol and shot the man in the back. The bullet passed through him, painting a vivid splash of blood on the wall.

She kicked the front door shut, drew down on the man with the cleaver and shot him, too.

She heard shocked voices from outside.

Anger.

Confusion.

She aimed at the door and fired three shots through it. She heard a scream from the hallway. One fortunate shot, maybe another if she got really lucky. It would give them something to think about, maybe slow them down a little.

Three slants of light cut into the room from the fresh holes in the door. She turned the key in the lock. It wouldn't keep them out—especially not with that shotgun—but even a few extra seconds might make the difference. She crossed the room to the bedroom door. She opened it, went inside and closed it.

There was nowhere to hide. Grace was cowering in the corner, as far away from the door as she could manage.

"We need to leave," Beatrix said.

"Triads come? For my sister?"

"Yes. We need to get out."

There was a crash from outside as the men in the hallway tried to force the door.

Beatrix crossed the room, unlatched the sash window and pushed it all the way up. She returned the Glock to her waistband and beckoned Grace over to her.

The girl was frozen still by fear. "If we stay here, they will kill us. Understand? We must go. *Now*. Do you understand?"

The girl swallowed, her larynx bulging, but she nodded that she did.

36

There came a tremendous boom from the other room. That was the shotgun blowing out the lock. They had seconds now.

There was a rectangular metal frame for the drying of washing bolted to the wall beneath the casement, and her window box rested on the sill. Beatrix pushed the box off so that she could climb out of the window without being impeded by it. There was a pause and then a crash as it shattered against the ground below.

"Get on my back."

Grace came over and passed her arms around Beatrix's neck. She locked her right hand around her left wrist and wrapped her legs around her waist. She was heavier than she looked.

Beatrix held onto the ledge with her right hand, bent her knees and pushed up. The fingers of her left hand found the next ledge up, her boots slithering and sliding on the bricks until they stubbed against an uneven finish. Grace held on, her forearms locking around Beatrix's neck almost too tightly. She reached up with her right hand, transferring her weight. The masonry had been weakened by the weather, and the first ledge she reached crumbled to a rough dust in her hand. She stretched across in a desperate lunge and, just as her momentum failed and gravity hungrily claimed her, her fingers closed around a protruding metal stud.

She heard a shout from the room below them.

Come on.

She shot her arm up again, scrabbling for the bracket that held a rusting waste pipe to the wall. She transferred her weight to it and the pipe tipped backwards, the retaining screws nearest to her popping out of rotting masonry and skittering off the wall as they tumbled away from them. Beatrix closed her eyes, knowing that she was committed and that there was no way for her to get off the pipe with Grace on her back. The girl screamed as the sudden backwards jerk loosened her legs from around Beatrix's waist and, for a moment, she was left to dangle there. Her locked wrists dug into Beatrix's windpipe. The metal screeched, but the remaining screws held and their plunge was arrested.

Beatrix gritted her teeth.

"Hang on."

She wrapped her legs around the pipe, reached for the section above her head, and started to shimmy up it. The screws and brackets groaned with the added weight, but they stayed in place.

She reached for the lip of the roof. She probed for a handhold, found a boxy air-conditioning unit and laced her fingers around the lattice of a protective grate. Grunting with the effort, she hauled herself up and fastened her left hand around an exposed pipe and pulled so that the two of them rolled over the parapet. She righted herself quickly and scouted the roof. It was just as she remembered it. No one up here with them. *Not yet, anyway.*

"We've got to get over there," she said, pointing across to the other roof.

The girl's eyes bugged out. "We cannot."

The ascent had terrified her.

What Beatrix was proposing would make that look like a cakewalk.

She couldn't worry about that. If they stayed on the roof, the men would climb the stairs and there would be nowhere for them to go.

She had five rounds left.

They had a shotgun and at least two pistols.

They were badly outgunned.

They had no choice.

Grace walked over to the parapet and looked down.

"I cannot."

"They'll kill you if you stay here," she said.

The girl blanched.

"Hold on tight, just like before. You'll be fine."

Beatrix stepped up to the edge, the tips of her toes just over the lip of the roof. The wind picked up and, despite knowing that it was impossible, she had the impression that the building was bending and swaying. She dropped down so that her legs hung over the parapet. She turned back to Grace and, finally sensing that she really didn't have a choice, the girl hurried over and looped her arms around Beatrix's neck again. Beatrix reached down and took Grace's legs, positioning them around her waist and pressing them tight.

The girl felt snug on her back.

It wouldn't be just like before, of course. The ascent had been more natural. Grace had been able to bear her weight with her arms and anchor herself with her legs. This time, she would be upside down. It would be harder for both of them.

Beatrix hoped that she would be strong enough.

She bent down and lowered herself to the wire and the cable. She gripped them with both hands, locked her ankles around them and let gravity swing her around so that she was hanging upside down. She felt Grace's body go taut with terror, her grip constricting around her throat and waist. She started to pull herself away from the parapet. The wire was looser than it appeared, and it bowed down and then started to sway from side to side as she continued farther out.

They were halfway when she heard the boom of the shotgun from behind her.

The door to the roof.

She paused, looping the crook of her left elbow around the wire and reaching back between her body and Grace's body until she felt the butt of the Glock at her back. She drew it as she saw the men emerge from the housing. There was no easy way to aim, so she reached out and pointed with the pistol, loosing off two quick rounds in the vague direction of the triads. The pistol kicked and the bullets winged away. Two misses, but the men ducked beneath the parapet. Something for them to think about, such as it was.

Three rounds left.

She held the gun to her side, pointing away from Grace, and told the girl to take it.

She grasped the wire with both hands and started to pull again.

A pistol barked and a round whizzed overhead, missing by a few feet.

Almost there.

Another shot, and then the boom of the shotgun.

Almost there.

A patch of wall disintegrated in front of her.

Something hot and sharp scraped across her arm.

Fragments of dry brickwork spattered over them.

Beatrix pulled harder, slithering across the wire.

The building on the opposite side of the gap was within touching distance. She craned her neck around and looked; there was a window two feet below them. "Hang on," she said.

She rearranged her grip, uncrossed her legs and let the momentum of the sudden swing carry her feet first to the glass. She kicked out, shattering the panes, and hooked her foot against the top of the aperture. "Get inside," she muttered. The effort of holding her body steady tore at her biceps and the muscles of her shoulders. Grace did as she was told. She slithered down Beatrix's body until she was able to rest her weight on the sill and then dropped into the room beyond.

The shotgun boomed again.

Beatrix reached ahead on the wire and yanked herself closer to the wall. She let go. Her feet dropped down onto the sill, slipped off, and, for a moment, she thought she was going to fall. The window rushed by her face before she reached out and grasped the frame with both hands. Her legs slammed into the wall beneath the window. There were fragments of glass caught in the putty and they sliced into her fingers and palms. The blast of pain forced her to let go with her left hand. Pain screeched down her right arm, too. Her grip was loosening until Grace appeared above her and reached down with both hands, grabbing Beatrix's wrist and anchoring her.

She grabbed the sill with her left hand, scrabbled the

toes of her boots against the disintegrating wall, clambered up and fell inside the room.

She assessed. It was a bedroom; a futon on the floor, a bookcase. The room was empty.

She looked down at her hands. Her left was lacerated, three bloody tracks running across the fleshy part of her palm and into the lower joints of her fingers, but her right wasn't as badly cut as she had feared.

She took the gun from Grace, turned back to the window and looked out. The four triads were at the parapet. She drew down on one of them and squeezed off a round. It found its mark. The man clutched his gut, stumbled over the parapet and toppled into the void beyond. Beatrix watched as he plunged down, slamming through a makeshift wooden roof and then crashing into a chicken run, the mangy birds scattering and squawking their dissatisfaction.

The three survivors drew back and then ran for the door.

She was almost dry. *Two rounds left.*

"We need to hurry," Beatrix said to Grace. "We need to beat them to the bottom."

37

B
eatrix yanked the door open and led the way into the room beyond. It was empty. There was a cloth on the table. She took it, tore it down the middle, and wound it around her left hand to try to stem the blood.

The door was locked, so she drew back and kicked, shattering the lock so that she could pull the door open. The hallway outside was similar to the one in the building that they had just escaped, and she navigated accordingly. There was an elevator shaft with a flight of stairs that wrapped around it. She knew that the elevator would be too slow, so she started down the stairs. Grace followed behind. Beatrix took them two at a time, drawing away from the girl. She reached the bottom first, pressed herself against the wall and peeked out. The road outside was busy with pedestrians and traffic. The entrance to her building was flung open and the first of the three men appeared there, glancing out with caution on his face.

Grace reached the bottom. Beatrix took her hand and led her to a small storage room that reached into the space beneath the stairs. She pressed the girl against the wall until they were both out of sight of anyone who might come in through the door.

She waited.

The door opened.

Voices.

Three different voices. Angry. One voice angrier than the others, barking orders in Cantonese.

She heard footsteps clattering up the stairs.

Two sets of feet.

Two men going up.

She waited.

The third was standing guard below.

She held up her hand to tell Grace to stay where she was, took a breath, and then slipped out of cover. The third man was standing with his back to the stairs, looking out into the street below, a meat cleaver in his hand. He hadn't seen or heard her. She moved to him, looped her right arm around his neck, placed her left on his temple and yanked his head up and to the right. His neck broke with an audible crack and his body went limp. She dragged the corpse backwards and dumped it in the alcove. Then she pressed herself against the wall, out of sight of the stairs once more.

She heard the sound of footsteps coming down from above.

She waited until it sounded like they were on the final flight, leading down to the lobby.

"Li?"

Beatrix turned out of cover. The two were halfway down to the lobby.

"Li?"

Two rounds left. She couldn't afford to miss.

She fired. The triads collapsed and slid down the

remaining few steps. Beatrix grabbed the nearest man beneath the shoulders and dragged him into the storage room. She returned for the second man. Grace stared at the three bodies with her hand clasped over her mouth.

"Come on," she said, taking the girl's hand and leading her into the busy street outside.

BEATRIX TOOK Grace back to the building they had just escaped.

"What are we doing?"

They were out of sight of the street. Beatrix paused and turned the girl to face her.

"Grace, listen to me. They were looking for something."

The girl frowned.

"Did your sister hide something?"

She shook her head, confused.

"They said something about a video."

Grace paused. "There is something." A frown crinkled her brow as she searched for the right word. "Something for computer."

"Do you know where it is?"

"Yes. I show you."

Beatrix dared not trust the lift, so they climbed the stairs. She moved as quickly as she could.

They reached the landing. The door to Beatrix's apartment was badly damaged. The area around the lock had been blown out by the shotgun blast, and other holes studded it from where she had fired through it. Facing it, the door to Grace's flat was still open. It, too, was damaged from the kicking that it had received.

Beatrix went inside first. It had been turned upside

down. Drawers had been emptied out, the chairs over-turned, pots and pans thrown about in the tiny kitchen. Grace scurried over to the bedroom, lifted the futon and pushed it against the wall, and knelt down. She pushed down on one of the floorboards and one end popped up. She slid her fingertips beneath it, lifted it clear and reached into the cavity beneath.

She took out a small waterproof bag.

"Here," she said. "My sister put this here. I saw her. Is it important?"

Beatrix took the bag. Inside was a thumb drive.

"It might be."

Grace nodded. Beatrix put it in her pocket and led the way back outside.

She went back into her flat, telling Grace to wait on the landing. The two dead men were sprawled across the floor, blood and brain matter congealing around their shattered heads in gory halos. The apartment was rented under a false name, and she only ever paid cash. It would be difficult to trace it back to her and she didn't have time to dispose of the bodies. They would have to stay here.

She gathered her bag and packed the things that she knew she would need. She removed her hardback copy of *Bleak House* from the shelf and opened it up. Two magazines for the Glock were nestled inside a niche that she had carved into the pages. She ejected the spent magazine and pushed in one of the fresh ones.

She put the second magazine into her pocket, collected Grace's bag, put the pistol back inside her waistband and took one final look around.

Keep moving.

You'll never settle down.

Not until you find Isabella.

She went outside and led the way down the stairs to the street below.

38

Beatrix and Grace stopped at a pharmacy. Beatrix bought a bottle of disinfectant, a pair of tweezers and a packet of surgical strips. Then they stopped in the nearby McDonald's where Beatrix bought Grace a Happy Meal, told her to stay at the table and eat it, and then went into the bathroom. She unwound the wrap from her left hand and examined the damage beneath. Now that the blood had stopped, it did not look as bad as she had feared. The cuts, although deep, had missed the tendons, and she had full movement. She held her hand over the sink and, gritting her teeth, emptied the disinfectant over it. She examined the flesh carefully, using the tweezers to pull out the tiny fragments of glass that had lodged there, and then sealed the cuts with the surgical strips. She opened and closed her fist and flexed her fingers. The damage was minimal. She had been lucky.

She led the way to Sheung Wan and took a room at the Sohotel. The place catered to backpackers and those on a budget. The room was small, just over a hundred square feet, with wall-to-wall windows doing a little to make up for the lack of space. Beatrix knew the area. Possession Point, the spot where the British landed in Hong Kong in 1841, was in nearby Hollywood Road Park, now a pleasant green space where locals practised *t'ai chi*. Sheung Wan was also within walking distance of the Macau Ferry Terminal for outlying islands, and was served by an MTR station. If they needed to get out of Hong Kong in a hurry, there would be plenty of options.

Beatrix made sure that Grace was comfortable and then told her that she needed to step out for a moment.

The girl's eyes went wide with fear. "Where are you going?"

"I'll be five minutes away. Don't worry, Grace. I'm the only person who knows where you are. The triads won't find you if you stay here. Can you do that?"

"How long will you be?"

"An hour. No more."

The girl's jaw stiffened and she nodded.

"Stay in the room," Beatrix repeated. She took the Do Not Disturb sign, opened the door, and hooked it over the handle. "Don't open the door. Not for anyone. Okay?"

She nodded again.

Beatrix smiled at her, patted her pocket to confirm that she still had the thumb drive, and left the room.

THE HOTEL WAS at 139 Bonham Strand. Beatrix asked for directions to a place where she could access the Internet. The woman behind the desk suggested the business centre, but Beatrix asked for somewhere outside the hotel. The woman shrugged, and, with a little buzz of amused disdain, pointed out of the front door and south to Aberdeen Street.

Beatrix thanked her and walked the six hundred metres to the 908 Cyber Café.

She paid for a terminal. There was no time to use the Facebook dead-drop. There was a payphone on the wall in the back of the café and she used it to call Chau, telling him where she was and that she needed to see him. Use of an insecure phone line was something Beatrix would not usually allow, but, if ever there was a time to break convention, it was now.

39

Chau arrived thirty minutes later.

"What is happening?"

She explained how the triads had visited the apartment block again and how, after they had forced their way into her flat, she had killed them all and escaped.

"All?"

"I didn't have much choice, Chau."

His face went pale and she saw his fingers begin to tremble against the table.

"How many?"

"Six."

"Six!"

She nodded.

"I cannot clean *six triad!*" he hissed.

She leaned forwards against the table. "I don't want you to clean them, Chau. They will have been found by now. I'm not proposing to go back there."

"Then you must leave Hong Kong." He frowned for a minute, becoming even paler as he recognised the consequences. "Maybe *I* must leave Hong Kong."

She reached across and gripped his wrist. "Calm down, Chau. I need you to relax."

"How can I relax—"

"Because it's not very likely that Ying will know who I am. He's never seen me. The men he sent to find the girl are all dead. They can't describe me to him, and, even if they could, how would he know who I am?"

"Blonde western woman, very dangerous, good with a gun? I think he will guess."

"He won't know yet."

"Then he will ask your landlord."

"My landlord has never seen me."

"Then he will ask your neighbours. They will have noticed. You are different. You will stand out."

"We're fine for now, Chau."

"For now?"

"For now."

He looked at her with suspicion. "Why do I think I am not going to like what you are about to say?"

"Those men were looking for something at the flat. That's why the first man was there. I think I have it."

She reached into her pocket and pulled out the thumb drive.

"What is on it?"

"I have no idea."

She took the stick and pushed it into the computer's USB port. It detected the drive and displayed the single file that had been stored there.

It was labelled in Mandarin:

趙

It had a *.mov* extension and a suggested duration of three minutes.

"What does it say?"

He squinted at the screen. "It is a name. Zhào."

"Mean anything to you?"

"No. It is a common name."

Beatrix had chosen a computer in the corner of the room that was not overlooked and, after glancing over her shoulder to double-check, she clicked the file. The default video viewer opened and the video played.

The footage showed a bedroom. Beatrix paused for a moment before she realised that she recognised it. It was the bedroom in Grace's apartment. She recalled the patterned sheets on the futon and the picture of a vase of flowers that had been hung on the wall. The camera was placed in the corner of the room and was at a low height. She guessed that it had been concealed in something; a bag, perhaps. A blind had been pulled down over the single small window and the room was dark. The camera was not particularly good and it struggled to adapt to the dim light.

A woman came into frame. She sat on the edge of the futon and reached down to take off a pair of high-heeled shoes.

"You know her?" Chau asked.

Beatrix nodded. It was the woman that she had seen in Grace's apartment. The girl's older sister.

A man's legs came into frame. A conversation commenced in Cantonese.

"It is small talk," Chau said for Beatrix's benefit. "They seem to be familiar with one another. He calls her Liling."

"And him?"

She caught the woman saying the name just as soon as she had asked.

"Zhào."

Chau turned to her, an expression of befuddlement on his face. She ignored him, her attention fixed on the screen.

The man's legs retreated into shot as he moved away from the camera, revealing more of himself. He was wearing a suit, and shoes that had been polished to a high sheen. He sat on the bed next to the woman and reached forward to work his shoes from his feet. He was looking at her, his face obscured, but then he turned and looked right at the camera.

"It is *him*," Chau breathed out.

"Who?"

"Zhào Gao. He is businessman. Very important. Very rich. Influential. There are rumours he works with triads."

They watched for another minute as the two of them undressed each other. The café had restrictions on what you could watch and Beatrix had no interest in drawing undue attention to themselves if the proprietor happened to notice what was on the screen. It was obvious what was about to happen. She paused the footage just as Zhào was looking into the camera again.

"You think he knows the camera is there?"

"No," Beatrix said. "It's hidden."

Chau was agape. "Zhào's company depends on his image. He is a family man. But this..." His voice trailed away.

"Whoever he is, someone set him up. That's why they filmed it. It's either her acting alone or someone else is behind it. Probably Ying."

"I could understand it if it was her. He is rich. Extortion would be very profitable. But *Ying?* Why?"

"Same reason. Blackmail. Or, if Zhào was working with the Wo Shun Wo and they needed to keep him in line, he could be threatened with this."

"But the woman had the file?"

Beatrix nodded as she closed down the video player.

"And now she's either dead or on the run because of it. And it's going to get her little sister killed."

"She is not our problem," Chau said, his voice clipped and taut.

"No. She is. I'm not just going to abandon her. We need to help her get away."

"To where?"

"She has family on the mainland."

"Then give her the money for bus ticket and be done with it."

Beatrix sighed, fighting impatience. Chau was fundamentally a good man, but he was also a coward with a selfish tendency towards his own preservation. She had no illusions about that. If his life depended upon it, he would serve her up to Ying or to anyone else who was threatening him. That was a good reason for the separation between them both that she insisted upon, and for the frequent reminders she gave him that she was just as dangerous as the men they served.

"Her sister got her into this," she explained with exaggerated patience. "Liling has been working for the triads. Liling has been working for Ying. Liling got into trouble. Not Grace. It's not her fault."

"And neither is it *our* fault, nor our responsibility. Send her away. That will be that."

"Her sister could be dead, but maybe she isn't. Maybe she's still out there, hiding. But she won't be able to stay hidden for long, and you can bet Ying will want to know where she is even more now that his men have been killed. The girl's an addict. You think she won't tell him about her little sister if he pushes her even a little? Maybe she tells him all about the relatives on the mainland. You think Grace will be safe there?"

Chau bit his lip, then shook his head. "No."

"I can't take the chance of sending Grace away until I know, for sure, that she will be safe. He'll think that she has this footage. He'll find her, bring her back, and find out what happened. And if he finds her, maybe she tells him about the Jackie Chan lookalike who worked with the blonde Western woman to clean up the dead body in her apartment. Maybe he comes and asks what you know about what happened."

"But she didn't see me."

Beatrix knew that she was close to persuading him. Self-preservation was his pressure point. A lie would be the final gentle nudge he needed. "She was watching through the peephole when you came to clean her apartment. She saw you, Chau. She can describe *you*."

The trembling got worse. "You said I was *safe*. You said—"

"You are safe, as long as the girl is safe."

He started to get to his feet. "I... I... have to leave."

She took his wrist again and held it. "No. Where would you go?"

"I... I..."

"You don't need to run. We can control this situation." She took the stick from the USB port and tapped her finger against it. "We have *this*."

"What do we do?"

"I think it's time I met our employer."

40

B eatrix watched as the funicular climbed the side of the Peak. Grace was sitting at the table next to her, turning a straw this way and that in the glass of lemonade that Beatrix had bought for her. The girl had become a little surly, staying in the hotel for the last few days. That wasn't surprising. It was a small room and there was very little to do save for watching the television and the counterfeit Disney DVDs that Beatrix had bought from a kerbside tout.

Beatrix had persuaded Chau to meet with Ying. The rendezvous had been this morning, on the deck of the Star Ferry as had become their usual *modus operandi*. She would typically have observed the meeting, but she had stayed with Grace instead. She had instructed Chau to be fastidious in ensuring that he was not surveilled, and then—and only then—if he was satisfied that he was alone, meet her here. She would have to trust that he had exercised the necessary caution, but she had the Glock in her bag in the event that he had not.

She watched as Chau climbed the ascent to the top of

the Peak. He stopped halfway, as she had instructed, and she observed the people that were following behind him to see whether any of them stopped too. No one did. If he was being followed, it was by a team. And she saw nothing to suggest that was the case.

She relaxed, but only a little.

He approached the table.

He looked down at Grace. "Is this her?"

"This is Grace," Beatrix said.

The girl looked up at him and smiled. Chau, who looked as if he was about to say something gruff and abrupt, held his tongue.

"Hello, Mr. Chau. Thank you for helping me."

Chau managed to smile back down at her.

"Grace," Beatrix said. "Mr. Chau and I need to speak. We'll just be over there. Do you want anything to eat?"

"No, thank you," she said. "I am fine."

Beatrix stood and led Chau to a table where they could talk without the girl overhearing them.

"Well?"

"He will see you."

"What did you tell him?"

"What you told me to say. That you have the video he is looking for."

"And what did he say?"

"He was unhappy."

"But?"

"He did not say no. He said you should come to the Nine Dragons. Do you know where it is?"

She knew his club and said that she did. "When?"

"Tomorrow. Noon."

That made sense. The place would be empty at that time of day.

"Will you go?" he asked.

"Of course."

Chau nodded. She noticed that he was fretting with a hangnail on his right thumb.

"Chau," she said. "This will soon be finished. I'll sort it all out. But, while I'm gone, I need you to look after Grace."

"And then?"

"If the meeting has gone well, the heat will be off. I'll drive her to Tianjin."

"You know how far that is?"

"Two thousand kilometres. I know."

Chau suggested that she should fly, but she had already dismissed that. She knew that Control and the analysts of Group Three would be looking for her, and she had no interest in making that search any easier. Driving, and staying off-grid, was preferable.

"What now?" he asked.

She looked back at the table. Grace was gazing out over the incredible vista, an expression of wonder on her face. *She might never have been up here before*, Beatrix realised. *What would have been the point?* Her own horizon was hemmed in by circumstance; her prospects offered a much narrower world than the one that was laid out from here.

What would be the point of tempting herself with things that she could never have?

"Come to the Sohotel in Sheung Wan. Get a room. Stay in the hotel. Don't leave; not for anything. Don't open the door. Don't answer the phone. I'll leave at ten in the morning. I'll need you to stay with Grace until I get back."

"Yes," he said.

"Thank you, Chau. I appreciate it."

41

They took a taxi to the Sohotel. Chau reserved a room on the same floor as the one that Beatrix had taken before taking Grace to her suite. He took the girl up in the elevator and let her lead the way. The room was bland and boring, with nothing to distinguish it from any other hotel that Chau had stayed in. A bed, a bureau, a television... that was it.

The girl went over to the bureau, took the remote and switched on the TV. She surfed over to *TVB J2*. A cartoon was playing, and she sat on the edge of the bed to watch.

Chau took the opportunity to look for anything that Beatrix might have left behind, but there was nothing. They had worked together for months and she was still an enigma to him. He knew nothing about her, save that she was carrying a weight of sadness on her shoulders. She was good at pretending to be someone else, but that was something that she had not been able to hide.

〰

THE GIRL LOOKED up from the TV show she had been watching. "Mr. Chau?"

"Yes, Grace?"

"I'd like a drink."

"A soda?"

"Yes, please."

"I saw a machine outside. I'll go and get a couple for us. Don't open the door—okay?"

"I understand," she said.

Chau went to the door, opened it, and went out into the corridor. The vending and ice machines were in an antechamber on the way to the elevators. He went inside, looked at the machine and the collection of garishly-coloured cans behind the glass. He put in his money and selected a Future Cola and a Jianlibao. The mechanism rumbled, the cans rolled forward and thudded down into the tray. Chau reached inside, collected them, and turned to leave.

He saw the three men as they went past the entrance.

They were dressed in cheap tracksuit tops, jeans and sneakers.

Triads.

Chau felt a churn of nausea in his gut.

Fuck.

He waited and then put his head out into the corridor. The men were outside the door to room 225. Two were armed with pistols and the other held a meat cleaver.

Chau was partially obscured by the trolley bearing fresh towels and linen that had been parked in the corridor by the cleaners who were servicing room 223.

He froze.

He didn't know what to do.

His little .32 Kel-Tec bulged in his pocket, but he knew that he wouldn't be able to use it to take down the three men before one of them, at least, was able to get a shot off at him.

What was his other option?

To flee.

But that would be a betrayal. Beatrix had given him one task: to guard Grace. It was a simple task—elementary—and he had accepted it gladly. He had been trying to impress her since they had started to work together, and here was a good opportunity to demonstrate that he could be trusted.

And he had failed.

He reached into his pocket, the tips of his fingers brushing up against the steel barrel of the pistol.

They hadn't seen him.

Maybe...

The man at the front of the trio took a key card from his pocket, slid it into the reader, waited for the clunk of the lock as it released, and opened the door. He went inside, followed by one of the others. The third man stayed in the corridor. There was a moment of silence, a child's scream, and then the sound of the scream as it was muffled. There was the sound of a scuffle, with something heavy thudding against the floor.

Chau gritted his teeth.

Who was he kidding?

What was he going to do?

He was a failure.

Chau backed away, turning and walking as quickly as he could to the elevator lobby. He pushed open the door to the stairs and hurried down, taking them two at a time. He stopped at the bottom, opening the door a crack and looking out to ensure that there were no more triads in the reception and, satisfied that there were not, he pushed it all the way open and walked quickly through the dimly lit space and into the midmorning brightness outside. He walked for as long as he dared and, once he was twenty metres from the entrance, he broke into a trot, and then into a flat sprint.

42

T he Nine Dragons was a cheap, tatty, and thoroughly down-at-heel sort of place. The entrance was below ground, accessed by way of a steep staircase that was guarded by a doorman who stood behind a lectern.

Beatrix walked up to the staircase, glanced down into it to fix it in her mind, and then walked on.

She circled the building, following the block formed by Lockhart Road, Tonnochy Road, Jaffe Road, and Marsh Road until she had skirted it front and back. In addition to the main entrance, there was a ramp that led down to a basement where goods could be delivered. There was also a metal fire escape that had been fixed to the rear of the building. There was no way of saying whether either of those exits would be passable, but it might be useful to know that they were possibilities.

She returned to Lockhart Road and the front of the club. She descended the stairs. One of the walls was decorated with posters of '80s film stars and the other was mirrored, floor to ceiling.

Beatrix paused at the lectern.

The doorman was a big man with a cruel face. He was wearing a cheap-looking white sweatshirt with the club's name embossed on the breast, a pair of black slacks and cheap patent leather boots. "Club closed," he said.

"I know."

"What you want?"

"I'm here to see Mr. Ying."

The man looked down at her sceptically. "He not here."

Beatrix glared at him with unmasked impatience. "Yes, he is. Tell him that Mr. Chau's friend is here. And that she doesn't like waiting."

Slow realisation dawned over his face. "*You?*"

She wondered how much he knew. "Go and tell him before I lose my temper."

The man told her to wait and hurried around the corner into the club.

She felt vulnerable. It went against all of her instincts to walk into a place like this without a weapon. Ying, and the men he led, were dangerous and amoral. He would not hesitate to kill her. After all, she had been killing for him for the last six months. She was visiting him on his turf, in a place with which she was unfamiliar, without anything to defend herself apart from the contents of the memory stick and the leverage that might provide her. She had to hope that she hadn't overplayed its importance.

The doorman returned.

"I search," he said, nodding at her.

"Fine."

He patted her down, sliding his hands up and down her ribcage and then frisking her legs.

"At bar. He see you now."

BEATRIX FOLLOWED the corridor around the corner and entered the club. It was a large wide room dominated by a dance floor and a mirrored bar. There were low tables and cheap leather sofas set around the perimeter and, beyond the dance floor, a series of dark booths. A TV suspended above the bar was playing a kung fu movie. The film was muted, and the only sound came from a room behind the bar where bottles and glasses rattled and clanked as they were rearranged. A Filipina was collecting empties in a wire mesh tray.

A man was sitting at the bar with his back to her, drinking a cup of tea. His face was visible in the mirrored wall to the side of him.

"Mr. Ying," Beatrix said.

She recognised him from the Star Ferry. He was in early middle age, his face prematurely marked with lines around his nose and eyes. His hair was parted down the middle and was perfectly black, with not even the slightest hint of grey. He was wearing a mauve tracksuit top, a white T-shirt beneath that, and a pair of jeans. He turned to her, his face impassive and cold. A gold necklace glittered in a spotlight that shone overhead. His eyes were like flint. There was no pity there. No emotion at all. An occupation such as his, not so different from her own, had a tendency to cauterise all empathy and feeling.

"You are the woman who works with Chau?"

"That's right."

"The *ghost*."

He cocked an eyebrow, just a little. Chinese society was patriarchal, and the masculine world of the triads especially so. Beatrix doubted that Ying approved of her, although it wouldn't have been possible to question her efficiency. She had demonstrated that six times; seven if you counted Donnie Qi.

"What is your name?"

"You can call me Suzy."

"Suzy." He nodded, his cold eyes staying on her. "What brings you here?"

"That doesn't matter. And there's no point asking anything else about me. I value my privacy."

He smiled at her reticence. "You are very good, Suzy. I have been satisfied with the work that you and Chau have done for me."

"I'm pleased to hear that."

"Our friend Mr. Doss, for example. Tell me, how did he die? He was poisoned, yes?"

"That's right."

"With what?"

"Something that disagreed with him."

He nodded and made an appreciative clucking noise.

"No more questions," she said.

He nodded his assent. "You are a very impressive woman. The pay is good, yes?"

"Sufficient."

"Better than sufficient, I think. It is *generous*. And it makes it difficult to understand why you have done what you have done." He indicated to the stool next to him. "But I am sure that we can sort it out. Please. *Sit*."

She felt a twist of nerves. "No, thanks. I'll stand."

He waved away her rebuff. "I do not care about the men you killed, the men who went to the apartment. You did me a favour. They failed. I do not tolerate failure, so I had no further use for them. It is the fact that you are doing this to me now that is troubling. You are not a failure, Suzy. Far from it. You are very useful to me, and now I cannot use you again."

"I'll have to learn to live with the disappointment," she said. "Look. Let's get to the point, shall we? This is about Liling and Zhào. I don't care if she set him up or whether you did. I don't care about the video, and I don't care about him. None of that matters to me. But I do care about the sister."

"Yes. The girl. Grace."

"Your men would have hurt her, and I wasn't prepared to let that happen."

"And so you killed them? All of them?"

"They attacked me. Did I have a choice?"

"You could have brought the girl to me. We could have found a solution without this unpleasantness."

She felt like telling him that she wasn't a fool—that she wasn't born yesterday—but she held her tongue. "Grace is innocent in all of this. She doesn't have to be involved."

"I'm assuming she gave you the video, then?"

"She knew that Liling had hidden something. She found it and gave it to me. It isn't her fault. She is not to be hurt."

"Who said I would hurt the girl?"

She couldn't restrain herself this time. "Come on, Ying," she snapped. "Don't waste my time. She has *nothing* to do with this. She didn't see the video. She hasn't copied it."

Ying was intransigent. "How can I believe that?"

Beatrix placed her hand on the bar, opened it, and pulled it away again.

She left the thumb drive there.

Ying cocked an eyebrow, but made no move to take it.

"You have watched it?"

"Yes."

"And copied it?"

"Of course."

"Then why do you give this to me? If you still have the contents, we still have a problem, do we not?"

Beatrix knew that they would reach this juncture eventually. She could give Ying the drive, but, as he had already said, that meant nothing. It was the file that was important, and there was nothing to say that Beatrix hadn't copied it a hundred times.

"Do you play chess, Mr. Ying?"

He shrugged. "I prefer *mahjong*."

"This is a stalemate. You can threaten me. I can threaten you. But neither of us will act because we know that would force the other to act. So we'll do nothing. Won't we?"

Ying laid his hand across the thumb drive and rapped his fingers against the bar. He looked at her, trying to intimidate her with his icy gaze. It didn't work. Beatrix held his eye until he gave up, presenting her with another cold smile. He flicked his finger and sent the drive across the bar so that it slid up to her hand. "I am afraid that I disagree with you. The situation is not as even as you think."

Beatrix frowned and took a step back. She had no idea what Ying meant. He said something in Cantonese and the doorman and another man appeared at the exit. She clenched her fists, looked back at Ying and then to the bar behind him. She instinctively looked for a weapon. There was a corkscrew nestled between a clutch of cocktail sticks in a holder. Not great, but it would improve her odds a little if the situation demanded it.

Ying took another sip from his tea and then replaced the

cup in the saucer with deliberate care. He turned his head and nodded to the two men. The doorman beckoned a third man into the room. The man had Grace with him. He was holding a fistful of her collar and he slung her ahead of him. The girl stumbled and sprawled onto the floor.

Beatrix was distracted and didn't notice that Ying had slid down from the stool. He sucker-punched her on the jaw and, for a moment, the lights spun. She stumbled back two steps and braced herself on the bar. She was closer to the corkscrew now and she reached over to grab it, clasping it tightly in her fist with just the last inch and a half pointing out between her index finger and forefinger. She spat out a mouthful of blood and turned back to Ying.

"Do not," he said, nodding to the corkscrew. He flicked his eyes back at Grace. The man who had thrown her down now had a cleaver in his hand.

"Are you sure you want to do this?" Beatrix said.

"No threats. You are not in a position to make them."

"I'll kill you. *All* of you."

"No, you will not."

The dizziness dispersed. "What do you want?"

"I know you could not give me every copy of the file. If you did, and I believed you, I would kill you. You know this. *I* know this. But I can see that you care for the girl. You cannot use the file while I have her. But, by the same logic, I cannot harm her, either." He took another sip of his tea.

"So what do we do?"

"We do nothing. You keep the file, I keep the girl. You disappear from Hong Kong. I guarantee that she will not be harmed."

Beatrix gritted her teeth.

"But, before you leave, there is one thing I need you to do."

"Is that right?"

"I want Chau. He, too, has defied me. He disposed of the first man to visit the girl when he should have told me what had happened. You are a *gweilo*, Suzy, but he is Chinese. His crime is worse and, for that, he must die. But he was not at the hotel this afternoon. He left the girl alone. That was negligent, but it saved his life. For now, at least. He trusts you. You have twenty-four hours to find him and bring him to me."

"And if I don't?"

"Please," Ying said. "I have said that I would not kill her, but there are other fates. She is pretty. There are men who pay well for pretty young girls. You do not need me to explain, do you?"

Beatrix looked from Grace to the three men behind her and then back to Ying. She had no options. No cards left to play. Chau had failed her. All he had to do was keep the girl safe, and he had failed. She looked back to the girl. She was terrified. Beatrix knew that it was with good reason. Ying had risen through the ranks of the Wo Shun Wo, and that would require a ruthless amorality. He had sanctioned her murder of Donnie Qi because he could see the benefits that would accrue to him: less competition, and the ability to call upon her services. It wasn't amorality, she corrected, or at least not just that. He was psychopathic.

"If you touch a hair on her head, you know what I'll do to you?"

Ying waved the threat away. "You have one day. Find Chau. If you do that, I promise the girl will not be touched. If not?" He shrugged. "You will find her in one of my Kowloon brothels. I cannot guarantee that she will be as pretty—or as innocent."

She knew there was no point in trying to bluff with what

she might do with the information contained on the memory stick.

Ying had trumped her.

He wouldn't murder Grace.

What he was threatening was much worse.

He would hurt her. A little at first, and then a lot. Her life would be made into an unimaginable Hell. It would be better if she was dead.

Beatrix turned and walked away from him. Grace looked up at her as she approached.

"I'm not leaving you," she said, loud enough for Ying to hear. "I am coming back."

Grace sobbed as she reached out and grabbed Beatrix by the ankle.

She reached down and gently released her grip.

"I'm coming back."

SHE CLIMBED the stairs to Lockhart Road. It was bright outside and the light lanced into her eyes. The noise of the busy street outside was clamorous, a confounding din after the quiet of the subterranean nightclub, but she didn't stop. She turned into the stream of pedestrians and started to walk. She was heading towards the MTR station at Wan Chai, but that was something of which she was only peripherally aware.

Think.

There had to be an angle.

She looked down at her watch.

Just past midday.

She selected the timer, set it for twenty-four hours and started it.

There had to be a weakness, somewhere that Ying was vulnerable.

She just needed to find it.

She left the Nine Dragons behind her and vanished into the crowd.

PART III

43

Beatrix looked at her watch and waited as the seconds went by.

23:45:15.

23:45:14.

23:45:13.

There were twenty-three hours and forty-four minutes for her to do what Ying wanted, or Grace would suffer the consequences.

She pushed her way through the bustle of Wan Chai. *First things first.* She had rented a post office box in Tsim Sha Tsui earlier, before she had gone to meet Ying. She knew that she would not be able to take her pistol with her to the meeting, so she had put it in a jiffy bag and left it in the box. She went into the building, collected the envelope and took it outside with her. She found a quiet spot in a nearby park, took the Baby Glock from the envelope and pushed it into the waistband of her jeans. She had an extra magazine, too, which she stuffed into her pocket.

She set off again for the Internet café that she normally used. She paid for an hour and took her usual spot in the corner, where it would be difficult for her to be observed. She opened Facebook and navigated to the page she and Chau used whenever either of them needed to send the other a message. She used the message that would tell Chau that she wanted to meet him at the Tian Tan Buddha statue on Lantau Island at 3 p.m.

She closed the window and opened another. She navigated to Google and typed in the name of the businessman who had appeared in the footage that Ying wanted so much.

Zhào Gao.

Several hundred results were returned. The first was a profile from Forbes. She opened it and read.

Gao was born in 1946 in Wuxi, Jiangsu province. His father was the founder and president of the Mandarin International Trust and Investment Corporation, China's largest investment company. He formed MITIC to attract the foreign capital and skills needed to expand China's business interests and to modernize its ageing industries. The corporation operated like a capitalist enterprise: it ran a bank in competition with government banks, arranged loans, sold bonds in overseas markets, invested in and imported equipment for Chinese businesses, and owned businesses in other countries.

When his father died five years previously, Gao had succeeded him.

Further searches suggested that Gao was suspected to have triad associations in Hong Kong and China. Allegations of criminal involvement had been ruthlessly suppressed by cadres of highly paid lawyers. He was said to be the most litigious man in China. Eventually, editors decided that the scoops they might get could never be worth the financial headaches that would result from pursuing them. Gao effectively browbeat them into submission.

Beatrix quickly navigated to Dropbox and satisfied herself that the footage of Gao's tryst with Liling had been successfully uploaded to her account. She cleared the cache, purging the browser's history, and logged off.

She set off for the harbour.

44

The ferry to Lantau, otherwise known as Mui Wo, operated from Central Pier Six, next to the Star Ferry Pier on Hong Kong Island. Beatrix paid for a return ticket and embarked.

She checked her watch. It was a quarter past one. If Chau was going to come, it was unlikely that he would have had time to catch this particular ferry. That suited Beatrix. She wanted to be at the rendezvous in plenty of time. Arriving late to a meeting was rude and, more relevant, it reduced the odds that you would be the one to walk away afterwards. She would get there first, scout the locale, and set up in plenty of time to make sure that, if he arrived, he was not being trailed. She had given him a simple task to perform and he had let her down. She would leave nothing to chance.

She walked to the bow of the ship. Chau was not aboard. She found a space at the rail where she would have a good view for the trip across the harbour. It was a fast crossing, scheduled for an hour, and Beatrix tried to relax a little. She had an idea what she was going to have to do, but she needed Chau's help to put the plan into effect.

THE FERRY NUDGED up against the dock. She disembarked and took Bus No. 1 to Tai O, changing to Bus No. 21 for Ngong Ping. A cable car transported visitors from here into the hilly interior of the island. Beatrix paid, waited in line, and then took a space inside a cramped car. She was confident that she was not being followed herself, but that did not absolve her from the responsibility of checking.

The Tian Tan Buddha was one of Hong Kong's main tourist attractions. It was perched high in the hills and stood over thirty feet high. Its prodigious size lent it the name by which it was more well known: the Big Buddha. It was part of the Po Lin Monastery and, as Beatrix read from an inscription placed on the trail that led up to the base, at 250 tons it was the biggest seated bronze Buddha in the world. The trail from the Ngong Ping village to the Buddha was flanked on both sides by smaller statues of the Twelve Divine Generals, each symbolising an animal from the Chinese Zodiac, armed with distinctive weapons.

There were several hundred people gathered around the base of the statue. They were served by a number of street vendors, and the smell of the food reminded Beatrix that she hadn't eaten since breakfast. She bought fried noodles and fish balls served in a Styrofoam cup and ate quickly, washing them down with a bottle of extortionately expensive water.

A long flight of steps led up from the base. Beatrix climbed. She passed a set of six Bodhisattva statues, the saints who gave up their palace in heaven so that mortals might find places themselves. It took five minutes to reach the top, but from there she was offered a majestic view over the lush greenery of Lantau Island, the shimmering South China Sea and the flights gliding in and out of Hong Kong Airport.

She turned and, as she looked back down the stairs, she saw Chau. He was wearing one of his ridiculously garish Hawaiian shirts, the print standing out among the more sensible garb of the tourists around him. He looked horribly flustered, looking back over his shoulder every few paces. His weathered face bore the unmistakeable signs of fear. She knew that he was perpetually on the edge of fright, but the events of the last few hours had toppled him over the boundary and into full-blown panic.

She concentrated on the people around him. Most were tourists, with some locals spread among them. She had taught him to make regular stops to make it easier to discern a tail, but her lessons went unheeded, and he hurried on regardless. That made it very difficult for Beatrix to be sure that he was alone. He passed the final pair of Divine Generals and then, thankfully, he did stop. Beatrix scoured the people behind him. None of them stood out. Of course, if he was being followed by more than one person, it would be easy enough for one of them to hand him off to another, but she had seen nothing to suggest that the triads were that sophisticated when it came to tradecraft. Still, she reminded herself, there were so many of them...if they wanted to follow him, it would be difficult for her to know.

Nothing else for it.

She needed to talk to him.

He set off again, climbing the 260 stairs to the top of the monument.

She hurried down to the middle tier, waiting out of sight

and letting him continue up the stairs. She waited, saw that no one was following, and then ascended again herself.

He reached the final tier. He was out of breath, his ragged respiration audible even when she was twenty feet away. She came up behind him, placed her open palm in the small of his back, and with a quiet, "Walk," impelled him onwards.

"Beatrix..." he started.

"Walk, Chau."

"I am sorry!"

"*Walk.*"

She knew that he had always been attracted to her, and that the attraction was underscored by a healthy fear once he had realised her capabilities and her willingness to implement them. She had never tried to reassure him on that front. It was useful that he was frightened of her. It was particularly useful now. She had no time for his bad puns and innuendos. This was all business.

She led him to a quieter space at the rear of the Buddha. The day was clear and there was a vast view out across the island to the South China Sea beyond. She nudged him over to the rail that guarded the drop from the dais to the jungle below.

"What happened?"

"I am sorry," he repeated pitifully.

"Tell me."

"I was gone for five minutes. There was no minibar. Girl said she was thirsty. You told me not to call anyone, so I go down to get drink from reception."

"I told you not to leave her."

"It was five minutes, that is all."

She bit her tongue to forestall the denunciation. "And then?"

"I came back. There were three men outside room."

"And?"

"And?"

"What did you do, Chau?"

"There was nothing I could do," he said plaintively.

"You had your gun?"

"Yes."

"I remember you shooting three men before."

"That was different," he protested.

It was different, she allowed. She had disabled two of those men already.

"I am sorry," he said again. "I am very, very sorry."

She took a breath, trying not to think about the knot of tension and frustration that sat in her gut like a fist of ice.

"Beatrix? Please, talk to me."

"It doesn't matter," she said at last. "I shouldn't have left you. Either of you. I didn't think they would be able to find you."

"Someone at hotel," he offered. "A white woman and a Chinese girl. It would be unusual. The little horses are everywhere. Ying asks and someone tells him."

She wanted to snap at him, to tell him that she knew that it was her fault for being so stupid, and that she knew that she was stupid to assume that they would be able to move through the city unobserved. The little horses were the most junior triads. They were the kids on the street, the drunks and the drugged—anyone who might offer a little information in anticipation of the reward that might come his or her way. She had been stupid for leaving Grace under Chau's protection, but there was no profit in dwelling on what she had done and what she *should have* done. She couldn't change any of it now. She had to move forward. The circumstances were laid out clearly enough. Ying had made his move, and now it was her turn to make hers.

"I need your help."

"Anything," he said, although the nervousness in his voice was difficult to miss.

"The man on the video."

"Zhào Gao?"

"I need you to find out where he is."

He frowned. "How could I do that?"

"I don't know," she said, with a flash of irritation. "You said you had a contact in the police?"

"Yes. But—"

"Make some calls, Chau. We need to find him."

He looked dubious. "I will try."

"This is important, Chau. We have to move quickly. Ying gave me twenty-four hours."

"For what?"

"To bring you to him."

His mouth gaped open. "But, you—"

She sighed impatiently. "I'm not going to do that, Chau."

"What are you going to do?"

"Mr. Gao needs to see the video."

"What good will that do?"

"Ying is just a *Dai Lo*?"

"Yes."

"Just a local boss?"

"Yes."

"I need to see his boss. Maybe Gao can set that up for me."

45

J ackie Chau delivered. He called two hours later to say that Zhào Gao would be in Hong Kong this week closing a deal, and was staying at the Shangri-La. The police kept an eye on important businessmen like him, and a small bribe had been enough for Chau's contact to provide the tip. Beatrix called the Intercontinental and, using a *nom de guerre*, reserved a room. It was expensive, but she didn't care. It was close to the Shangri-La and convenience was going to be more important than parsimoniousness. Then she made her preparations.

First, she told Chau that she was going to need two fake passports with visas that allowed onward passage into China. She knew that he had contacts that he could use. It was simple administrative fraud, the wheels greased with a small bribe. She told him to take the cost plus ten percent out of the significant amount that he still owed her. She told him that she would need the passports quickly, within twelve hours. He clucked his tongue, suggesting that would add to the price, but Beatrix told him to take whatever he needed from her money. She didn't care. She just wanted it done.

She visited the mall and purchased a simple, stylish black cocktail dress, a pair of high-heeled shoes and a Louis Vuitton bag that was big enough to hold her sneakers, a change of clothes and her Glock. She bought a razor-sharp kitchen knife. Then she bought a wig made from natural black hair and a pair of clear glasses. Finally, she bought a prepaid cell phone with a data allowance.

She checked into her room at the Intercontinental, stripped to her underwear and went through into the bathroom. She put on the short bob wig and arranged it until she was happy with how it looked. Then, she took the cell phone and downloaded the video of Zhào Gao from her Dropbox account. She reviewed the footage again, fixing his appearance in her mind. Satisfied, she put the phone into the Louis Vuitton bag along with her Glock and the kitchen knife.

When she was done, she put on the black dress and the clear spectacles. She regarded herself in the full-length mirror that was fixed to the back of the wardrobe door.

She looked good.

More importantly, she looked *different*.

She collected her bag, locked the door and had the bellboy hail her a cab for the Shangri-La.

BEATRIX TOLD the driver to stop a block away from the hotel. She collected her things, paid him, and bought a packet of cigarettes and a lighter from the kiosk opposite. She wasn't much of a smoker, beyond her self-medicating her demons with the local hashish, but she knew that she might need an excuse to stand outside during surveillance, and a cigarette was as good an excuse as any to be outdoors.

The Shangri-La was a fine hotel. It was situated on prime Kowloon real estate and rooms started at $600 a night. There was a line of exclusive taxis outside, waiting to be ushered forward by the bellhops. Limousines jockeyed for space, ferrying their occupants to the front door where the men and women were immediately fawned over by efficiently obsequious staff. She walked to the door with a confident stride, nodding at the doorman who opened the door for her, and made her way into the lobby.

The room was huge. Stunningly impressive. Three storeys tall with four massive crystal chandeliers cascading from the distant ceiling. An old banyan tree had been nurtured in the wide space before the reception desk. Voices were quiet and reverent. Staff circulated with brisk orderliness. A grand piano was positioned at the far end of the room with an arrangement of architecturally impressive blooms in a crystal vase. Sofas and Chinese rosewood chairs were arrayed around small tables, guests tipping waiters as they delivered trays of tea and coffee. A double-wide staircase swept up to the next floor.

She made her way farther inside, assessing the security. The doormen looked vigilant, but the room was big enough that she could put distance between herself and them. Discreet omnidirectional security cameras were fixed to the ceiling, and she could see that the coverage would make it impossible to find a blind spot. *Never mind*.

She located the elevator lobby and found an empty sofa that had the right combination of discretion and position. It was close enough that it offered an unobstructed view of the elevators, yet not so close to the desk or the doors that she would attract too much unwanted attention.

There was a copy of the *South China Morning Post* on the table in front of the sofa. She picked it up and pretended to read, all the while looking over the top of the pages and examining the comings and goings in the foyer.

A waiter in a neat black uniform stood smartly to the side of the sofa. "Can I get you anything, madam?"

She looked at his name badge—Raoul—and smiled at him. "I'd love a cup of tea, please."

"Of course, madam. What would you prefer?"

"Earl Grey."

The man smiled, said that he would be right back, and set off.

Beatrix kept her attention on the elevators and examined the faces of the men who were emerging from them. She had fixed Gao's appearance in her mind and was confident that she would recognise him, should he appear.

The clientele here all smelled of money. The men were dressed in expensive suits, many of the older ones accessorising with girlfriends who were improbably young. The women clicked and clacked across the marble floor on immoderate heels, dressed lavishly well. It looked like the perfect kind of place for someone like Gao to stay, but there was no sign of him.

Beatrix hoped that Chau's intelligence was accurate. Every minute she spent waiting for the man was a minute less for Grace.

Raoul returned with a silver platter and a mug of tea. He poured it for her and left it on the table. He handed her the chit; she paid and added a five-dollar tip. He acknowledged her generosity with a shallow nod and left her alone again.

She didn't touch the tea for the first ten minutes and, when she finally sipped it, it was starting to cool. That didn't matter. It was only a prop. She wasn't thirsty, and if she drank too much, she would need the bathroom. That wasn't possible when she was the only operative conducting the surveillance.

The tea was stone cold when she sipped it again.

And then she saw the man she was waiting for.

Zhào Gao was in a group of five: him, two young girls, two guards.

He was reasonably tall for a Chinese, with a slender build. He was in his late sixties, but he looked younger. The skin on his face was taut, an obvious indication that work had been done. As one of the girls put her hand on his elbow and said something to him, the smile he gave her did not crinkle his brow.

They paused at the desk. Beatrix went by them, nodding her thanks as the doorman opened the door for her. She took the cigarettes from her bag.

A stretch Hummer was bullying its way to the front of the queue of taxis. She scoped it out quickly: a black paint job that glittered in the light, big truck tyres and twenty-inch custom chrome rims, blacked-out windows to all aspects, and hazard lights blinking on and off.

A Land Rover Discovery followed.

Chau's gaudy Mercedes CLA was parked half a block away. She saw the flash of red paint against the side of the road.

Beatrix lit the cigarette and put it to her lips as the door of the hotel was opened for the group, the doorman giving a full bow. She stayed twenty feet away. A driver emerged from the Hummer and opened the door. Gao and the two women got inside. The Discovery pulled up behind the limousine and the two guards climbed inside.

Beatrix took out her cell phone and called Chau.

"*Yes?*"

"Gao's on the move. You see the Hummer?"

"*Yes.*"

"Follow it. I'll be behind."

She put the phone away and strolled to the two cars before they could pull away. The Discovery was new, and immaculately clean inside and out. The three men were big and she heard them speaking in German as she passed the open window. *Private security*, she thought. *Would they be armed? Very likely.* She would need to neutralise them regardless of whether they were or not. She reached the Hummer just as it was rolling away. The back windows were opaque, but one had been opened a little. She could hear raucous conversation from inside before the vehicle pulled into traffic and the laughter was absorbed into the constant hum of the city.

Chau followed. He was completely unsuitable to mount a successful surveillance pursuit, but, since he would have been even less suitable to run the surveillance inside the hotel, she had concluded that it was the lesser of two evils.

She dropped the cigarette into a drain, flagged down a cab, gave the driver a fifty, and told him to follow Chau's car.

46

Chau relayed the location of the Hummer. They were headed north. He told her that he had guessed their destination when they were half a mile out. When he reported that the Hummer had stopped outside the Lisboa, he did so with some satisfaction. He said that it was a triad gambling club, tolerated by the police because the management were exceptionally generous in the size of the kickbacks that they made so that they would look the other way.

"What about the Land Rover?"

"*There is parking lot. It is there.*"

"And the men?"

"*There are street vendors. Men have stopped for food. Must be hungry.*"

"Fine. Drive on, park up and then come back on foot. You know what to do."

She told the driver to stop, got out and walked the rest of the way.

∾

BEATRIX SAW THE THREE MEN. They were sitting at a picnic table, eating from three cartons of noodles. They had arranged themselves so that they were facing the casino, able to observe the comings and goings. She heard German again. They were laughing and joking. They had the look of soldiers, with large builds and short cropped hair. One of the men had a cell phone on the table. Beatrix guessed that they would wait here until Gao needed them. The casino would have its own security. They would only be required again when he came out. He would call and they would resume their duties.

The parking lot was behind them. The Discovery was taller than the other cars around it and she found it without difficulty. It was parked so that it could not be obstructed should they need to quickly drive away, but it was far enough away that she knew that they wouldn't be able to see her if she was careful.

There was a Mercedes SLK parked alongside it. She ducked down to a low crouch and made her way between the two vehicles. She would have liked to have been able to pop the bonnet so that she could get to the engine, but that would have been too risky. Instead she reached into her bag, taking out the knife and slashing the rear tyre. She moved to the front of the car and slashed that tyre, too. Air hissed out as the tyres deflated, the heavy car slowly lurching to the side. Staying low, Beatrix went around to the other side of the car and slashed those tyres, too. Ensuring that she was unobserved, she dropped the knife back into her bag and stayed below the line of the cars until she was several spaces away from the disabled Land Rover. Then she stood and made her way back to the casino.

The three men were still at the picnic table.

THE CASINO WAS EXCLUSIVE. The door was staffed by two immaculately turned out guards, and Beatrix couldn't be sure that they would let her inside.

She skirted the building, eventually finding a door that looked as if it was used by the staff and suppliers that were making deliveries. There was a keypad lock on the door. Two staff members, wearing uniforms with the casino's livery in gold brocade, were smoking cigarettes outside.

Beatrix took her own cigarettes from her bag, put one between her lips and lit it. She took her cell phone and pressed it to her ear, pretending to make a call. She paced back and forth, raising her voice in anger. The two members of staff regarded her, shared a comment in Cantonese that she couldn't translate, and then went back to their cigarettes.

She made sure that she was watching when the two stood, treading the cigarettes underfoot. One of them entered the code on the keypad. 3526. Beatrix saw it clearly, waited until they had gone inside, waited another minute, and then entered the code herself.

The lock popped and the door opened.

She went inside.

47

The casino was heavy with smoke, the atmosphere thick with the scent of perfume and alcohol. Beatrix found it dizzying and a little nauseating as she passed out of the corridor that led to the bathrooms and into the main room. The place was as exclusive as she had expected it to be. It comprised two large rooms. The first room had four poker tables. The second room had two roulette wheels and three blackjack tables. A lobby between the two rooms was equipped with a luxurious bar with a granite surface, the shelves behind it stacked with premium-brand spirits. Beatrix went to the bar and ordered an orange juice. The barman served it with wordless efficiency, took her twenty-dollar bill and did not return her any change.

She observed. The chairs around the tables were all occupied and each table bore a small fortune in stacked chips. The clientele was a mixture of Chinese and foreign nationals and the atmosphere was excitable and tense. She could hear the rattle of the balls as they were spun around the roulette wheels, and the clatter of chips as they were tossed into the middle. Results were met with exclamations of pleasure or distaste. The bigger wins were greeted with whoops and cheers, but these were no more than occasional. The trend was for rueful sighs and philosophical comments as the house won again and again.

The men wore suits, whilst the women paraded in cocktail dresses much like her own. Beatrix was glad of the outfit and heels. She would be able to stand a little scrutiny, but she knew that she could not afford to draw unnecessary attention to herself. There were surveillance domes over each of the tables and she knew that their footage would be analysed by staff looking for anything suspicious. There would be members of staff in the crowd, too, keeping an eye on things and making sure that the casino's losses were kept within acceptable boundaries. They would regard the guests with appraising eyes. She nursed her drink and concentrated on fading into the background.

She assessed the layout of the establishment. She knew that there was a way out through the back, but she didn't plan on using it again. There were doors to her left and right for the male and female bathrooms. She guessed that the door behind the bar must lead to a storeroom. A flight of marble stairs led down to the main entrance and the street outside.

Beatrix considered her options. She only needed a moment alone with Gao. She knew that she could be persuasive, and she also knew that he would be pliable once he saw the video that she had downloaded to her phone. It might be possible to do it in the casino. That would be a lot easier than the alternative. Perhaps, if he went to the bathroom, she could follow and intercept him. There would be an attendant inside. If she was going to speak to him, it would have to be in the corridor. She would have to persuade him very quickly before he could summon security.

She mulled it over and dismissed it. *Too risky. Too many variables.* It would need good fortune, and she wasn't in the business of relying on luck.

She moved through the room with the poker tables and into the room with the blackjack and roulette. She passed the cashier's desk first. The man, owlish in wire-framed spectacles, sat behind a screen with piles of notes and chips arranged on shelves. She saw notes of all denominations, mainly HK $500 and $1000 bills. The cashier did not appear to have anything with which to defend himself, but she suspected that the guards nearby were armed.

Gao was sitting at one of the roulette wheels, the two girls on either side of him. She walked up. The wheel, table and chairs were on a raised platform, surrounded by a rail that reached as high as her stomach. There were others watching and Gao was putting on quite a show. He was presiding over a generous stack of chips and they watched him push several thousand dollars' worth to the centre of the table, spreading them over a handful of black numbers.

Beatrix watched as the croupier collected the ivory ball in his right hand. The man gave the wheel a controlled twist clockwise with the same hand, and then flicked the ball around the outer rim of the wheel anticlockwise, against the spin. He called for final bets. Gao smiled at his girls, flipping each of them a five-hundred-dollar chip and grinning as they leaned over the table to place them on their lucky numbers.

The ball settled. Black. The croupier scraped the chips across the table, divvied up the appropriate winnings, and passed them back again. Gao had won.

Beatrix didn't look too closely at Gao. She didn't want

him to notice, but she did want to get an idea about him and how he operated. *Was he drunk? High? What was his attitude like? Aggressive? Relaxed?* She assessed it all, and then, when she had been there long enough, she faded back to the bar. She could still watch the proceedings at the table from there.

A man sidled up to her. "Hello," he said.

She ignored him.

"Haven't seen you here before."

She ignored him again.

He didn't take the hint. "Let me buy you a drink."

The interruption was unwelcome. The last thing she wanted was to make a scene, and so she relented. Perhaps it could be played to her advantage. The man, whoever he was, looked comfortable here. He appeared to be English. Perhaps he was a regular. She could have a drink with him. He might make for some useful cover. The alternative was to stay on her own, and that would start to look odd.

"Orange juice," she said.

"Nothing stronger?"

"I don't drink when I'm playing."

"What's your game?"

She put a smile on her face. "Roulette. Yours?"

"Same."

They watched the table as they sipped their drinks.

"You know him?" he asked her.

"Not really."

"His name is Gao. Filthy rich. Multi millions. *Billions*, probably. Investment."

"He certainly likes throwing his money around."

"Likes to put on a show. Bit vulgar, if you ask me."

"I think I did read something about him once," she said. "Not very complimentary."

The man leaned in and spoke conspiratorially. "The thing about the triads? Listen, you want to know a secret? Everyone here is involved with the triads, one way or another. That orange juice you're drinking? That's cash we just laundered for them."

She pretended to be a naïf. "This is a triad place?"

He laughed at her ingenuousness. "They own everywhere. Hong Kong. The whole bloody peninsula belongs to them."

She was about to tell him that she would take another orange juice when Gao swore loudly, pushed away from the table and stood.

"Oh dear," the man said. "Someone's not very happy."

She had been distracted, but it was obvious that he had lost. He cursed again, barked invective at the croupier and made for the exit. A member of staff hurried after him, trying to get him to stay, but Gao ignored him.

Beatrix reached into her bag and took out her phone. She sent the prepared text.

NOW.

She didn't know whether she would have enough time. She had expected to have been able to give Chau notice, but that would have meant that Gao had given her an indication that he was about to leave, and he had surprised her. It looked like she was going to have to rely on Chau's initiative, and that wasn't something that filled her with confidence.

"Where are you going?" the man said to her.

"Nice to meet you," Beatrix said. "I'm late for an appointment. Thanks for the drink."

48

The limousine was parked in front of the entrance. Chau was standing on the same side of the road, fifty feet to the north. He was smoking a cigarette, and pretending to hold a conversation on his cell phone. She was relieved. He was exactly where he was supposed to be and doing exactly what she had told him to do. He saw her come out of the casino and started to proceed along the pavement in the direction of the limousine.

Gao was on the pavement, the two girls close behind him.

Beatrix had an elevated position on the steps and could see to the picnic tables and the parking lot beyond. The three bodyguards were running for the Discovery.

They had been caught off guard, too.

Beatrix smiled at the two doormen as she descended the stairs.

She reached into her bag.

The chauffeur stepped out of the front of the Hummer and opened the rear kerbside door.

Gao paused to let the two girls get into the car. They

giggled as they ducked down and slid into the cabin. Beatrix caught a glimpse of crystal tableware, shards of light glittering off a chrome ice bucket. A blacked-out partition separated the driver from the passenger compartment. That was good. She paced herself carefully so that she was on the pavement beside the chauffeur just as he closed the rear door and turned to get back into the car himself.

He didn't get the chance.

"Excuse me," she said.

He paused and turned back in her direction. "Yes?"

She nodded down at her bag. "One of those girls left this inside."

The suspicion melted from the man's face. "Here," he said, holding out his right hand. "Give it to me."

She pulled her hand out of her bag, the Glock clasped in a loose grip. Her index finger was inside the trigger guard, the trigger pressed up tight against the pad of her index finger. The chauffeur's eyes bulged and he took a step back, his foot slipping off the kerb so that he stumbled back against the frame of the door.

The two doormen clocked what was going on and started down the stairs.

"No," Chau said, pulling his little Kel-Tec and waving it at them. The doormen stopped halfway to the pavement.

Beatrix reached for the chauffeur and, with her left hand, grabbed his jacket and yanked him away from the car. He fell over onto his knees and she kicked him in the ribs with the point of her shoe. He gasped in pain and folded his arms around his chest.

"Now, Chau."

Beatrix had gambled that, if they were quick enough, Gao would not realise what was going on outside his car. She had been pleased that the two girls were there to accompany him. They would make for an excellent distraction. She opened the rear door and slipped inside. The limousine was a riot of bad taste. It was equipped with three mirrored LCD TVs, stainless-steel headliners, and twinkling fibre optics on the ceiling and around the full-length champagne bar. It had two large bench seats facing each other and another that extended between them along the side of the car that was flush against the kerb. Gao was sitting in this seat, his back to the action outside. The girls would have been able to notice it had they been looking, but one was occupied with trying to open a bottle of champagne and the other was nuzzling into Gao's neck.

The girl with the champagne saw her. "Hey!" she protested.

Beatrix heard Chau shut the front door and the engine throbbed as he fed it revs.

"*Get out!*" the girl said to Beatrix, and then screamed as Beatrix showed her the Glock.

"Goodbye." Beatrix nodded to the open door and waved the gun at them.

The girls quickly got the picture. They grabbed their clutch bags and stumbled out into the street.

Gao cursed in Cantonese and started to rise. Beatrix turned the gun on him.

"Sit."

He sat down again.

She crouched and reached for the door, yanking it shut just as Chau let off the handbrake and pulled away.

eatrix sat in the rear seat at ninety degrees to Gao, but close enough to reach out and touch him should she need to. She regarded him and carried out a quick assessment. He was angry and confused. Beatrix could sympathise. He had lost money at the roulette wheel and now his plans for the rest of the evening had taken an unexpected turn for the worse.

He jabbered angrily at her in Cantonese.

Beatrix ignored him.

Chau accelerated and the automatic locks clicked, securing the doors from anyone outside the vehicle. Keeping the gun trained on Gao's head, Beatrix turned and looked back through the rear window. She saw the chauffeur on the side of the road. The two doormen were next to him, one of them with a cell phone pressed to his ear. They needed to move quickly. They would report the hijack to the police and a car as ostentatious as this would be easy to find, even in a city that was as flush with excess as Hong Kong.

They rushed by the parking lot. Beatrix craned her neck around and saw the crippled Discovery. It was crawling onto the road, all four tyres completely flat. The bodyguards were out of the game.

Beatrix would have been more confident if she had been driving, but she couldn't have trusted Chau to keep Gao under control. This could only be a two-person job, and he had to be the driver. She needed him to follow through.

Gao spat out another burst of invective that Beatrix was unable to translate. She didn't need to. She could guess what it comprised: indignation, threats, bluster. She knew Gao's type. He was an important man, used to getting his own way. This would be an outrageous imposition. Perhaps he thought that he could shout and threaten his way out of it? If he did, he was mistaken. Next, he would try to buy his way out, asking her how much she wanted. That wouldn't work, either.

He fired another volley of abuse at her and, when that had no effect, he tried to raise himself out of his seat. Beatrix was ready for that. She turned her hand ninety degrees, reached across the cabin and drove the butt of the Glock into his nose. He fell back onto the seat again, blood running from his right nostril onto his upper lip. He reached up with his fingers and dabbed at it. She turned her wrist again so that the barrel was pointing straight at his head and put her left finger to her lips. *Quiet.* He looked at her with newfound fear and was silent.

The Hummer was too big and the traffic too dense for Chau to drive quickly. He proceeded with care instead, following Jaffe Road onto the tangle of on and off ramps that gave access and egress to the main highway that ran east to west across the island. He picked up speed a little, passing the Wan Chai Sports Ground, the Royal Yacht Club and the Police Officers' Club. Eventually, they reached the docks and Chau turned off just before North Point Ferry

Pier. He swung onto Wharf Road, passing beneath the thicket of cranes that serviced the freighters delivering and collecting goods from the port.

Beatrix turned to Gao. "I'm sorry about this. I would have made an appointment, but things are urgent and I doubt that you would have taken it."

He replied with another flurry of furious Cantonese.

"English, please. I know you speak it."

He glared at her, but switched languages. "You seem to know a lot about me."

"I do."

"Then you know that this will get you killed."

She held up the gun again. "You're in no position to make threats. And it's rude, especially when I'm here to help you."

"To *help* me?"

"You'll agree in a minute."

"Who are you?"

"That doesn't matter. What matters is what I want to show you, and what it means for your immediate future."

His eyes flashed. "What do you mean?"

"Here. Look."

She took the cell phone from her Louis Vuitton bag and tossed it onto the seat next to him. The video file was open on the screen, ready to play. She watched his face as he looked down, an expression of irritated curiosity to start with, but, as he looked at the still image, he must have remembered where it had been shot and what the footage might contain. His eyes widened and she saw him swallow.

"Play it."

He didn't look away as he pressed his finger to the screen. The soundtrack was tinny through the phone's cheap speakers, but more than clear enough for the nature of the transaction to be audible. Gao stared at the screen, unable to take his eyes away. He watched it for twenty seconds before he pressed his finger to the screen again to stop it and handed it back to her as if it was suddenly scalding his fingers.

"You've seen that before, haven't you?"

He looked out of the window, his jaw clenching and unclenching. His skin had a blotchy funereal pallor.

He didn't answer.

"I'm guessing it was emailed to you. The girl—what was her name?"

"Liling."

"That's right. And Liling tried to blackmail you with it, didn't she?"

He folded his hands in his lap and looked down at the floor of the limo.

"Look at me," she said. He did, and she gestured with the Glock. "If you don't answer my questions, I'll shoot you in the knee. Do you understand?"

He nodded.

"What did she do?"

"She emailed it to me and said that it would be sent to the press if I didn't pay her. One million US. That was her price."

"And?"

"And if I had paid her, what good would that do me? The whore would still have the video. She would come back for more and I would be in the same situation again. I am a family man. My company relies on family values. Chinese values. This would be...it would be very destructive. My companies would suffer. Jobs would be lost."

"And so you told your triad friends."

He nodded. "She brought it on herself," he said, as if that

was justification enough for what Beatrix now knew must have happened to Grace's sister.

"They killed her?"

He looked away.

Beatrix slapped him with her left hand. "Answer the question."

"They said that they would make the problem go away. They said it was finished."

"But she didn't have the video on her."

"No. But they said that they would be able to find it."

She laughed without humour. "They *tried*."

"You knew Liling? She gave it to you?"

She held up the gun again. "See this? It means I'm asking the questions."

"So, what is this? You are going to blackmail me now? How much do you want?"

"I don't want money."

"Then what do you want?"

"Just your help. You are a very wealthy and influential man, Mr. Gao. Well connected in the Hong Kong underworld. Would that be a fair assessment?"

He shrugged uncomfortably.

"I am afraid I have a dispute with someone from the underworld. His name is Mr. Ying. You know Mr. Ying, I believe. He is responsible for the *whores* you enjoy so much." She used his word, loading it with bile and daring him to look away from her. He did, and she slapped him again. "Liling used to work for him. You do know Ying, don't you?"

"Yes," he said bitterly.

"He was the man you went to for help?"

"Yes."

"And he killed Liling."

Quieter, "Yes."

She took the phone and held it up. "Did you ever wonder how this was filmed?"

She could see the penny drop. For a smart man, he was remarkably slow on the uptake.

"It wasn't Liling. *Ying* filmed this to use against you in the future. Liling tried to take advantage of it, but he is responsible for it. He is not your friend, Mr. Gao."

"And you are?"

"No. But Mr. Ying has something that I want. I have something that he wants. Unfortunately, what I want is worth more to me than what this footage is worth to him, and he knows that. I do not have the advantage. He has asked me to do something that I am not prepared to do. But if I don't do it, he will hurt someone who has already suffered enough. Someone who doesn't deserve to be caught up in all of this."

"So what do you want from me?"

"I want Mr. Ying out of the way. I imagine that's something you would like, too?"

He gave a small nod, as if even the act of acknowledging it was treacherous and dangerous.

"I can make that happen, Mr. Gao. But to do that, I need help to get to him. That's where you come in."

"What help?"

"Mr. Ying is a *Dai Lo.*"

"Yes?"

"And I need to speak to the Dragon Head."

He spoke fearfully. "Mr. Yeung?"

It was the first time that she had heard the name. Even Chau didn't know the identity of the boss.

"I need to talk to him. You need to make that happen."

50

Beatrix waited in the hotel room.

She changed into trousers and a T-shirt.

She made preparations for what she hoped would come next.

She looked at the practicalities of getting across the border.

She packed a bag with the things that she would need, then she distracted herself with two hours in the mall, buying the things that she thought that Grace might need.

She bought train tickets, in soft sleeper class, a four-berth cabin for them to share, and returned to the hotel.

Chau delivered the fake passports that she had requested: a British one for her and a Chinese one for the girl. Hong Kong was not treated as part of the mainland for immigration purposes, so her passport had been stamped with a Chinese entry visa. It would allow her to stay in China for three months. Grace's passport would allow her to stay indefinitely. They both looked authentic, and she was confident that they would get them safely out of Hong Kong.

She sat cross-legged on the bed, maintaining the Glock

and counting her ammunition. Two magazines. Twenty rounds. She hoped that would be enough.

She stared at her watch. Time passed. She stared at her phone, willing it to ring. It didn't. She paced the room. Hours passed. She exercised, pumping out a thousand sit-ups and another thousand crunches until she was covered in sweat. She stared at the phone. She checked that it was charged.

Still nothing.

The deadline came and went.

HER TELEPHONE finally rang two hours after the deadline had expired.

"*Hello?*"

"Who is this?"

"*I am a friend of Mr. Gao.*"

His English was accented just a little. She didn't recognise the voice. "Mr. Yeung?"

"*Never mind who I am.*"

It didn't matter, and she didn't care. "You know where the girl is?"

"I do."

She wanted to tell him that he was late, that he should have called hours ago, that the delay might have cost Grace her innocence, but there was no profit in doing any of that. She bit her lip between her teeth and then said, her voice hard as iron, "Where?"

"*Mr. Ying has many brothels in Kowloon. I understand you visited one before Mr. Qi's untimely demise?*"

"Get to the point. Which brothel is it?"

"*It is on Jordan Road. Find Jaguar Shoes. It is a front. The brothel is above. The girl is held on the third floor.*"

"How well guarded is it?"

"*Reasonably well. But not so well that it would be an impediment for someone such as you.*"

The man had a slightly supercilious tone, and laughter danced at the edges of his words.

"I don't know who you are, but, if you are lying to me, I'll find Gao again. Before I kill him, I'll make him tell me who you are. And then I'll kill you."

"*I am not lying. We have been watching you. I have no doubt you mean what you say, and I believe that you would try to do it, too. We respect someone with the dedication to do what they promise. Good luck in Kowloon, although I do not believe you will need it.*"

The line went dead.

Beatrix took her Glock and spare magazines and hurried to the door.

BEATRIX RODE the MTR to Jordan Station. She was carrying her bag and the bag that she had packed for Grace. It was eight in the evening by the time she emerged at street level, and the area was bathed in neon. Jordan Street was a narrow canyon, with tall buildings on either side making it feel claustrophobic. The walls were disfigured by air-conditioning units and enormous hoardings. Lines of red flags were strung overhead and lanterns were suspended between the lamp posts. Glowing signs advertised FOOT REFLEXOLOGY and CITY HAIRDRESSING. Scores of handwritten notices written on Day-Glo cards were plastered onto the facades of the shops. They advertised girls from Russia, China, Hong Kong and Thailand. Prices were scrawled next to the nationalities. There were karaoke bars, saunas and massage parlours. Grocery shops offered racks of postcards. Pedestrians idled, some walking down the middle of the street. Traffic growled and horns sounded. Crashing dance music played from the open doorway of a mobile phone shop. The night was close and oppressively hot, the air full of smog that clotted her nostrils and stung the back of her throat. Overhead, the sky was a mass of blacks and purples and, in the distance, a peal of thunder sounded.

A storm was coming.

Beatrix paused outside the shoe shop. A shutter obscured the window, but a door next to it was open. A fluorescent arrow pointed into the shop, promising "Free Preview. Many Different Countries/Girls. Taste Excitement. Less 50%." The doorway was obscured by a curtain of multicoloured beads. The unit next door was more brazen. Three bored women sat on the floor in cheap lingerie. A red light flickered overhead.

She scouted up and down the street. There was no other way inside. Music pulsed. A gaggle of drunken *gweilos* staggered down the middle of the street, drawing the ire of the taxi driver whose cab they were blocking. He leaned on his horn. They swore colourfully in return.

Thunder boomed again, closer this time, and the first fat gobbets of rain splashed onto the asphalt.

Beatrix was sick with trepidation. There was a tightness in her muscles that she recognised: the anticipation of violence. Ying's deadline had passed four hours ago. She returned to the doorway. There was no point in being subtle, and she was in no mood. She didn't know whether she was too late. Grace might not have the luxury of subtlety.

She stepped up to the bead curtain. She swept it aside with her right hand as she reached into her bag for the Glock with her left.

51

The door opened into a small hallway with a flight of stairs directly ahead. A desk was crammed against one wall, leaving barely enough space for it to be passed. A blowsy, broad-shouldered woman—the *mamasan*—was at the desk. She was reading a dog-eared paperback and looked up as she heard the tinkling of the beads.

She said something in Mandarin. A query and then, as Beatrix dropped the bags and advanced, a protest. Beatrix made no effort to translate, but it didn't matter. She stepped up to the desk and punched the woman square in the face. She toppled backwards and fell off her stool. Beatrix slid around the table, crouched over the woman and punched her again. Her eyes rolled back and closed.

She transferred the Glock to her right hand, slipped her finger through the guard and put a little pressure on the trigger.

The stairs were bare, with pictures of J-Pop stars plastered to the wall.

She climbed.

The first-floor landing was larger than the hallway downstairs. There was a long sofa upholstered in stained red fabric. Five girls sat on it. They were all in their underwear, and they looked up with a boredom that curdled into hostility when they saw that she was not a customer. Hostility turned to fear as they noticed the Glock. There were four doors off the hallway. Beatrix heard grunting from behind one of them, the creaking of floorboards and the rhythmic bang of a headboard as it clattered against a thin plaster wall.

The man on the phone had said the third floor, and so she climbed.

The second floor was the same. It was lit by a row of lights with orange shades. A woman with badly dyed hair sat on a wooden stool and hid her face behind a newspaper. Another four doors, with noise coming from behind two of them. One of the doors opened and a Chinese man stepped out into the hallway, hoisting up his trousers. He saw Beatrix, and was about to say something, but then he saw the Glock in her hand and thought better of it. He pressed himself against the wall as she walked by. Beatrix glanced inside the door and saw a naked woman, wiping herself, her clothes draped over the end of her bed.

She climbed. The higher she got, the more vulnerable she felt. More people between her and the exit. *No time to worry about that.* The building didn't look as if it had a fire escape. The only way out was to go back down the stairs. She wouldn't have long to get Grace and get out. Someone would have seen her. The woman downstairs might come around. The man who had come out of the bedroom. The girl inside. The girls waiting for trade. Any of them could raise the alarm.

She reached the third floor. It was the top of the building. Another hallway with four doorways.

She raised the Glock, approached the first door and opened it.

Empty.

She tried the second.

A man and woman, both naked, asleep on the bed.

The third.

It was locked with a deadbolt.

She slid the bolt back and opened the door.

A bed, a dresser and a single wooden chair. A large fern in a planter. A round mirror on the wall. Faded wallpaper, peeling in places, pustulated with mould.

A girl was on the bed, sitting against the headboard, her legs drawn up beneath her chin.

"Grace."

She moved her head and looked across the room. She was expressionless. If she recognised Beatrix, she did not show it. Beatrix saw the purple contusion across her cheekbone. It extended all the way down the right side of her face to her chin. She was wearing a simple red dress with thin straps and Beatrix saw another bruise on her right shoulder, the discolouration running down her torso until it was hidden beneath the fabric.

Her anger kindled.

She heard an angry voice from the ground floor.

She made her voice as soft as she could. "Grace."

The girl turned her head away and stared at the wall.

Beatrix heard the sound of feet pounding up a staircase below.

She stepped into the room, took the girl by the wrist and pulled, gently easing her off the bed.

She heard more voices. Doors opened and slammed. An outraged protest.

Beatrix led the way out of the bedroom. The second door was open now, the naked man she had seen before looking at the stairs. He heard Beatrix and turned. She shook her head, showed him the Glock, and indicated that he should go back inside. He did. The door closed again.

She held Grace's hand and led her down the stairs, the pistol held out before her. She descended into the first-floor hallway. The women were still there, and their attention swung away as two men ascended from the opposite side. They were wearing tracksuit tops and jeans and they had cleavers in their hands. One man had tattoos on his face. Beatrix shot him first, adjusted her aim with a flick of her wrist, and shot the other. The pistol was small, but it was unsuppressed and it barked loudly. The women screamed and scuttled as far away from her as they could. She led Grace across the hall to the stairs. The girl stopped at the bodies. Beatrix stooped and picked her up, her left arm holding the girl against her body while she held out the pistol in her right.

"Put your arms around my neck."

Grace did as she was told and held on.

Beatrix negotiated the final flight of stairs. The woman she had knocked out had disappeared and her table had been overturned. Beatrix paused at the foot of the stairs and collected the two bags that she had left there. She listened. She heard the noise of the street outside, cars passing, raised voices, an argument. She stepped around the table and parted the curtain of beads. There was a car parked at the kerb that hadn't been there before, blocking the flow of traffic. The car was empty. She waited for another five seconds, scanning left and right, but she saw nothing.

She put the Baby Glock in her bag and, still carrying the girl, merged into the flow of pedestrians.

52

Beatrix hurried with Grace to the MTR. She took the girl to the public bathroom and, behind the locked door of a cubicle, encouraged her to change out of the dress. Her body was horribly bruised. She tried not to look at the marks as she helped her to dress in the jeans, t-shirt and thin jumper that she had bought for her earlier.

Beatrix led the way onto the concourse, bought tickets for them both from the machine, and descended to the platform. There was a short wait for the next train. Beatrix walked away from the entrance to the platform and turned so that she was facing it. There had been no time to check that they were not being followed, and she knew Ying well enough to know that he wouldn't react well to what she had just done. She concentrated on keeping herself under control, suppressing the seething anger that was urging her back to the brothel to murder every last pimping bastard that she could find.

The train arrived.

They rode the Tsuen Wan Line north to Yau Ma Tei and changed to the Kwun Tong Line.

Beatrix could not stop herself from asking the question. When they were seated again, she took both of Grace's hands in hers.

"What did they—" She stopped, unsure of how to ask the question that she needed to ask. "Did they make you do anything?"

Grace stared back at her. She didn't speak. Her face was blank, like a mask. There had been light in her eyes before. They had sparkled when she laughed, even after everything that had happened to her. But the light was gone now, extinguished. It was a more eloquent answer than anything she could have said.

Beatrix drew the girl to her and hugged her. Grace shuffled across the seat and moved awkwardly into Beatrix's embrace, stiff and unresponsive. Beatrix held her and waited for her to relax, but she did not. Beatrix felt the sting of tears in her eyes and, immediately after that, the burn of fury. All of her rage—the drips of poison that she had been collecting since Control's agents had torn her life straight down the middle three months ago—overflowed the inadequate vessel into which she had been collecting it.

The train rumbled north to Kowloon Tong. They disembarked and Beatrix led the way to the East Rail Line and the final run to the border at Lo Wu.

"Don't worry," she said, hating herself even as she said it. "It's over now. I have you. They can't get to you. You're *safe*."

Grace's voice, when she finally spoke, was as blank as her face.

"You said that before."

The repudiation stung bitterly. She couldn't be angry about it.

The girl was right.

What had happened was her fault.

Chau had erred, but it was at her direction.

It was *her* fault.

53

The checkpoint was a short distance from Lo Wu station. Beatrix led the way, gripping Grace's hand tightly in hers. She waited until the platform was clear before she took the Glock, the magazine and the knife and dropped them into an empty trash can. She hoped that she wouldn't need weapons now, and she wasn't about to risk taking them across the border.

The crossing was straightforward enough: two buildings connected by a long bridge. They made their way across it and descended the stairs into a large hall with a long queue of people, waiting for passport control. Beatrix handed over their passports and arrival cards and waited for them to be checked by the surly guard. The woman stared at them, bored beyond words, before she grunted something unintelligible at her.

"Excuse me?"

She repeated it. Beatrix's Mandarin wasn't good enough to translate it.

Grace replied for her. The guard asked another question. Grace answered again and the guard pushed their passports back over the desk so that Beatrix could collect them.

Beatrix knew not to wait. She kept a firm grip on Grace's hand and walked straight ahead until they were out of the main doors and outside.

"What did she say?"

"She ask who you were. I said you were friend of my mother."

"Well done."

The girl didn't reply and, in moments, the glazed look returned to her face.

Beatrix looked around.

China.

They were in a large public square with Shenzhen Railway Station on one side and Luohu Commercial City on the other. She led the way to the railway station.

"You said you had relatives in Tianjin," she said. "Your aunt? If you want, I'll take you to her."

The girl didn't reply.

"You can't stay in Hong Kong. It's not safe. The man who"—she paused, clenching her teeth—"took you; he is dangerous. And he won't just let you stay. You have to leave now. I'm sorry, but...there's no other choice."

She just looked at her feet and let Beatrix lead her on.

"Grace, talk to me."

"It is fine," she said. "I understand. But you do not have to come with me. I can go myself."

"*No,*" Beatrix retorted at once. "I'm coming, too."

I've let you down once.

I'm never letting you down again.

THE TRAIN from Shenzhen to Beijing was scheduled to take thirteen hours. It was known as the "*Jingjiu*" and ran non-stop. The bullet trains that the Chinese were so proud of did not yet serve this marathon route and, as they approached the platform, Beatrix saw the locomotive. It was blocky and powerful, with brutal lines that looked nothing like the sleek trains that she had seen in the gushing advertisements. The train, a quarter of a mile from end to end, was comprised of sixteen carriages painted in high-gloss white with blue racing stripes.

Beatrix took out their tickets and showed them to one of the female attendants. She shone a regulation smile at Beatrix before directing her to the third carriage along. Another similarly glossy attendant took over when they reached the correct car, showing them inside to their sleeper compartment.

Hundreds of passengers aboard this train were wedged into seats designated only as hard or soft. Beatrix had bought tickets in soft sleeper class, a separate compartment with bunks and antimacassars and a loudspeaker in the ceiling playing music that proved impossible to turn off until she pulled the grille away and yanked out the wiring. The compartment had four bunks, each of which was furnished with a mattress that was significantly more comfortable than those in the "hard sleeper" compartments. They had room, so they were able to choose whether to sleep on the upper or lower bunk. They both chose the lower and sat quietly as the train rolled out of the station, and stayed there for another thirty minutes until Beatrix suggested that they find the dining car for some food.

"That would be nice," Grace said.

Beatrix felt that she was finally making progress.

The dining car was pleasant, with neat tables covered with starched white tablecloths and comfortable seats. They ordered rice and vegetables and looked out of the window into the darkness as they ate them, the gloomy landscape rushing by.

They had been eating in silence until Grace rested her chopsticks across her bowl and asked Beatrix what she was going to do.

"What do you mean?"

"Where will you go? After this?"

"Back," she said.

"Hong Kong?"

She nodded.

"Why? It is not safe for you, too, is it?"

"I can look after myself, Grace."

"Stay in Beijing. Or go somewhere else. Why go back to Hong Kong? Triad will find you."

She watched the emerald-green paddies rushing by on the other side of the glass, and thought about how going back was a foolish move. "I have a friend there," she said.

"Mr. Chau?"

She nodded. "I told him I would protect him if he helped me find you, and he did. I have to see him. I'll try to persuade him to leave."

"And if he will not?"

"That'll be up to him. His choice."

"But *you* will leave?"

She paused at that. The smart thing to do would be to get away, to put a thousand miles between her and Ying, and try to forget all about it. And yet...and yet, she couldn't do it. She knew that she would never be able to forgive herself if she ran. Ying had done something unconscionable. She had killed men for much, much less. He owed a debt for that, and she would collect.

There would be blood.

"Beatrix? You will leave?"

"Yes," she lied. "I think my time in Hong Kong is done."

54

They transferred to a second train for the connection to Tianjin. They arrived at midday, hot and sticky after the air conditioning in the train broke down. Beatrix paid for a cab to take them to the village on the outskirts of the city where Grace's aunt lived. The car pulled up outside a pleasant row of houses on a hill, with a view into a valley where the tiers of a pagoda could be seen. A wire that was heavy with paper lanterns had been strung across the street. Children played happily in a patch of scrubby grass.

"Is this it?"

"Yes," Grace replied. "My aunt's house is over there."

"Here." Beatrix handed her the bag with the things that she had bought.

The girl reached for the door and, as Beatrix thought she was going to open it and go without another word, she paused, her fingers trailing on the handle. She turned back and Beatrix saw that she was crying.

"Don't," Beatrix said, taking Grace by the shoulder. "It's fine now. You'll be fine."

"Thank you."

She smiled. She wanted to apologise for what had happened to her, but she didn't know how to say it.

Grace took her hand. "You are sad, Beatrix. I can see it in your eyes. I hope that you can be happy."

She pulled the handle, pushed the door open and stepped down onto the dusty street.

The driver turned. "Miss?"

"The station."

The man put the car into gear and pulled away. Beatrix turned and watched through the rear window. Grace had paused at the gate to one of the houses. She waited there until the car reached the corner that would take it out of view, raised her hand in farewell and then disappeared.

55

Beatrix didn't know when the decision became a decision. It had been in the back of her mind for a while, she realised, lingering there like an illness waiting for the right time to take hold.

When had it been transformed from a possibility to a certainty?

From an abstract prospect to an inevitability?

It didn't matter. Beatrix became aware of the decision as she rode the train south again. The train was leaving Zhengzhou.

She had found the little packet of opium in her bag. She wasn't even aware that she had brought it with her, and her first thought was to chide herself for doing something so stupid. Bringing it across the border was asking for trouble. If she had been arrested, it would have been the work of a moment for Control to locate her. That would, unquestionably, have been that. Her second thought was that she must dispose of it. That would be the sensible thing to do, to throw it from the train window into the landscape beyond.

But, even as she accepted that was true, she had known that she would be unable to do it.

The dealer in Wan Chai had given the little envelope to her as a sample. She had dismissed his offer. Opium was not for her. But the voice in her head had whispered its sweet insinuations—had told her that she was wrong, that it was for her; it was perfect for her. It told her that it was just what she needed to help her forget about Isabella. That same tiny voice, impossible to silence, had continued throughout the long journey north and now on the return trip back to Hong Kong.

Did she want to forget about Grace and what had happened to her?

Did she want to forget the blankness in the girl's eyes?

She *did*.

She wasn't sure what the rules were for smoking on the train, but there were no alarms that she could see. She yanked the stiff window upwards until it was halfway open and the wind was rustling the curtains. She collected her bag from the opposite bunk and took out the packet. She pulled out the opium and rubbed it between her fingers. It was tough and fibrous. She pinched off a small piece and rolled it into a ball, which she dropped into the bowl of the cheap metal spoon she had taken from the dining carriage. Beatrix set it alight with her lighter. It smelt unusual, like fresh plant sap. She blew it out at once, lowered her head over the smoke and inhaled deeply through her nose.

The fumes hit her like a sledgehammer.

She slumped back against the wall of the bunk.

Her thoughts evaporated like mist.

She concentrated on the smoke, the ebb and flow as it entered her lungs and then her veins. She felt herself falling into space. The compartment, the train, the monotony of the endless landscape; all were obliterated as dreams that were not really dreams, but visitations, filled her mind. She heard the clack of the rails, and then fragments of conversation. She saw absent friends. She saw Grace. She saw her husband, Lucas, and her dear Isabella. They formed part of a raucous procession behind her closed eyelids.

Then she heard another voice. It shook her awake, and she realised it was her own murmuring, her conversation with someone who wasn't really there.

She might have been slumped there for five minutes or five hours. She had no idea. She came around again to the sound of an angry voice. Harsh, guttural Mandarin, and a fist crashing against the door.

She forced open her eyes and, still light-headed and woozy, slapped herself on the cheek.

She stood on unsteady legs and slid the bolt in the lock. The guard was standing outside. He spat out a stream of quick-fire Mandarin that she couldn't understand. Seeing her confusion, he turned and pointed out of the open door. The train had pulled into a platform, and a sign—translated into English—read Shenzhen Station. She heard the music. The long-haul expresses always broadcast a triumphal or sentimental song when they arrived at their destinations. She recognised the saccharine "Fishing Junks at Sunset."

They had arrived.

Hours had passed.

Beatrix suddenly felt nauseated and, pushing by the guard, she bent double and vomited out of the open door and onto the platform. The man watched, perplexed, as she was sick again and again, eventually heaving on an empty stomach.

When she finally felt in control of herself, she went back into the compartment and collected her bag. Once she had made sure that the rest of the opium was stowed safely inside, Beatrix fled into the night.

56

Hong Kong was the kind of place where you could get whatever you wanted, whenever you wanted it. There was no night and no day, but only the light of the sun and the light of the neon. It had been a simple enough thing to find what she needed. The man who had sold her the opium had smiled a knowing smile as she returned and asked for more. He told her that she would enjoy it more if she experienced it properly. He had told her to return that same evening and, when she did, he had taken her to a fetid alley that lurked behind the high wharves of the Kowloon harbour.

Beatrix tried to remember the winding lefts and rights of the journey and knew that she would struggle to find it again on her own. The entrance was found at the end of a flight of steps that led down to a black gap like the mouth of a cave. She passed down the steps, worn smooth in the centre by the ceaseless tread of feet. There was a single flickering bulb above the door. The man knocked. An eye appeared in the peephole, and then locks were turned and the door opened to them. The man said nothing; he just stepped aside.

Beatrix climbed the stairs to a long low room, thick and heavy with brown opium smoke.

They called them *Hua-yan jian*: flower-smoke rooms. It was a romantic vision and did not accord with reality. It was dark and difficult to make anything out. She saw bodies stretched out in strange poses; bowed shoulders, bent knees, heads thrown back, and chins pointing upward. Those who were awake and cognisant turned to look at her with glassy, hostile eyes. Out of the black shadows there glimmered little red circles of light, alternating between bright and faint, as the burning opium waxed or waned in the bowls of the metal pipes that were held to the lips of the smokers. The majority of the men and women here were quiet, lying in idle repose, but some kept up low conversation with themselves or with others. There were mumbled imprecations, sighs of torpor, and snores from those who had lapsed into addled sleep. Beatrix saw the small brazier of burning charcoal at the other end of the room. One of the wizened old men paid by the triads to administer the den was crouched before it, his elbows resting on his bent knees and his jaw resting upon his two fists, staring into the fire.

She paid for a 'premium' space. For an extra ten dollars she was guaranteed a place on the floor, as well as the privilege of having her pipe prepared for her by the ex-patriot Indian who ran the den. It was late and, although she did have a spot to lie down, all the best places had been taken. These were against the wall, where you could lean back without falling over. There was also what the Indian called the 'VIP section', an exclusive end of the floor near the brazier that had a mattress wedged up against the corner by a window. This cost twenty dollars, and was also taken.

She didn't care. She would make do.

"Ya-p'iàn," the Indian said in a hushed and reverent tone.

Opium.

57

Time passed.

Beatrix returned to the den again and again. She lost track of the days. She wasn't really sure how long she had been smoking. *A week? Two weeks?* Everything was smoothed out. Worries disappeared. Concerns were forgotten. Time became an abstract concept.

She closed her eyes and let her thoughts drift, buffeted along by the warmth and dizzying caress of the opium. It obliterated her memories. She forgot about Grace. She forgot about Ying. She even forgot about Isabella. She forgot about the hopelessness of it all. Each new breath of the sweet-smelling smoke rubbed away a little more detail until all that was left of her recollections was a mess of scenes, pictures and images that made little sense.

"Hey."

She dived deeper and deeper, leaving her worries and regrets above her where they couldn't trouble her any longer.

"*Hey.*"

She felt a hand on her shoulder, shaking her, gently at first, and then much harder.

She opened her eyes and blinked until she could see again.

It was a middle-aged Chinese man.

"What?" she mumbled.

"Your phone. Your phone. It ringing."

She heard it now and reached into her pocket. She answered it and pressed it to her ear.

"What?"

"*Where are you?*"

It was Chau.

"What do you mean?"

"*You said you wanted to meet. The money?*"

"No, I didn't."

"*Yes, you did. You called me.*"

"When?"

"*Yesterday.*"

Had she? She didn't remember.

"*You said three o'clock on the ferry. It is four. Where are you?*"

Had she said that? *Really?* It was possible. She thought about it some more and remembered that she had wanted to see him. The money. He had money for her. She wanted the rest of what she was owed. There was a lot, and she was going to need all of it. She had called him. He was right. She had.

"Where are you?"

"*Kowloon. Where you said. Where are you?*"

"Sheung Wan."

"*You want to come to me?*"

She paused, trying to clear the fumes from her brain. "No. Be in Sun Yat Sen Park in an hour."

58

Chau was waiting next to a small Buddhist shrine that was strewn with the flowers of the locals' frequent offerings. The street was full of kerbside vendors, doing a brisk evening trade. There were clouds of pungent smoke, the sizzle of hot oil and a wide variety of morsels.

Chau was sitting at a wooden picnic table. He was picking at an open paper bag of fried grasshoppers. She went over to him and sat down. There was a bag at his feet.

He indicated the insects. "You want?"

"No, thanks."

They watched as a local hooker approached the shrine and deposited an offering amid the detritus that had already been left there.

"She ask for busy night with pleasant customers," he said.

They watched the girl as she made her prayer, turned and walked away to rejoin the busy street.

"The girl?" Chau asked. "Grace?"

"Safe."

"Where?"

"She's safe, Chau. Leave it at that."

"What about us?"

"What *about* us?"

"What are we going to do? Ying is looking for us."

"Do what you want. Move away. Stay here. I don't care."

"He will kill us if he finds us."

"Didn't you hear me? I said, *I don't care.*"

He looked at her with concern. "What is the matter, Beatrix?"

"I'm done with all of it, Chau. Ying. The triads. *All of it.*"

"What about me?"

"You're a big boy."

He looked at her as if she had slapped his face.

"I'm sorry, Chau. It's just...I'm tired. I'm tired of all of it. We took care of Donnie Qi and now we've got Ying. The triad..." She shook her head. "It's like a hydra. You chop off one head and two more grow back. We can't keep fighting. Look. You've got money now. We made a lot, right? Use it. Go away somewhere. Never come back."

"You're giving up?"

"You can call it that if you like."

His eyes narrowed as he regarded her. "What is wrong with you?"

"Nothing."

"You are high. You are on drugs!"

She waved it off.

"No," he persisted. "You are. Your eyes. I know signs. You are high."

She stood. She felt a blast of shame. She didn't want to admit what she had been doing, and that all she could think about was going back to do it again.

"You are leaving?"

"My money?"

"Here." He nodded to the bag at his feet.

She reached down and took it. She didn't bother to check it was all there.

"Thank you, Chau."

"For what?"

"For this. And for helping me with Grace. I appreciate that. You didn't have to do it."

"You can't just leave me!" he protested pitifully. "Ying will kill me."

"Then *go*," she repeated. "Go to China. Go anywhere but here." She put out her hand and, after a moment of hesitation, he took it. "Goodbye, Chau."

She turned her back on him and walked away.

59

Time passed. Beatrix visited the *Hua-yan jian* every evening. Sometimes she would stay for an hour and other times she would stay all night.

Each pipe removed her from her worries and anxieties, but when she awoke, they were all there again as if they had never been away. They developed. Like cancers, they mutated and spread. Her memories, far from being erased, became malignant reminders of her failures.

She found that, as she cared less and less about herself, she cared more about what had happened to Grace. She was unable to forget the girl. The look in her eyes, when she had taken her from the brothel, haunted her dreams. Even the depth of her narcotic slumber was unable to cloak it. She remembered Grace's tears as she had left her outside her aunt's house. She remembered her thought, fully realised now, that the girl had been robbed of her childhood. Beatrix's anger, never completely extinguished, had flickered back into life. She could control the flame with each new pipe. But as soon as she revived, it was like a gust of pure oxygen had been directed onto the restive embers and it flared once again.

And then, one day, she found that she had diverted from her usual path to the den. She found herself in Wan Chai, on Lockhart Road, opposite the Nine Dragons. It was incredibly foolish of her—she had no weapon, for a start—but she had been drawn there, unable to resist. She bought a baseball cap and a pair of sunglasses from a street vendor and put them on.

There was a karaoke bar opposite the club. The place had an open façade and she had taken a seat there, nursing a drink for thirty minutes as she watched the comings and goings on the other side of the street.

The idiocy of what she was doing finally dawned on her, and she had just scattered enough change on the table to cover the check when a car drew up alongside the club and Fang Chun Ying stepped out. She angled her head away and watched through the big mirror that was fixed to the wall behind the bar. He was with two of his lieutenants, a broad smile on his face as if he was without a care.

Beatrix waited until he had descended the stairs into the club, collected her bag and left the bar.

She took out her phone, opened a browser window and navigated to the Facebook page that she and Chau used to communicate with one another. She stopped so that she could type.

MEET ME. SAME PLACE. 9PM.

CHAU WAS WAITING at the same picnic table in Sun Yat Sen Park, wearing the same ridiculously garish Hawaiian shirt that he had been wearing before. He was looking in the other direction, out into the harbour, and she took a moment to stop at one of the street vendors so that she could buy him a packet of fried grasshoppers. She paid the vendor and took the food to the table.

"Chau," she said.

He started with alarm. "Beatrix, I did not see you."

"Because you always have your eyes closed," she said.

"I did not think we would meet again."

"I've had a change of heart. Here. Peace offering."

She gave him the fried grasshoppers.

"Thank you," he said, but he left them untouched. "What is it, Beatrix? I am confused."

"You didn't leave."

"I think about it, but I do not know where to go. But I know you are right. I cannot stay."

He's nervous, too, she thought, but that was not out of character for him. He was a nervous man by disposition. And, she reminded herself, there was no reason why he would have expected to hear from her again. He would have anticipated bad news, perhaps something that would have repercussions for him.

"Maybe you can."

"Stay?"

"Maybe." She indicated the bag of insects. "You're not going to eat those?"

He pushed them to the middle of the table. "I am sorry. I have lost my appetite. What are you talking about?"

"Ying. I saw him."

"*What?* Where?"

"The Nine Dragons."

"Why would you go there?" he said, his eyes bulging with panic.

"I don't know. I had an itch. Needed to scratch it."

"Did he see you?"

"What do you think, Chau?" she chided. "Of course not."

"So?"

"So I've changed my mind. I can't let a man who has done the things that he has done—the things that he is *still* doing—breathe the same air as my daughter. He needs to *go*, Chau. Do you understand what I mean by that?"

"Of course. How?"

"That's why we're talking. I need you to help me."

He shook his head violently. "No, Beatrix—"

"Relax, Chau. You have to do very little."

He started to stand. "I have to do *nothing*."

"*Sit down*." Her eyes were full of cold fire. She knew that his fear of her was all she needed to control him.

He sat. "What do you want?"

"I watched him. He's well guarded. As far as he's concerned, I'm still here. He'll be careful until he's sure I'm gone."

"So?"

"So there has to be *somewhere* he lets his guard down. His home, his mistress, a restaurant he likes to visit. Somewhere he feels safe. Do you still have your police connection?"

"Yes," he said. Chau was friendly with an officer in the Organised Crime and Triad Bureau of the Hong Kong Police Force. The officer was bent and could be easily bought.

"Speak to him. Tell him you want to know everything he knows about Ying. I want his routine. They'll have had surveillance on him at some point. They probably still do. And then you tell me what he tells you. I'll look at it and pick out the weak spots. That's the first thing."

"The second?"

"I need a weapon."

Beatrix had ignored the urge to smoke that night. She had used some of the money that Chau had given her to rent a cheap hotel room. The room was palatial in comparison to the den and she managed five hours of almost uninterrupted sleep and awoke to feel more refreshed than she could remember.

When she opened the Facebook group, she found there was a message for her from Chau.

MIDDAY. SAME PLACE.

CHAU WAS WAITING FOR HER.

"You still want Ying?"

"I do."

He looked terribly nervous. "I...I..."

"What, Chau? You *what?*"

"Then I know how it can be done."

"Really?"

"Like you say—I have friends, Beatrix. I ask."

"The police?"

"No. Friend in Wo Shun Wo."

"You never mentioned him before."

"There was never reason to mention him. He says that Ying plays poker every Wednesday night. There is a warehouse he owns. The game is there. Four other players play with him. Old triad friends. High stakes. He will be there tonight."

"Where is it?"

"It is on Ap Lei Chau. Lee Nam Road."

"Security?"

"Some. But it is Wo Shun Wo, Beatrix. No criminal is going to rob them, and police are not going to raid triad poker game. Triads own underworld and own police. What do they have to fear?"

Me, Beatrix thought. *They have* me *to fear.*

But she knew that Ying would be careful, and she didn't dismiss the potential for security quite as readily as Chau did.

"Your friend. Is he involved?"

"He will be there. He is croupier. He will leave a door open for us if we pay him well enough."

"How much?"

"Not too much. Don't worry about that, Beatrix. I sort it. I benefit, too."

Beatrix considered the possibilities. It was a golden opportunity. Somewhere quiet, out of the way. No one to get in the way. Somewhere he would feel safe and secure. That was all good. But there would be security. It would be easier, but it wouldn't be easy.

Chau reached down and collected a bag that was resting by his feet. He passed it around the table to Beatrix. She opened it and put a hand inside. There were two pistols wrapped in oilcloth inside.

"I don't need two," she said.

He looked at her and tried to put a little confidence in his voice. "I will help."

"*Really?*"

He nodded. "When Ying is gone, things better for both of us. The other players will be armed. Two of us will stand a better chance than one."

That was true. "You have to be sure, Chau. *Completely* sure."

He held her eye. "I am sure, Beatrix. This will work. The end of problems for both of us."

61

Beatrix took a taxi to the address Chau had given her. Ap Lei Chau was also known as Aberdeen Island, and Lee Nam Road was near the docks. It was south-west of the main island, and the taxi passed over the four-lane bridge that connected the two before skirting the busy central district for the industrial zone to the south. She had the driver stop half a mile away, paid him and got out of the cab. She waited until he had pulled away, and started to walk.

Lee Nam Road was a narrow two-lane highway that was pressed in on one side by the shoulders of the warehouses and office blocks, and by the sea on the other. There was a concrete berm topped with a wire-mesh fence and, beyond it, Aberdeen Harbour and the East Lamma Channel.

Ying's warehouse housed a legitimate business that supplied ice to bars and restaurants around the city. Beatrix scouted it from the other side of the street. The building was right up close to the street, with trucks bearing the business's livery parked at the edge of the road. A large roller door was open and a truck, backed halfway into the interior, was being loaded. She counted six members of staff. A seventh man was lounging against the wall, smoking a cigarette as he glared dolefully at the comings and goings outside.

She walked on. More warehouses. Lots of trucks. The sound of freight being hefted around, the reversing-alarms of lorries and the busy hum of forklifts. She stopped at the end of the street and watched as the freshly loaded truck was driven away.

She set off in the direction from which she had arrived, pretending to hold a conversation on her cell phone. She assessed the entrances and exits. It was a single-storey building. There were two long windows on the ground floor, both obscured by lowered blinds. There was the roller door, large enough for a truck to pass through. That, she guessed, would be closed and locked as soon as the day's business had been concluded. It would be too noisy to open and she discounted it as a means to get inside. The main door for those on foot was to the side of the roller door. *A frontal assault?* If there were guards, that would be where they were concentrated. She discounted it. *Too risky.*

She walked on a little more. There was an alleyway between Ying's warehouse and its neighbour. She saw another door next to a row of industrial bins. It was open.

Chau's contact had told them that was how they would get inside. He would leave it open for them.

That was more promising.

There was nothing about the place that looked out of the ordinary. It looked like a working, legitimate business. She had no doubt that Ying was involved with several such setups, all around the city. He would need a mechanism to launder his illicit money. This would be as good as any.

She walked to the terminal at Lei Tung and rode the bus

back to Hong Kong Island. She had already started to plan. Could she trust Chau's intelligence? There was no reason why not. He had just as much motivation to do away with Ying as she did.

No, she corrected herself. Almost *as much*.

He hadn't looked into Grace's eyes like she had.

But he had enough motivation. Ying wanted Chau dead. He had been living a frightened existence ever since Ying had threatened them both. He knew, better than she did, what the man was capable of. He stood to recover his liberty with the *Dai Lo* out of the way. This was his home. And he had more of a reason to live than she did. He was invested.

So *how* would she do it?

Beatrix reassessed. Ying and another five men would be there. Maybe guards, too. She could gamble and do it alone, but she stood a better chance with Chau's help. She would need someone to cover the others while she secured Ying. She had been wary of Chau's offer, but now she found that she agreed with him. It wasn't ideal, but nothing had been ideal ever since she had landed here. She would make do.

62

They took Chau's Mercedes to the island. Beatrix sat in the back and made sure that both guns—a Walther P5 for her and a Browning Hi Power for Chau—were clean and ready to fire. She hoped that getting Ying out of the building could be achieved without violence, but she was not prepared to gamble on that. If it was necessary to shoot, the last thing she wanted was for there to be a misfire.

She told him to drive as near to the warehouse as he could. Parking was not easy, but they found an empty space fifty feet to the north.

She gave the Browning back to Chau and told him to pay attention.

"I'm going to go in first and I'm going to do the talking. I want you to stand by the door and cover them. I doubt they will be particularly frightened by having a gun waved in their faces, so we're going to be firm and to the point. Businesslike. I'll get Ying and bring him out. You stay and cover the others, then get back to the car. He'll travel in the back with me. You drive."

"I understand. Where do we take him?"

"There's empty land on South Horizon Drive. We'll take him up there and put him in the trunk. I'll drive from then on. We'll take him somewhere we can make him disappear." She looked at him sternly. "Is that all clear, Chau?"

"It is."

"You do *exactly* as I say. There's no room for variation."

"Exactly as you say." He looked pale.

She knew she needed to reassure him. "Nerves are fine, Chau. I'll do most of what needs to be done. You'll just need to cover me."

"I know. I got it."

THEY LEFT the Mercedes and Beatrix led the way down the street. She saw nothing that gave her any reason for concern. The business's trucks were parked at the side of the road, forming a narrow corridor with the building into which small pools of illumination were thrown by the street lights overhead. The roller door was shut and secured by a hefty padlock. The main entrance was shut. As they walked next to the door, she glanced in through the glass panel. The small reception room was dark, save for a sliver of golden light admitted by the gap beneath an internal door that must have led into the warehouse.

Someone was inside.

They walked on until Beatrix was satisfied, then turned and walked back.

The alleyway was dark, but Beatrix could see that the side door was ajar.

Beatrix took two balaclavas from her pocket and tossed one to Chau. "Put it on," she said.

He nodded and pulled the balaclava over his head, unrolling it all the way until all she could see was the glitter of his black eyes and his thin lips. She did the same.

Beatrix led the way. They advanced into the alleyway.

She reached the door.

She paused there and listened. It was quiet inside. She curled her hand around the Walther P5 and gently pulled the door fully open.

Inside was a short corridor. It was dark, save for the light that limned the edges of the interior door at the end of the corridor. Beatrix stepped inside. Her heart beat a little faster. She tamped it down with measured breathing. The adrenaline was good; it would keep her sharp, but she needed to be in control.

She turned her head. Chau was behind her. He held his pistol ready.

She was ready for violence, if that was what was needed; fast, sudden, volcanic violence that would inspire anyone who might doubt her to think again. She would shoot if she had to. She wasn't fearful of it. It would be an automatic reaction if she found herself in a situation where she determined it was necessary.

She reached the door and paused again. She couldn't hear anything from the other side.

She turned to Chau, about to tell him to be ready to move, and looked right into the barrel of his raised pistol.

"Do not move."

"You've got to be joking."

"No joke."

She shook her head. "Seriously? You're double-crossing me? *You?*"

His face was obscured by the balaclava. "You ask me to choose between him and you. I choose him. You are a junkie. I know. I see the signs. How can I trust a junkie? How can you protect me when you don't even care about protecting yourself?"

A bitter little smile kinked the edges of her mouth. "You idiot, Chau."

"Take off balaclava and open door."

She pulled it over her head. She wondered whether there would be any chance of getting to him before he could fire, but she concluded that it would be too risky. He had cautiously taken two steps backwards, increasing the distance that she would have to cover. The corridor was narrow, too. The chances of disabling him before he could shoot her were slim.

She cursed herself.

Chau, of all people.

He had fooled her.

63

"Door, please, Beatrix. Open door."

She turned the handle and opened the door. The room beyond was empty.

There was no table, nor any chairs. No sign of a poker game. No sign of Ying.

"Into room, Beatrix."

She did as she was told.

Two men were standing behind the door. They closed it and came forward. One of them said, "Hands behind back."

"You're a dead man, Chau."

He kept the gun trained on her. He was a hopeless klutz, but she knew that he could use it. She had seen him kill before. He was capable of a lot when his back was against the wall. "I am sorry. I have no choice. Now, please—do as he says."

"Have you listened to a single word I've said?"

"I have no choice. Your hands, Beatrix. Do as he says, please."

Beatrix had no choice. She put her hands behind her back and the man who had spoken pressed her wrists together so that the bracelets he held could be fitted. She was pushed into the middle of the room. She turned to get a better look at Chau. He had taken off the balaclava. The colour had drained from his face.

"I'm still going to kill Ying. And now I'm going to have to kill you, too, Chau."

Ying stepped out of a room at the back at the mention of his name. He laughed. "Ignore her, Chau. She is in no position to make threats. I am certainly not afraid of her."

He took off his tracksuit jacket. He was wearing a white T-shirt beneath it. A heavy gold chain sparkled in the overhead spotlights. He laced his fingers together and made a show of cracking his knuckles.

Beatrix knew she was about to take a beating. The only question was how bad it was going to be.

"You have caused me many problems, Beatrix. And it is a shame. Really. Now, before we can continue, Chau is going to apologise to me. Isn't that right, Chau?"

She saw Chau swallow and knew what was about to happen. He went to the table, took a white handkerchief from his pocket and opened it. He took his left hand, the one missing a joint of the little finger, and spread it out atop the handkerchief. One of the men who had been waiting for them took a box cutter from a shelf and joined him at the table. Chau closed his eyes, sweat beginning to run freely down his face. The man extended the blade of the cutter and rested the edge below the remaining knuckle of the same finger.

"Are you sorry, Chau?"

"Yes, *Dai Lo*. I am sorry."

"Are you *very* sorry?"

"I am."

At a nod from Ying, the man sliced down with the knife

and severed the finger at the knuckle. Chau had faced the loss of his finger after insulting Donnie Qi, but Beatrix had intervened to save him then. *Funny how life can be*, she thought. His destiny had been predetermined. She could have intervened or she could have stayed in her chair. It would have made no difference to him. The result would have been the same.

For her, though?

Things would have been very different. She was paying a heavy price for trying to prevent an inevitability.

The universe was laughing at her. It was all a big, cosmic joke.

The blood drained from Chau's face and he looked as if he was about to faint. He took a second handkerchief and held it around the bleeding stump. Then, he wrapped the severed knuckle in the first handkerchief and presented it to Ying with a deep bow.

"I apologise, *Dai Lo*."

"You see," Ying said, "because he has apologised, I am prepared to spare him. He will be able to work for me again, too. You want to know what his first job will be?"

"I can guess."

"Yes, I am sure that you can. He will make you disappear when we have finished punishing you for your insolence."

Ying reached into his pocket and pulled out a pair of brass knuckledusters. He slipped the fingers of his right hand through the holes, adjusting the rounded grip until it was settled, and punched it into the palm of his left hand.

Beatrix tested the cuffs. They were solid. There was no prospect of being able to get out of them.

She braced herself for what she knew was coming.

It was going to be one of those days.

Ying punched her in the face.

It was more than just Ying. The two men joined in, too. They laughed and joked as they beat her. They were like animals. They kicked or punched, moving out of the way so that another could get in close enough to kick and punch, before swapping places again. She dropped to the floor so that she could bring her knees up and try to protect her organs. White flashes sparked across her vision. She blinked through the starbursts and saw them standing over her, feet raised to kick and stamp. She closed her eyes. She had her chin pressed up tight against her chest. She switched off her mind, but she remained conscious throughout. The boots to her head and sides were alternated with strategically aimed blows to the mouth, ears and kidneys.

There was a pause and she heard Ying issue what was unmistakably an order, and then Chau responding diffidently. Ying repeated what he had said and she heard feet, shuffling closer, and then felt a half-hearted kick. "Harder," she heard Ying order, in English this time. "Kick her *harder*. Show her what it means to interfere in Chinese business."

She opened her eyes and looked up at him. There was something animalistic in Chau's face. There was pain, from the finger. There was relief, no doubt because he felt that his inclusion in this little game signalled that he was well and truly back within the fold, but there was something else, too. Something base and primal. His diffidence was gone, as if shorn away with every fresh kick. There was fury in his eyes. *Why?* Because she had constantly rebuffed his clumsy advances? Because she frightened him, made him feel less of a man? A strong woman, like Beatrix, might have seemed like an affront to his masculinity. Now he was resetting the balance.

She rolled over and made sure that they could see how weak and pitiful she looked. She wanted them to see. Pride was an irrelevance now that would get her killed. And, although she was not afraid of death, she was reluctant to surrender to it without taking Ying and Chau with her. So she played the part. She mewled and coughed, letting them know how terrified she was.

She had no idea how long the ordeal lasted. Long enough for them all to work up a sheen of sweat, and enough that, when they were finally done, they were all breathing heavily.

Ying said something in Mandarin. His two goons picked her up and dragged her to the back. She let her head hang down low, but not so low that she couldn't pay attention to her surroundings and where she was going. She tried to tune in again, to get a sense of what their plan was. She was happy for them to think that she was subdued. She could have spat out the blood in her mouth, asked them if that was all they had, but all that would have done was to hasten her end. She was surprised that they hadn't killed her already. Maybe Ying wanted to have a little more fun at her expense before he finished her off.

They dragged her along a corridor, a door on either side. There was a flight of stairs descending at the end.

She found a little strength from somewhere and parlayed that into a wisp of hope.

Maybe they would get lazy.

Maybe they would make a mistake.

Maybe they would take off her cuffs, take their eyes off her for a minute.

Maybe, maybe, maybe.

Who was she kidding?

64

The stairs led to a basement. Her legs wouldn't support her, and so they had to drag her instead.

She glanced up. There was a passage with several doors. They took her to the one at the far end and opened it, tossing her inside. She landed on her chest, her chin striking a glancing blow on the concrete floor. Her vision dimmed again. The door was slammed shut, and the light disappeared. Complete darkness.

She lay on the floor for a minute. She could feel her face swelling. Her lips had been split, her left eye was starting to close, her nose was stoppered with clots, and her body was bruised from head to toe. She took careful breaths, unsure whether she had broken any ribs.

The room was freezing. It took her a moment to join the dots. They had tossed her inside an industrial freezer. *Was it switched on?* She couldn't say. If it was, she wouldn't last long. She didn't mind. This was a respite from the beating. A death from hypothermia would be pleasant, compared to what might have happened to her. She knew the symptoms. Shivering, and then tiredness, fast breathing and cold or pale skin. More violent shivering until the hypothermia worsened further, delirium, a struggle to breathe or move, and then the loss of consciousness. That all sounded civilised in comparison to what had just happened, and what was likely to happen later.

She squeezed her eyes shut and tried to think around the pounding in her head.

Chau.

Fucking *Chau.*

She couldn't believe that he had sold her out.

The more she thought about it, though, the less she blamed him. She knew that she was in a mess. The opium. She was smoking too much. She wasn't sleeping or looking after herself. And who, when presented with a partner who clearly had no interest in her own self-preservation, would willingly go up against a man like Ying?

She wouldn't.

She had given him two choices.

First, to work with her. The odds of success were slim. Even if she had been able to dispose of Ying, who was to say that his vendetta against them would not have been adopted by another? *No*, she admitted. *The first choice was not attractive.*

The second choice? For Chau to go to Ying and offer the *Dai Lo* the one person he wanted more than himself. Beatrix Rose, delivered to him all wrapped up with a bow on top. For the small added consideration of *yubitsume*, he had been restored in Ying's good graces. Beatrix wouldn't have staked very much on the chances of that being a particularly long and mutually rewarding relationship—she would have laid better odds on him turning up in the harbour with his throat slit—but one proposition clearly offered better prospects than the other.

He had made the same choice that she would have made.

That did not mean that she was minded to be clement. Beatrix had never been big on forgiveness, and there were consequences with a choice like that. For now, though, that was moot. She was beaten, cuffed and dumped in a deep freeze. Chau probably felt pretty good about himself and the decision that he had made.

She tensed against the bracelets, but they held firm and the pressure on her swollen wrists made her wince. She lowered herself onto her side and rested her head on the floor. She closed her eyes. She was tired. The last thing that she could remember before she surrendered to the cold was the face of her daughter, but then that, too, was lost.

65

Beatrix opened her eyes. She thought that she had heard something outside. She couldn't see anything, not even the faintest sliver of light. She concentrated her attention on her hearing. She closed her eyes and held her breath.

There. A footstep?

She got her feet beneath her and pushed herself backwards until her shoulders were wedged up against the shelves on the far wall. *Were they coming back again?* She expected another beating. Her exposed ribs and head felt dreadfully vulnerable. She drew her knees up to her chest, trying to make herself as small a target as possible.

She strained her ears.

She couldn't hear anything now.

Had she imagined it?

"Hello?" she called.

There it was again: the sound of a soft footstep.

"Hello?"

She heard the sound of metal tapping against metal and then the sound of the handle on the freezer door being turned. She gritted her teeth at the sound of the bottom of the door scraping against the floor as it was pushed open. Light spilled inside and she saw the silhouette of a man. She didn't know what to expect. *The start of another beating?* The man who was now inside her cell was probably preparing to rain kicks on her defenceless body. Or was it to be something else? Perhaps the men would take turns to take advantage of their *gweilo* pet. Perhaps that was why there was just one man, and why he was quiet. The muscles in her shoulders tensed as she tested the cuffs again. They were solid, the bracelets cutting into her swollen flesh.

She was tempted to tell him to get it over with, but she wanted him to think that she was weak and beaten. She didn't want to show anything that might suggest that she had any fight left in her.

The man drew closer.

When he spoke, it was little more than a whisper. "Suzy?"

"What do you want?"

"I have a message from Michael Yeung."

He knelt down before her. Beatrix did not recognise him. He was dark haired and had furtive eyes.

"What message?"

"He want to help you."

"Why would he do that?"

"He say Ying goes too far. Cannot be trusted. And Zhào Gao very angry with him." He paused. "If I release you, what will you do?"

"I'll kill him."

"That is good. And then?"

"And then what?"

"What will you do after you kill Ying?"

"All my scores will be settled."

"Mr. Yeung say he want to work with you."

She didn't reply.

"You do not want to?"

"You ever heard the expression 'once bitten, twice shy'?"

"Mr. Yeung is not like Qi or Ying. He is *professional*."

She coughed. She could feel blood in her mouth. She spat it out onto the floor. "Good for him."

"But you talk to him?"

"Fine."

She felt a hand on her shoulder, gently impelling her to lean forward. She did, and then felt the hand between her shoulder blades and then down to her hands. Something cold and metallic brushed against the inside of her wrists. The man gave a small grunt of exertion, and then she heard the rattle of the chain as it was cleaved in two.

She looked beyond the man. The cell door was open. The corridor outside was lit by a strip light and she saw a flight of stairs, leading up to the ground floor.

"You must hurry. They will come back. We must be quick."

The man put his arm around her shoulders and helped her to stand. She shrugged him off. She was bruised and tender, but nothing was broken. Her body was serviceable.

"Where is Ying?"

"He is at his club. Nine Dragons. We are watching him. We will tell you where he goes."

The man bent down and picked up a bundle. He gave it to her. It was a dishcloth. She opened it. There was a Ruger LC9 Pro 9mm pistol inside.

She assessed her injuries again. She wasn't going to be running marathons any time soon, but she could walk and she could point a gun. It would be enough.

The man indicated the pistol. "Will this do?"

She nodded. "I'll kill Ying on one condition."

"What is it?"

"I said all my scores would be settled. That wasn't quite true. I need you to help me settle one more."

"Of course. What would we have to do?"

"Give me Jackie Chau."

"Who?"

"The man who betrayed me."

"I do not know this man."

"Tell your boss if he wants to work with me, he needs to find him."

66

Fang Chun Ying owned a lot of property across Hong Kong, but his favourite was the apartment in The Altitude, the new building that had recently been constructed on Shan Kwong Road in Happy Valley. It was on the fifteenth floor and offered panoramic views of the city, the bay and the lush greenery that clothed the hills of Kowloon that the locals called the Nine Dragons. It was a uniquely spacious apartment that had been created by buying two adjacent properties and knocking them through to create one especially large space. It was a short walk to the jockey club and it typically accommodated the rich *gweilo* workers who staffed the law and accountancy firms and banks in Central. It did not please Ying that the Westerners were the only ones who could afford the prime real estate, yet it gave him pleasure that it was not beyond him. It was a benchmark. Purchasing it was a validation, a sign that he had succeeded on their terms as well as his own.

His driver pulled up alongside the entrance. Ying had business to transact in the morning, and he told the man that he expected to see him at nine. The driver's name was

Chang, and he had known him since childhood. He trusted him completely. Chang bid him good night and waited in the car until Ying was safely inside the building.

He rode the elevator to the penthouse. The lift opened directly into the apartment.

He took off his jacket. He saw that it had been spattered with the woman's blood. His mouth curled into a sneer of distaste. He went to the mirror and saw that he had her blood on his neck, too, and another splash on the inside of his wrist. He was hot, too, shining with malodorous sweat. It made him think of the woman. For someone with so fearful a reputation, it had not taken them long to reduce her to a snivelling mess on the floor. They would leave her to contemplate her end and then return to put her out of her misery tomorrow. Chau had guaranteed that he would make her disappear. He knew that Chau did good work. He had been impressed with his burgeoning reputation while he worked for Donnie Qi, and had admired the work that he had since done for him.

He had admired Beatrix's work, too. He had admired that even more. It was a shame that their relationship had come to such a sorry juncture. She was a very useful tool. It wasn't easy to find someone as skilful and reliable as she had been. What had happened was unforgivably wasteful, but things were as they were. There was no sense in dwelling on the past.

He needed a shower to wash the sweat and the blood away. He went through into the bathroom and turned on the water. He went into his bedroom, undressed and wrapped a towel around his waist.

"Hello, Ying."

67

Ying spun around.

A woman was sitting in the armchair that faced his bed. It was dark and difficult for him to make out the details of her face, but he recognised her voice.

It filled him with fear.

He had a pistol on the dresser. He edged toward it.

"Don't," the woman said. She had a pistol aimed at him. There was only ten feet between them. She couldn't miss.

"Beatrix. You got out."

"Evidently."

"How did you find me?"

"I have a new patron."

"You do?"

"Mr. Yeung. I think you know him."

"*Of course* I know him," he snapped.

"He is disappointed in you. Zhào Gao is a friend—you were blackmailing him. Yeung said your greed threatened triad business."

"It was not like that. I will speak to him. I will explain."

"He doesn't want to speak to you. In fact, he asked me to get rid of you."

"I give you money. *Lots* of money. You take it and leave Hong Kong. I give you my word you will not be stopped."

She got up. The light fell on her face and he saw just how badly they had worked her over. She was bruised, one eye was closed, and there was dried blood around her nostrils. She walked over to the sliding door that opened out onto the balcony. It was already ajar, the wind rippling the thin gauzy curtains. She moved the curtains aside and pulled the door until it was completely open. Then she beckoned him to come to her.

He did as she asked.

"You want money?"

"Come onto the balcony with me, Ying. We can talk about it."

He stepped out into the cool night air.

"How much do you need?"

"I don't want your money. Turn around."

"Why?"

She levelled the gun and stepped up, pressing the barrel between his eyes. "*Turn around.*"

He did and, before he could react, she had taken his right arm by the wrist and yanked it all the way up his back. The sudden pain was excruciating and, in an attempt to lessen it, he leaned over so that his torso was bent over the balustrade.

"*Please*...I tell you what you need."

"Why don't you tell me about Grace."

"The girl?" He gulped the words out.

"Do you have a daughter, Mr. Ying?"

"Yes. Two."

"How old are they?"

"Ten and twelve."

"You need to help me understand, then. If you have girls, ten and twelve, why did you do what you did to her?"

The words spilled out before he had a chance to consider them. "She is just daughter of whore. She end up whore herself one day. Why do you care?"

The pressure on his arm increased. "Say *that* one more time."

"Say what?"

"Call her a whore. I *dare* you."

He gritted his teeth against the pain. "I am sorry. Where is she? I will apologise to her."

"She is a long way away. Safe."

She leaned her body against him so that she could increase the pressure on his arm. She pushed up. She felt strong. Full of muscle. The balustrade was like a fulcrum, his weight slowly tipping him over. He felt his feet rise above the floor, just the tips of his toes touching the concrete.

"Why did you do this, Ying? You knew what I would do. You brought this on yourself."

"I help girl," he begged. "Please. I give her money. I give you money, you give it to her—you do what you like with it. *Please*."

"She doesn't need your money."

"Girls like that, you buy and you sell. I buy her happiness. Her sister was whore. She will underst—"

She leaned forwards, pushing up with both hands until Ying's elbow popped. He screamed, a primal exclamation as unbearable pain flashed into his brain, but Beatrix did not relent. Instead, she clamped her right arm between his legs and heaved him so that he was balanced across the balustrade. He begged, looking down at the vast drop to the street below, but even as he did, he knew that she had never intended to spare him. She lowered her shoulder and pushed, tipping him all the way over the edge and out into the void. He fell, aware of the wind whipping around his flailing limbs and the roar of terror that he recognised, belatedly, as coming from his own throat.

His body slammed into a parked car, bounced ten feet into the air, and then came to rest in the ornamental gardens that he had once so admired. His body was arranged face up, a dozen bones broken, his vertebrae crushed. He gazed up at the ziggurat that stretched high above him, the distance that he had fallen. He tasted blood in his mouth and his breath wouldn't come. He heard the wail of a car alarm and a woman's horrified scream before everything coalesced into one long hiss of static. Darkness bled at the edges of his vision, and then closed in, swallowing him whole.

68

J ackie Chau liked to pretend that he was not an extravagant man. But when he was honest with himself, he would admit that he had a few vices, some of which could be expensive. He did like to treat himself. He could have flown economy, but the flight to Toronto was long and, since he could afford it, he had decided to go first class.

He had never flown first class before.

He was in the British Airways lounge. He had forsaken his usual garish attire for a suit and a white shirt that had been cut from reassuringly expensive cloth. He arrived an hour before his flight departed, took a drink in the bar, and allowed the gushing staff to pander to him.

He had heard about Ying's death. His friend in the police had contacted him six hours ago. The story was that he had killed himself. They said that he had thrown himself off the balcony, but Chau didn't believe that. Ying had no reason to kill himself. He had been murdered.

She had murdered him.

It had to be her.

He had no interest in waiting around to find out.

He was hungry. He wanted something pleasant to eat before the flight took off. He sat down and looked through the menu. He ordered the sushi rice prepared with red vinegar in the traditional *edomae* style and the octopus with *daikon* pickle and wasabi. A discreet waiter appeared as soon as he rested the menu on the table and Chau gave the man his order. The waiter complimented him on his taste and left him with the wine menu.

The sommelier arrived to make recommendations and Chau settled on a glass of champagne. The Bruno Paillard Nec Plus Ultra was the most expensive on the menu at HK$4,000, but he chose it regardless. He had the money, and he felt like pushing the boat out. And, after all, he was celebrating a new beginning.

The bottle arrived, the cork was popped, and a glass was poured for him. He sipped the champagne, letting the flavour dance across his tongue. It was exquisite.

He was enjoying a second sip as the waiter returned to the table.

"There is a telephone call for you, sir. A question about your luggage."

"What question?"

"I'm awfully sorry. They say that they've found something inside it. They've had to take it off the plane."

Chau felt a tremor of apprehension. *They'd found something?* There was nothing in his luggage besides clothes and toiletries. Chau thanked the man, folded his napkin and left it on the table, and made his way back to the reception. The woman behind the counter directed him to a telephone that had been left for him on a table. He put it to his ear.

"Hello?"

No reply.

"This is Chau. Hello?"

Still nothing.

He turned to the woman. "There's no one there."

"I'm very sorry, sir. Let me call them back."

He put the receiver down. "They just asked for me?"

"Yes," she said. "Your luggage. They wanted to check something with you. I'm really very sorry. I don't know what's happened."

He left the telephone and went back to his table. The staff had discreetly cleaned the crumbs away and folded his napkin. He sat and allowed the waiter to arrange it across his lap.

He raised his glass and toasted himself.

Gom bui.

It meant 'dry the cup'.

To starting over.

Second chances.

Clean slates.

He took a long sip.

CHAU WAS hungry and the food was good. He set about it quickly. When he was done, he finished the champagne and looked at the dessert menu. He wouldn't normally, but, he reminded himself, this was a special occasion.

There was no way he was going to stay in Hong Kong. *No way.* Once he had determined that he needed to leave, there had been only one destination. Toronto had a large Chinese community. There had been an exodus north from California during the depression. Chau's brother, Rickie, lived there with his family. The two of them had never been very close, but Chau knew that he would take him in until he was able to get himself sorted out. He had never travelled outside of China before, but he had always enjoyed the pictures that his brother had sent to him. Clean streets, clean air. A different way of life. Quieter. *That*, he thought, was just what he needed.

"Hello, Chau."

Beatrix Rose sat down opposite him.

His feet scrambled beneath him as he tried to get away from the table.

She reached across and grabbed his wrist. "Stay. We need to talk."

"What..." he began, panicked. He had no idea what to say. "What about?"

"Did you enjoy your meal?"

"Yes," he said, uncertainly. He stammered a little, unable to quench his fear of her. "You were watching?"

"I've been watching you for three days, Chau."

"I didn't see—"

"Of course you didn't. I'm *the ghost*, right? That's what Ying said."

Her tone was heavy with sarcasm.

"I tried to teach you about counter-surveillance," she said, "but you were never a particularly good student. I said that it would be the death of you."

"What does that mean?"

"I told you to avoid routine. It makes things easier."

"For what?"

"For people who want to follow you, Chau."

He looked down and saw that his hands were trembling. She looked down, too, and shook her head.

"I'm sorry, Beatrix," he said.

She smiled at him. "For what?"

"For what happened to you."

"So why did you do it?"

"What choice did I have?"

"I said I would protect you."

"By smoking opium? No, Beatrix. You had given up."

She didn't answer and, for a moment, there was silence between them.

"How was the champagne?"

"It was..." He trailed off, looking at her questioningly. A void opened up in the pit of his stomach.

She smiled at him. "Celebrating your departure?"

"What have you done?"

"Never mind."

"What have you *done?*"

She ignored the question again.

It didn't matter.

He knew.

"Ying is dead, by the way."

"I know."

"He should have killed me the night you betrayed me, but I think he wanted me to suffer. I'm curious. How much did he give you to sell me out?"

"It wasn't about money."

"No?"

Chau started to sweat. His mind was racing. "He was going to kill us both. Why couldn't you have left girl alone? Things were going well. Business was good. You spoiled everything."

"Leave her?" She looked as if she was about to continue, but then she shook her head. "There's no point in explaining. You wouldn't understand."

He panicked. "Please, Beatrix. I am sorry. What have you done?"

He knew what she had done.

"Goodbye."

She began to stand, but he reached out for her wrist. "I saved your life."

"It might have been better if you had left me to die. I don't even think I'm grateful any more. Goodbye, Chau. You won't see me again."

69

The plane had only just levelled off at thirty thousand feet when Chau was sick for the first time. He grabbed a paper bag and vomited into it. It lasted for ten seconds and then, when he thought he was done, another heave brought up a mouthful of sticky bile. The bag was full.

A steward hurried over. "Sir? Are you all right?"

Oh yes, he had known. He knew exactly what she had done to him, but he had been too afraid to admit it to himself. What would have been the point? There would have been nothing that could have been done to save him. He remembered what she had done to David Doss, the man working for the HK Commission Against Corruption whom Ying had wanted dead. He remembered the poison that she had poured into his drink. It was too late now. The ricin was in his cells. He *knew*. He was going to die at thirty thousand feet, wrapped in the luxurious embrace of a first-class cabin.

"Sir? You're very pale."

He felt an enervating wave of lassitude. He tried to stand, but the weakness overtook him. He lost his grip on the seat ahead of him and he fell back. The steward looked down at him, saying something that he couldn't hear. The dizziness got worse, a spinning vortex that was playing tricks with his sight. He tried to pull himself up again, but fell back down a second time.

"Sir?" the steward said, trying Mandarin. "What's the matter?"

He tried to tell him that he had been poisoned—that the woman he had been talking to in the terminal building had done it to him—but he had no idea whether he managed to form the words. He became aware of a slow pulse of pain that beat in his gut, keeping time with his heartbeat. The pain became stronger, deeper and broader, climaxing in a crescendo so intense that he thought he was going to black out. The steward loosened his collar and called for help. The pain was all encompassing, but, in that small part of his brain that was still cognisant and aware, he realised that he had brought all of this upon himself. Beatrix had been wronged, and she deserved her revenge.

70

Beatrix waited in the observation lounge, watching the jets launch themselves into the night sky. She wondered which one was Chau's.

She wondered which one she would need to take to bring her closer to Isabella. A flight to London? Paris? Somewhere in America? She couldn't answer the question. She didn't even know which country her daughter was in.

She left the airport and went straight to the *Hua-yan jian*.

The delicious oblivion enveloped her. It was a divine indulgence. She thought of Chau for a moment, running from her and yet arriving dead at his destination. She felt incapable of regret. There was just the dense fugue of the drug. It made it impossible to take a grip on her thoughts. They slipped from her grasp, squirted away, dissipated. There was no point in fighting it. She closed her eyes and let the opium carry her away.

THE THICK BLACKOUT curtains were always drawn, but they

had been disturbed in the night and now they were open just enough so that the junkies could see the sun slowly rise over the city.

"Shhh," the man next to Beatrix whispered from his dingy mattress. "If you close your eyes, you can pretend it's not happening." Beatrix had quickly learned that the morning was a time for 'getting straight,' although good intentions were often quickly ignored when the moment of truth came: leave through the front door, blinking into the bright sunlight, or smoke more opium.

Beatrix was lying on the mattress, having collapsed onto her back when her latest hit had kicked in. She had the beginnings of a cold, the most obvious symptom of addiction. She felt sallow and sleepy. The high was the purest luxury, good enough to forget the down and then the vacuum that she would enter that would make her want it even more.

She saw three shadows at the entrance to the room. She blinked, trying to work out what was different about them. They stepped in and she saw them a little better. The one at the front was old, perhaps in his early seventies; the two at the rear were younger and holding handguns, both of them extended with silencers. The older man stepped carefully between the men and women laid out on the rough beds on either side of him. The men with the guns waited at the door.

The man stopped before Beatrix and crouched down so that he could speak to her more discreetly.

"Your name is Beatrix?"

She blinked. Something was wrong with what he had just said.

"My name's Danny Wu."

She realised what was wrong: he knew her name. He *shouldn't* have known her name.

"My name is *Suzy*," she said.

"I know your name is Beatrix. I'd rather begin our relationship in a place of honesty. May I use it?"

She looked up at him, trying to blink the somnolence from her eyes. Wu spoke with an American accent.

"I'm here on behalf of Michael Yeung. I expect you know the name?"

"Never heard of him."

The man before her was wearing a baggy shirt and a pair of cargo shorts. He looked out of place among the stupefied smokers arranged in states of disarray around him. He had a mess of grey hair that was shot through with streaks of silver. His skin was wrinkled, and lines radiated out from the edges of his mouth and the corners of his eyes.

"Mr. Yeung helped you with Ying. Do you remember?"

She looked around for the Indian. She wanted another pipe.

"Do you remember?" Wu repeated.

"He took too long."

"What do you mean?"

She knew she was slurring her words, but she couldn't help herself. "I told Gao I needed to find the girl quickly. Within a few hours. I had a deadline. He took too long. I missed the deadline. The girl paid for that."

"I'm sorry to hear that. Doing what you asked wasn't simple."

"Not my problem. I don't owe Yeung anything."

"But he saved your life. Ying would have killed you. It wouldn't have been pleasant."

She laughed without humour. "It's a shame he didn't."

She saw the Indian. He was in the corner, watching fearfully. The others, too far gone to realise or care who the interloper was or who he represented, remained where they were. Some watched with dumb faces, others smoked, others closed their eyes and floated away.

"Beatrix, please. Will you let Mr. Yeung help you?"

"I don't want any more of his help."

"Ying paid you a lot of money to work for him, and yet I don't see any sign of it looking at you now. You have nothing. I know that you've transferred a large amount to a firm of private investigators in England. What are you looking for?"

His words stirred her, just a little. It wasn't that he had found out information about her that brought him closer to the truth than anyone since she had fled from Control. It was that the mention of the investigators reminded her of Isabella and triggered the usual sting of longing and the dull certainty that she would never see her again.

"Or is it a person? Are you looking for someone?"

She looked away.

"If you need money, he will pay very well for a woman with your talent. And if you are looking to find someone, perhaps he can help with that, too. His organisation has men and women all around the world. And he has resources that are unavailable to others. I'm sure I don't need to elaborate on that."

He reached out a hand and rested it on her shoulder.

"At least let me take you somewhere else. The police are coming this morning. Soon. Do you want to be here when that happens?"

That registered with her.

"Where?"

"Are you hungry?" he asked.

She shrugged.

"I know a very pleasant restaurant. They serve excellent breakfasts. What do you say?"

Here it was again. Another crossroads.

Two choices.

The first choice. Stay where she was and, if Wu was telling the truth, wait to be arrested by the Hong Kong police. Control would locate her and send an agent. Even if she was released, they would find her. She was in poor condition, not fit to defend herself against an adversary like that. Staying here would be suicide. But maybe suicide wouldn't be so bad.

The alternative?

Go with Wu. Listen to him. Hear him out, even though she knew what Yeung's proposal would entail. She would be asked to kill, and offered money to do it.

She thought of Isabella. She was out there somewhere, a child kept from her mother. Beatrix could try to forget her hopelessness in the haze of the opium pipe, but the longing was still there. She had to keep looking. She couldn't give up.

And if she wanted to see her again, what else could she do?

She stood and almost toppled to the side. Wu put an arm around her waist and anchored her. The two heavies at the door made their preparations to leave. The other addicts watched with black, disinterested eyes.

Beatrix allowed Wu to help her out of the Hua-yan jian and into the bright, sticky, humid Hong Kong morning.

GET EXCLUSIVE JOHN MILTON AND BEATRIX ROSE MATERIAL

Building a relationship with my readers is the very best thing about writing. Join my newsletter for information on new books and deals plus all this free Milton and Beatrix content:

1. A free copy of Milton's adventure in North Korea - 1000 Yards.

2. A free copy of Milton's battle with the Mafia and an assassin called Tarantula.

You can get your content **for free**, by signing up here.

ALSO BY MARK DAWSON

IN THE JOHN MILTON SERIES

The Cleaner

Sharon Warriner is a single mother in the East End of London, fearful that she's lost her young son to a life in the gangs. After John Milton saves her life, he promises to help. But the gang, and the charismatic rapper who leads it, is not about to cooperate with him.

Buy The Cleaner

Saint Death

John Milton has been off the grid for six months. He surfaces in Ciudad Juárez, Mexico, and immediately finds himself drawn into a vicious battle with the narco-gangs that control the borderlands.

Buy Saint Death

The Driver

When a girl he drives to a party goes missing, John Milton is worried. Especially when two dead bodies are discovered and the police start treating him as their prime suspect.

Buy The Driver

Ghosts

John Milton is blackmailed into finding his predecessor as Number One. But she's a ghost, too, and just as dangerous as him. He finds himself in deep trouble, playing the Russians against the British in a desperate attempt to save the life of his oldest friend.

Buy Ghosts

The Sword of God

On the run from his own demons, John Milton treks through the Michigan wilderness into the town of Truth. He's not looking for trouble, but trouble's looking for him. He finds himself up against a small-town cop who has no idea with whom he is dealing, and no idea how dangerous he is.

Buy The Sword of God

Salvation Row

Milton finds himself in New Orleans, returning a favour that saved his life during Katrina. When a lethal adversary from his past takes an interest in his business, there's going to be hell to pay.

Buy Salvation Row

Headhunters

Milton barely escaped from Avi Bachman with his life. But when the Mossad's most dangerous renegade agent breaks out of a maximum security prison, their second fight will be to the finish.

Buy Headhunters

The Ninth Step

Milton's attempted good deed becomes a quest to unveil corruption at the highest levels of government and murder at the dark heart of the criminal underworld. Milton is pulled back into the game, and that's going to have serious consequences for everyone who crosses his path.

Buy The Ninth Step

The Jungle

John Milton is no stranger to the world's seedy underbelly. But when the former British Secret Service agent comes up against a ruthless human trafficking ring, he'll have to fight harder than ever to conquer the evil in his path.

Buy The Jungle

Blackout

A message from Milton's past leads him to Manila and a

confrontation with an adversary he thought he would never meet again. Milton finds himself accused of murder and imprisoned inside a brutal Filipino jail - can he escape, uncover the truth and gain vengeance for his friend?

Buy Blackout

The Alamo

A young boy witnesses a murder in a New York subway restroom. Milton finds him, and protects him from corrupt cops and the ruthless boss of a local gang.

Buy The Alamo

Redeemer

Milton is in Brazil, helping out an old friend with a close protection business. When a young girl is kidnapped, he finds himself battling a local crime lord to get her back.

Buy Redeemer

Sleepers

A sleepy English town. A murdered Russian spy. Milton and Michael Pope find themselves chasing the assassins to Moscow.

Buy Sleepers

IN THE BEATRIX ROSE SERIES

In Cold Blood

Beatrix Rose was the most dangerous assassin in an off-the-books government kill squad until her former boss betrayed her. A decade later, she emerges from the Hong Kong underworld with payback on her mind. They gunned down her husband and kidnapped her daughter, and now the debt needs to be repaid. It's a blood feud she didn't start but she is going to finish.

Buy In Cold Blood

Blood Moon Rising

There were six names on Beatrix's Death List and now there are four. She's going to account for the others, one by one, even if it kills her. She has returned from Somalia with another target in her sights. Bryan Duffy is in Iraq, surrounded by mercenaries, with no easy way to get to him and no easy way to get out. And Beatrix has other issues that need to be addressed. Will Duffy prove to be one kill too far?

Buy Blood Moon Rising

Blood and Roses

Beatrix Rose has worked her way through her Kill List. Four are dead, just two are left. But now her foes know she has them in her sights and the hunter has become the hunted.

Buy Blood and Roses

Hong Kong Stories, Vol. 1

Beatrix Rose flees to Hong Kong after the murder of her husband and the kidnapping of her child. She needs money. The local triads have it. What could possibly go wrong?

Buy Hong Kong Stories

Phoenix

She does Britain's dirty work, but this time she needs help. Beatrix Rose, meet John Milton...

Buy Phoenix

IN THE ISABELLA ROSE SERIES

The Angel

Isabella Rose is recruited by British intelligence after a terrorist attack on Westminster.

Buy The Angel

The Asset

Isabella Rose, the Angel, is used to surprises, but being abducted is an unwelcome novelty. She's relying on Michael Pope, the head of the top-secret Group Fifteen, to get her back.

Buy The Asset

The Agent

Isabella Rose is on the run, hunted by the very people she had been hired to work for. Trained killer Isabella and former handler Michael Pope are forced into hiding in India and, when a mysterious informer passes them clues on the whereabouts of Pope's family, the prey see an opportunity to become the predators.

Buy The Asset

IN THE SOHO NOIR SERIES

Gaslight

When Harry and his brother Frank are blackmailed into paying off a local hood they decide to take care of the problem themselves. But when all of London's underworld is in thrall to the man's boss, was their plan audacious or the most foolish thing that they could possibly have done?

Free Download

The Black Mile

London, 1940: the Luftwaffe blitzes London every night for fifty-seven nights. Houses, shops and entire streets are wiped from the map. The underworld is in flux: the Italian criminals who dominated the West End have been interned and now their rivals are fighting to replace them. Meanwhile, hidden in the shadows, the Black-Out Ripper sharpens his knife and sets to his grisly work.

<u>Get The Black Mile</u>

The Imposter

War hero Edward Fabian finds himself drawn into a criminal family's web of vice and soon he is an accomplice to their scheming. But he's not the man they think he is - he's far more dangerous than they could possibly imagine.

<u>Get The Imposter</u>

ABOUT THE AUTHOR

Mark Dawson is the author of the breakout John Milton, Beatrix and Isabella Rose and Soho Noir series.

For more information:
www.markjdawson.com
mark@markjdawson.com

Made in the USA
Columbia, SC
21 June 2020

11475167R00198